ROMEO'S DEFENDER

J. A. KOLLY

Order this book online at www.trafford.com
or email orders@trafford.com

Most Trafford titles are also available at major online book retailers.

Printed in the United States of America.

ISBN: 978-1-4251-8804-7 (sc)
ISBN: 978-1-4269-1535-2 (e)

Trafford rev. 09/18/2013

www.trafford.com

North America & international
toll-free: 1 888 232 4444 (USA & Canada)
fax: 812 355 4082

This book is dedicated to all the Shipmates that stood with me through tumultuous seas.

Chapter 1

TEACHER

I BECAME aware when the cradle began to descend. By the
time, the cradle settled in the center of the room, there were
already tiny tubes connected to the child. The tubes will carry
nutrients and most importantly the Element to the child. As the
cradle settled, the sides retracted and flattened. From the floor
came a corresponding bed, which stretched around the now
flattened cradle. The child will need more room as he grows. The
Elemental energy field keeps the child elevated 10 centimeters
above the bed as alternating energy wavelengths massage the
tissues stimulating growth.

It has been thousands of cycles since I went into stasis. I
waited patiently for the first thousand cycles. When no child
arrived, conserving the Element, I went into stasis. I am Teacher.
The Old Ones developed me to train a Defender. I am one of
many, but all other Teachers are in stasis. Our descending cradle
calls us awake. My one purpose is to develop a Defender. There
was a war, and the Old Ones needed warriors for defense. The
Teachers develop the warriors. The war was lost, but the planet
survived. I survived deep below the surface, waiting for my call.
The call has finally come . . .

I send a microscopic tendril down to the child's head.
It slowly enters the ear canal and passes easily through the
tympanic membrane. The tendril follows the auditory nerve to

the brain where it branches out establishing my home within the future Defender. The child has dreams, some pleasant of the beings that comfort him. Some frightful, following his separation from his mother, and what appears to be warfare on the surface of the planet. I calm his mind and take away his fears. In his memory, I can see the frightened woman that brought him to the dome. I can see her put a necklace with metal disks around his neck. The tender way she kisses him goodbye, I surmise the woman was his mother.

I watch over the child, as he grows. With our neural link, I begin his education. His species only uses a small portion of their available brain storage area, so it is easy for me to store large amounts of data in his brain that he can access later. His physical development is progressing at the nominal rate. I believe the Defender will be ready for training soon.

Chapter 2

EGAS INQUISITIVE

(Earth/Giann Alliance Ship)
(Research and Exploration Vessel)
Five Hundred Thirty-four AC. (After Contact)
(Two Solar Cycles earlier)

CAPTAIN Donald Phillips EGAF, (Earth/Giann Alliance Fleet), frowned into his cold coffee cup, and then gazed up at the planet filling the navigation monitor screen. He is a big man, in the tradition of the Welsh miners who were his ancestors. His muscled physique gives him the appearance of a younger man. The only clue to his age and experience is the graying hair at his temples.

The planet above is unsettling to Phillips, and after twenty-five solar cycles with the Fleet, Phillips found that feeling usually meant bad news. The Inquisitive has been in orbit around the planet for fourteen planetary cycles to gain information for exploration. So far, he had gotten more questions than answers. He did not like it, but then he was only the ship's Captain. Once in orbit, the Lead Scientist is in charge of the expedition, and Phillips is to provide security and support. One hundred and fifty years after the contact with the Giann, Earth and Giann standardized their calendars to describe years as solar cycles, months as lunar cycles and days as planetary cycles. This change better-suited space travel and communication between the two worlds.

This planet is a class M, with surface water and an oxygen/ nitrogen mix atmosphere. A touch less nitrogen than Earth or Giann, but the air was quite breathable. The two large symmetrical brownish appearing continents have plenty of small lakes, rivers and vegetation but they all have a slight rust hue. As the scientists that have been sending probes to the surface remark, "Different planet different colors." After all, we found long ago not all vegetation that produce oxygen are necessarily green. The wispy thin clouds that surround the planet speak of infrequent rain and an arid climate. The planet's designation was for its proximity to its Sol type star and reads R-67252-4. The additional number four on the end designated it as the fourth planet in the system. The other five planets in the system were the usual empty rocks, but the water on the fourth is what caught the interest of the EGAF Scout Vessel traveling through the system two solar cycles ago. The letter and the proceeding numbers were for where the planet was located. Since the letter was "R", the communications people took to calling it "Romeo", as per the military alpha/phonetic communications code. Besides fundamental plant and life like bushes and odd colored grasses, Romeo is deserted. The beautiful oceans have marine plants but the probes could find no animal life there either. *It is very odd indeed!* Phillips thought, *for such a desirable class-M planet. It's almost as if the ecology of the planet just started a few solar cycles ago.*

Then, there is the satellite. Noted upon approach, it was too small for a moon, and too close to the planet. It appeared to be a small round stone ball circling the planet. It has no apparent power source to keep its orbit and no detectable emissions. It was another puzzle that the scientists on board found so intriguing. Phillips did not like puzzles, particularly if those puzzles could endanger his ship and crew.

Phillips put down his cup and headed for the Science Deck; he was tired of waiting. Passing navigation control, he spoke to Ensign Nomarie behind the console. "Ensign, Lieutenant Commander Stil will take the Con." Nomarie looked up and responded as he noted the time in the ship's computer log. "Lieutenant Commander Stil has the Con, aye."

Lieutenant Commander Michael Stil, EGAF, is the Executive Officer of the Inquisitive. He also serves as the Ship's Security Officer. He is standing behind the communications console observing Chief Petty Officer, Bin a Giann crewmember, sending the daily reports back to EGAFC. (Earth/Giann Alliance Fleet Command), commonly pronounced, "Egaff-see," by the crew. Stil turned and acknowledged the order. "Ensign I have the Con."

Michael Stil, second in his class at the Fleet Academy, and now has served with the Fleet for fourteen solar cycles. Stil is a tall thin man with piercing blue eyes and quiet demeanor. He has a keen attention to detail and speaks with a clipped, Eastern, North American accent that suggests a New England heritage. Michael is now ambiguous about his career with the Fleet. His wealthy family was quite surprised when after graduating from Cambridge, he elected to go to the Fleet Academy. As his Father once told him, "Our family builds Starships, we don't man them!"

His family was even more surprised when after the Academy, Michael married Angela Brook. Michael met Angela while at the Academy, on Europa. She was working on her Doctorate in Geology at the time assisting Dr. Henry Chase with a field study on Europa. Michael was in love with Angela from the first moment he saw her. Angela was not stuffy and shallow like the society girls his mother preferred him to date. She was smart, beautiful and determined to make a difference in the universe. Angela had long, light brown hair, and the largest brown eyes that Mike had ever seen. At a little less than two meters tall, Angela barely reached Michael's shoulder, but when they are together they both say the match is perfect. Whether in shorts at a dig, or in a formal gown at a fundraiser, Angela has the poise and stature of a dignified Lady.

Dr. Angela Stil is now one of the civilian members of the expedition. Her specialty is Geology and her hobby is Alien Archeology. Angela is pregnant with their first child, and she is due to deliver any day. Michael hopes she will deliver aboard the ship, not that the physicians in the mobile hospital with the expedition could not do the job as well. The hospital is able to treat all medical problems for the three hundred members of the expedition that will embark to the planet. Stil would just feel better if his first-born was aboard the Inquisitive when delivered. Michael has been very careful not to relay his concern to Angela and cause her any additional anxiety.

Once on the planet, the expedition will be totally independent and self-sufficient. There are enough equipment and support personnel to supply the small colony for research and exploration when the Inquisitive eventually leaves orbit. Part of the research will be the research of any edible flora and the adaptation and incorporation of Earth and Giann plants and animals to the planet. Even if the agrarian experiments were to fail, the expedition would have enough supplies with replication to last more than twenty solar cycles, more than enough time for the Inquisitive or another ship, to return. The Inquisitive is one of the older hyper-light ships. Its maximum speed is just a little more than three times speed of light. At best speed, it still took over 18 lunar cycles to reach the Romeo system. The long length of the trip here, and the full scope of the expedition necessitated the voluntary inclusion of the expedition personnel's significant others, hence the full support facilities.

Taking the lift down from the Bridge three levels, Phillips reached the Science Deck, and walked forward past multiple compartments to what now is the Lead Scientist's Office in the bow of the ship. The large compartment with the equally large observation ports functions as a shared office for Dr. Chase and Dr. Pel. Phillips found the lead scientist, Dr. Henry Chase, in discussion with his Giann counterpart, Dr. Pel. Phillips believes that Henry Chase is the epitome of the collegiate scholar. Chase even dresses the part, with a preference for old-fashioned tweed suits instead of the modern synthetic jump suits, Van Dyke beard, and floppy cloth hats; he fits the bill as the dashing college professor.

Phillips has found Chase to be rather windy and self involved, but his bosses at the EGAFC say Chase is the best. Standing behind them is Dr. Pel's gray brother, Major Pel EGAFMC. (Earth/Giann Alliance Fleet Marine Corps) Major Pel is the Officer in Charge of the Marine contingent assigned aboard the Inquisitive. They are in intense discussion, Chase with his low oratorical voice and Pel, with the musical voice that comes from the translator worn like a necklace around his neck. Phillips entered the compartment and a crewmember working at one of the many computer workstations, stood and stated, "Attention on deck!" Phillips gave the obligatory response, "As you were."

In the old Navy tradition, Phillips knew if he did not give the "As you were", the crewmembers in the compartment would continue to stand at attention awaiting his instruction, and no work would be completed. The civilians in the compartment, of course, mainly ignored him. Phillips strode straight up to the group. "Well Dr. Chase, what's your analysis?" Chase rolled his eyes in irritation at the interruption and replied. "Well

Captain, the planet appears safe enough, but we do have some unanswered questions." Phillips saw the data sheets in Dr. Pel's hands. "There are unanswered questions? What do you mean?" Phillips looked back to Chase. "Is it safe for your party or not?" Chase looked at the slowly blinking dark eyes of Dr. Pel, and then turned to Phillips.

"I think the planet is safe, it's just that our sensors don't appear to be able to penetrate beneath the surface of the planet. We find no electrical magnetic emissions from the planet, any hazardous plant or animal life. However, when we attempt to scan beneath the surface of Romeo, it is just total interference. We can scan the other planets in the system down to their molten cores, but with Romeo, everything just stops on the surface. Then, there are also the small dome like structures, along with the unusual craters and scaring of the surface of the planet."

Phillips continuing to stare at him asked, "What kind of small domes? Are they artificial, or some type of natural formation?" Chase gestured to the large holographic generator in the center of the compartment. Suspended in the center above the generator is the holographic image of Romeo. Phillips, Chase and Dr. Pel walked over to the generator; Major Pel was not far behind. Chase pointed to the planet and began his lecture.

"Captain, as you can see, Romeo has two large continents and two oceans. The continents are symmetrical and run north and south to the polar caps. The ice caps at the poles are quite large and I believe that at one time the oceans were much larger. These large flat areas on the continents we believe at one time used to be large lakes. Running north and south from each pole, about five hundred kilometers in from each ocean, are the mounds, or domes."

Chase looked closely at the hologram, adjusted a dial, and then offered, "They are fairly small, even on maximum magnification, and I didn't notice them. Neither did the sensor staff. Dr. Pel was doing temperature gradient studies, and noted five spots close to the edge of the continent that seemed in perfect alignment exactly one thousand kilometers apart. They looked like little triangles, a little cooler than the surrounding soil, and as he watched they disappeared! Dr. Pel surmised that the disappearance must be due to the rotation of the planet and the angle of the sun. He ran the hologram backwards, and watched them slowly appear, and get larger as they approached the edge of the night side of Romeo."

Chase pressed other adjustment controls, and the hologram slowly began to turn backwards. Chase pointed at the globe. "Now, watch right here." Phillips concentrated on the spot, and Chase slowed the counter rotation even more. Then Phillips began to see it. It started as a tiny flattened line then slowly the point of a triangle appeared and got longer. The top point of the triangle got the longest just before touching the line of darkness of the night side. Phillips watched as Chase adjusted the hologram back to its normal rotation and speed. "So the triangles are cooler than the surrounding area because they are shadows."

"That's correct," nodded Chase.

"And since these shadows are triangular, whatever is causing the shadows is either dome shaped or triangular. But how can you be sure they are domes?"

Chase gave him a smug look, "It's just simple geometry. If they were triangles, as the planet rotated and we mapped the location as it traveled across our view, we would see the lines of the sides. It is like looking straight down the line of a cliff from an aircraft; you do not see the cliff, but you see a line. A rounded dome or mound would still give a triangular shadow, but if it matched the surrounding territory you wouldn't see anything from above."

Phillips looked at Dr. Pel, "And you surmise that they are artificial because . . ." All three spoke in unison. "They're exactly one thousand kilometers apart!" Chase continued. "Now that we knew what to look for, we looked closely at the edges of both continents and found that there are ten on each continent, five on each side." Phillips turned to Dr. Pel. "Do you have any idea, what these domes or mounds might be?" Dr. Pel raised his hands at his sides in a very human like gesture, and offered, "I have no idea." Phillips then turned to Chase. "What about the craters and scaring you mentioned?"

"Angela, I mean, Dr. Stil has been studying those. Excuse me Captain sometimes, I just forget she is not one of my students anymore. She is handling the geological scanning studies. Just a moment, I'll have her brief you."

Chase picked up his communicator from his belt and walked off. Phillips watched Dr. Pel go back to the hologram platform and then glanced at Major Pel, standing stiffly in the same position he was in when Phillips entered the compartment. Major Pel gave a slight bow of the head, "By your leave, sir." Phillips returned the nod, "Major Pel." Pel then gave another slight nod of his head, made a crisp military facing movement, and headed toward the exit hatch with a determined stride.

The Giann culture is a culture of twins: All Giann are born as twins one with light pigmentation like white or cream the other darker like gray. One is always smaller or slighter of build and the other always larger and stronger. There is no intellectual difference between the twins, but the smaller became the Scholars, Physicians, Teachers and Scientists. The larger Giann are the protectors and experts in the Giann Martial Arts. The larger Giann, whether white or gray, became the soldiers and laborers. Giann always travel as twin pairs, and with the Fleet are assigned together. The larger Giann have twice the strength of the Humans, and can survive in very adverse environments, which makes them very formidable soldiers or security personnel.

At the hatch, Major Pel stopped, and made room for the entrance of Dr. Angela Stil. Angela appeared to be slightly out of breath from the exertion of walking quickly in the last few days of her pregnancy. She gave Pel a warm genuine smile. "Why thank you Major Pel, you're so kind to a fat lady." Pel replied in his serious formal way. "You are welcome, Dr. Stil." He made another crisp facing movement, and left the compartment.

Angela walked towards Phillips, using that slightly waddling stride common to women in their third trimester of pregnancy. She quickly said, "I'm so sorry to keep you waiting Captain, but I had to visit the potty on the way here." Phillips smiled; he liked Angela, and thought that Mike Stil was a very lucky man to have married such a smart, talented and warm-hearted woman. Phillips gave a fake shocked expression, and chuckled. "The Head, Dr. Stil, you stopped in the Head!"

"Oh Captain, I spend so much time there these days, they should start calling it the Angela!"

That statement brought another chuckle from Phillips and a smile to some of the crewmembers working in the area. Phillips took Angela by the arm and guided her over to the hologram display. "Dr. Chase tells me you've been doing the research scans on what appear to be craters and scaring on the planet's surface."

"That's correct Captain, may I sit down?" Phillips pointed to an empty console chair. "By all means, Dr. Stil, by all means please sit." Angela sat down with a grunt, rubbing her protruding stomach in a motherly pregnant woman way, and began.

"Well Captain, when the ship first approached, the craters and the scaring were quite obvious, even without the scans. What we were interested in, is if they were natural phenomena, or if they are artificial in nature. You see, if the surface routinely gets pounded by meteor showers that get through the atmosphere, it wouldn't be a very healthy place to stay."

Phillips gave her a nod of understanding. "So I scanned a good variety of the craters on each continent, and I found they were all similar." Phillips squinted at the hologram. "Similar?"

"Yes, in the study of craters, let's say on Earth's moon, the one thing you find is the craters are all different. The difference is caused by the individual meteorites that hit it, and all of the different angles at which they hit. Therefore, you see, there are angled craters, and some that are round but slightly misshapen due to the trajectory of the collision. Straight-on collisions do happen, but perhaps, only one out of thousands. After all, they are hitting a curved surface."

"So, what makes the craters on Romeo so similar?"

"They are almost all straight-on collisions. Most of their debris fields lay around the craters in an almost perfect circle. That would be like a meteor shower hitting the planet from all the points of the compass at once!" Phillips looked thoughtful. "Why do you say all at once?" Angela changed her position in the chair and pointed to the holograph planet in front of them.

"The weathering, even on Earth's moon, craters weather. Even in an airless environment, over the planetary and solar cycles, the craters wear down from dust movement and erosion. The newest collisions have crisp new sides. The older ones are rounded and filled with sediment. On Romeo, all the craters have appeared to weather the same." Looking at Angela, Phillips summarized. "So that would totally rule out any natural phenomena."

"That's the conclusion I came to. There's also something else." Phillips straightened up. "What else?" Angela grunted and repositioned herself in the seat again.

"Although the surface is difficult to scan due to whatever is in the soil, I've picked up minute pieces of heavy metal lying in the debris fields around the craters." Phillips had one more question. "When you said all the craters have weathered the same, would you have any idea how old they could be?" Angela gave Phillips one more warm smile.

"Of course, that's my specialty! From the scan's computer simulations, I would say the event happened about three thousand to thirty-five hundred solar cycles ago. Of course, once I get down there and examine them myself, I bet, I could get that guesstimate down to within five solar cycles."

"Thank you, Dr. Stil, if you'll excuse me." Feeling he had gotten as much information as was available Phillips turned and left the compartment. Angela sat there, slowly rubbing her stomach and gazed at the holographic image of Romeo. "When, I finally get down there!" she muttered.

Phillips returned to the Bridge and upon entering walked over to Mike Stil sitting in a Bridge chair reviewing reports. Stil stood when Phillips entered the Bridge. "Commander Stil, please arrange for Officers Call at 1800 hours in the Wardroom. Please include the leading scientific personnel." Stil nodded. "Aye, Captain, 1800 hours in the Wardroom."

"I'll be in my Ready Room reviewing some of the scientific data if you need me."

After the Captain left, the Helmsman looked over Stil. "Good news, sir?" Stil paused and looked up at the image of Romeo on the navigation screen. "I'm not sure, I'm not sure at all."

Chapter 3

EGAFMC (TA), EUROPA

(Earth/Giann Alliance Fleet Marine Corps,
Training Academy, Europa)

WHAM! The energy bolt hit her body armor, directly in the middle of her chest. The blast knocked her into the air, and in the reduced gravity, back five meters. Midshipman Maryann Hall tried to regain her breath, and shake the stars out of her eyes. She slowly remembered she was in the large Tactical Training Center deep within Europa. The cave the size of a stadium had broken buildings, pillboxes and fortifications for offensive and defensive training. When her sight finally cleared, the face of Gunnery Sergeant Hin looking down at her greeted her.

The large Giann was anything but pleased, "GREAT, Midshipman Hall, THAT'S JUST GREAT! Your assault just got you killed and probably got your whole squad killed!" Hin reached down and with one arm pulled Hall to her feet. Gunny Hin bent over so her face with the large diagonal eyes was just centimeters from Maryann as she shouted. "JUST WHERE WAS YOUR HEAD DURING THE CLASS ON TARGET SUPPRESSION AND TACTICAL ASSAULTS, IN URANUS?"

The pun brought snickers and chuckles from the other Midshipmen in the squad, gathering around the pair. The large Giann turned quickly toward them. "WHAT ABOUT **YOU MAGGOTS**? THE CORPS IS A TEAM. WE ALWAYS WORK AS A TEAM. IF YOU USED HALF THE MIND THE CREATOR HAS GIVEN YOU, THE FLAWS IN HER ASSAULT PLAN WOULD HAVE BEEN IDENTIFIED BEFORE-HAND!"

Gunny Hin lowered her voice and spoke in a disgusted monotone. "It's your duty to think and work as a team. **IF,** and I do mean **IF,** you ever get out of this grammar school, you will be leading **REAL** Marines. They will be expecting you to keep them alive! Space is **NOT** a friendly environment. There **ARE** a lot of planets out there with a **LOT** of nasty ways to get you killed!" The Gunny paused and stared at them with unblinking eyes. "DO YOU HEAR ME?" The squad replied. "YES, GUNNERY SERGEANT, HIN!"

Hin lowered her voice, "Good, now, full environmental suits and outside, I want you people through the confidence course in armored suits, **twice,** before chow." The Gunny saw a slight hesitation, "NOW!"

The squad of Midshipmen broke and ran for the airlock and the suit room with another chorus of, "YES, GUNNERY SERGEANT HIN!" Hin thought to herself as she walked to the instructor's lounge. *I should have been a builder. I work with rocks anyway.* The Giann felt a response to her frustration from her twin that worked as a technician in Sickbay. *Now, now, I remember when you were a recruit!* Gunny Hin gave a mental shrug and went into the lounge.

The Giann are telepathic and although they have a mouth, do not possess vocalization organs or structures. For contact with other vocal species, the Giann designed vocal communicators that they wear like necklaces. When the Giann first used the new devices, they noticed discomfort in the Humans that they spoke with. It was just simply that their mouths didn't move when they spoke. Over a few solar cycles, the Giann learned to "mouth" the word they were producing thus eliminating the problem. This technique was especially important when speaking with the hearing impaired that were used to reading lips.

The Giann telepathy is specific to their species only. They normally only communicate with other Giann. However, there are documented cases of Giann that were in great distress telepathically reaching other species. Giann twins also have a special shared form of empathetic telepathy, not shared with other Giann. A Giann can always describe where the other twin is, and how they feel.

In the suit room, Maryann removed her helmet, shook out her short, brownish-blonde hair and reached back to unbuckle her armor. Maryann, though of medium build, has been athletic all her life. After college sports, she had thought she was in shape for Marine training, but she was mistaken. She gave a groan as the movement brought pain to her chest. A voice came from behind her. "Hey, Pug, can I give you a hand with that?"

John Phillips is one her best friends at the Academy. John's slim build and wiry muscular frame gives him an ease of motion that makes even the most difficult physical tasks look easy. His freckled light skin, green eyes, and reddish-blond hair, speak of his British ancestry. One night while studying, Maryann had confided in John that she was not happy with her face. She described her face as plain, round, with a small pug nose. John had laughed, because he could not believe such a smart, pretty and strong woman had a touch of vanity. John's nickname for her had been "Pug", ever since.

He gently helped her unbuckle her armor, and lifted it over her head. Maryann turned towards the mirror in the room, and unbuttoned the top two buttons of her tunic. Her chest was sore and she wanted to see if it bruised. John saw the large red, blue, and purple welt between the top of her breasts. "That looks nasty, maybe you should stop in Sickbay." Maryann buttoned up her tunic. "I'll be ok; what hurts more is that I blew it first time out as Squad Leader."

Chuck Mills, the massive ex-college football lineman from a university in Texas, was changing into his suit across from them. He gave a horselaugh. "Oooh, Hall, would you like me to rub some ointment on your chest?" Yolanda Pierce, a tall Black Midshipman next to Chuck, swung her suit quickly around, and the armored hand of the suit just happened to hit Mills right in the groin. Chuck doubled over, grabbing for his testicles. "Ow, you did that on purpose!"

Pierce continued putting on her suit. "Perhaps you should consider keeping your **ointment** to yourself."

Yolanda Pierce is a genius. Literally, at first the other Midshipmen wondered why a woman with the IQ of 196, and Doctorates from no less than three prestigious universities, would want to become a Marine. One morning during chow when Maryann explored the question, Pierce had responded. "This is a challenge for me that I can't find anywhere else. What about you?"

Maryann looked down into the congealed mess that the cook said was something on a shingle. She looked back up at Yolanda and said. "All my life I've been competing. I was a swimmer. I played volleyball. I ran track and played field hockey. I was never number one, the leader. In track, I ran third in a relay. I never won anything on my own. I want to be something else besides plain old Maryann the also ran." Since that short conversation, Maryann and Yolanda have been the best of friends.

John, ignoring Chuck's lack of wit turned to Maryann. "Hey we all make mistakes and besides, Hin was right, we should have all realized that assaulting a position without suppression grenades first is a mistake."

Midshipman Tan, the only Giann member of the squad, had already completed donning his suit and walked over with his helmet under his arm. The Giann initiated contact with Earth more than five hundred Solar Cycles ago. There was a lot of human concern after contact since before their arrival there were rumored reports of white or gray aliens with large diagonal shaped eyes abducting humans and performing all types of gruesome experiments on them.

The Giann admitted that they had observed the human species prior to contact for many solar cycles. They presented proof that the "experiments" were actually misunderstood. The Giann had in fact medically corrected any abnormalities they found in the people examined. The Giann had felt they were helping the people to live longer fruitful lives. The Giann made a global apology for the examinations and admitted they had mistakenly imposed upon the freedoms of another sentient species. Contact was initially fraught with fears and suspicion but over the years with free cultural exchange, the fears suspicion and concerns have all but evaporated.

Some people still view the Giann with suspicion but they are a small xenophobic minority. The most vocal are the members of the Galactic Peace Party. These people neither, represent the galaxy or seem to embrace peace. With an agenda of isolationism for Earth a wealthy tycoon, Wingate Toath leads them. Toath is a billionaire industrialist and a representative in the EGA Council. He devoutly believes that Earth should not have formed an alliance with the Giann. If Toath and his small group of, "like minded" people had their way there would not be any Giann deployed on Earth vessels. Giann now compose almost thirty percent of the Fleet and Marine personnel.

"That is correct Midshipman Hall; we were all negligent in our duties by not offering better advice, and pooling our knowledge." Maryann nodded and gave them a strained smile. "Thanks, guys." Hall then turned to Phillips. "I guess you're right. Now, could you give me a hand with this suit, Sailor Boy?" John smiled. Maryann has called him that ever since he told her that his father was Captain Donald Phillips, the Commanding Officer of the EGAS Inquisitive.

Chapter 4

EGAS INQUISITIVE

(1800 Hours)

THE Captain's Ready Room is a small multipurpose room just off the Bridge. Once again, the Ready Room goes back to ancient times when the ship's Captain had to be readily available to the Bridge in times of danger. Now used mostly for administrative duties the Ready Room still has a fold down bed so the Captain can sleep close to the Bridge. Before leaving his Ready Room for the Officer's Call, Phillips paused to look at the hologram on his desk. It is a holographic image of his wife Diane, and his son John. Phillips took the image himself. He was home on leave, and John was home from College. He had hoped that upon graduation John would go to the Fleet Academy, and become a Fleet Officer like the rest of the family. However, John had decided to go to the Marine Corps Academy instead.

Phillips had come from a long line of Fleet Officers that had ties all the way back to Briton's Grand Fleet of the Napoleonic Wars. Nevertheless, it was John's decision, and Phillips had to respect his son's choice. He has no doubt now that John will make a fine Marine Officer. Phillips entered the Wardroom. The Wardroom is where the ship's Officers take their meals and it commonly doubles as a large conference room for staff meetings. The ship's Master Chief called out. "Attention on Deck."

Phillips responded, "As you were," and proceeded to the chair at the head of the long central table. He looked around at the expectant faces at the table. "I called you here for the final decision about landing the expedition, and if we're landing, recommendations for the plan of action," Phillips let that request sink in then turned to Henry Chase, sitting to his left. "Dr. Chase, may we begin with you?" As all eyes turned to Chase, he cleared his throat, and began as if this was another student lecture.

"As you all know we have spent the last fourteen planetary cycles examining Romeo. We have been using sensor research, and had sent down planetary probes to gather soil, mineral, and atmospheric samples." Chase looked around the table, and then went on quickly as if just then realizing this was information that everyone knew.

"First, we found out why our sensors don't seem to penetrate the planet. We found that the soil contains a crystal like element that either blocks or interferes with electromagnetic energy. This element permeates the rock and the soil on Romeo. While the crystals appear benign, Dr.'s Wright and Sang in biochemistry have secured samples, and are currently working on further analysis. We have also found ten domes on each continent, five to each side."

Chase gestured to the holographic projector in the middle of the table. He worked his hands over a control pad in front of him. A close image of a dome appeared in the middle of the table. "We sent probes down to examine the domes, as well as to take a sample of them." The holographic dome in the middle of the table slowly began to turn as the mobile probe slowly circled the dome, recording the total object.

"You will notice that the exterior size of the domes is approximately thirty meters across the base, and they are only fifteen meters high. They appear to be made out of the same indigenous rock of the planet, except for one small difference."

Chase worked the control pad in front of him again, and the view of a boulder in front of the probe appeared. The soil around the boulder was reddish-brown with sprouts of a tough looking greenish-blue scrub grass, and a spindly bush with gray-brown leaves. As Chase worked the controls, a robotic arm came forward from the probe with a small diamond circular saw attached. The arm moved forward and made a slice through the boulder, creating dust and debris just as if cutting through a rock on Earth. Chase worked the control pad again. "Now, watch this."

The view was back to the probe in front of the dome. Once again, the arm of the probe extended with the saw. There were sparks and a great deal of smoke, and then the arm lifted. The saw blade was blackened, melted, and half its original size. The probe zoomed in at the point of contact with the dome. There was not even a scratch on the stone!

Chase worked the pad again, obviously enjoying his demonstration. The view again was of the dome, but this time the probe extended a small industrial laser. The laser fired and at the target sight, there was nothing! There isn't a burn mark from the heat or any mark at all. Chase worked the pad, and the dome was once again slowly turning in the middle of the table. Chase paused for a few moments to let the impact of the demonstration sink in then continued. "In addition we closely examined the dome with the highest visual magnification of the probe and found no cracks, scratches or evidence of an opening." Phillips turned to look from the hologram to Chase. "So what is it, and what does it do?"

Chase scowled slightly. "That's all the data we currently have. We do have more tests we can try when we are on the surface, but any speculation of what it is, would only be that, speculation. The only thing we know for sure is what it is not. That is a naturally occurring structure. As for what it does I would hazard a guess that it doesn't do anything." Now it was Phillips' turn to look irritated. "Dr. Chase would you or your people have any idea if those structures could be dangerous?"

Dr. Pel, next to Chase raised his hand. "Pardon my interruption; I would speculate that since there was no reaction noted to the actions of the probe. The domes may be benign." Phillips leaned forward in his seat. "May be, are you willing to risk lives on a **may be**?" Dr. Pel sat back in his seat with no further comment. Chase however, certainly was not done. "Captain, you're being unfair! We are doing the best we can under the circumstances. We don't have enough information to give guarantees, and we can't gain any further information **up here!**"

Phillips looked around the room and most of the civilian scientists were nodding their heads in agreement. For the most part the military personnel appeared attentive, but unwilling to give an opinion. Phillips gaze stopped briefly on Angela as she looked at the turning hologram, and unconsciously rubbed her stomach. Phillips then turned to Stil. "Lieutenant Commander Stil, may I have your recommendations please?"

Stil, whom had been watching Chase, sat stiffly upright with a slight look of surprise. "Sir, with all due respect, I don't believe I need to mention our mission here is the research and exploration of Romeo. From the point of view, relating to security my opinion is that currently none of the information shown presents a danger to the Inquisitive or the crew. I do however recommend starting surface exploration with a limited number of personnel chosen by Dr. Chase, and accompanied by Major Pel, and some of his

Marines." Phillips nodded and turned to Major Pel standing quietly behind his twin. "Major Pel, may I have your input please?"

"Sir, I can have two squads available at Dr. Chase's pleasure."

Chase perked up in his seat as if to protest but Phillips cut him off. "Dr. Chase, please realize you have won your point, but I'm responsible for the security of the expedition as long as the Inquisitive is in orbit. If you go down, the Marines go with you." Chase nodded sat back in his chair and made a "As you wish" motion with his hands. Phillips pleased that they accepted the proposal moved on to the next issue. "What is the plan for the satellite?"

This was Angela's department. "Captain I've been working on the data from the satellite, but as you know there is very little. It is about five hundred meters across and too large to bring in the ship for examination. We have had about the same luck with the robot probes as they have with the dome. I am not a good candidate to get in a suit to do the closer examination of the satellite, so my assistant Connie Holmes will be going out tomorrow." Angela gestured towards her husband. "Michael will provide a security shuttle, a crew and two technicians to accompany Connie. She will try to get a surface sample if possible."

Phillips looked at Stil who just nodded in agreement. Phillips then looked around the table. "Well if there aren't any other issues . . ."

It was just then that Angela began to scream!

Chapter 5

EGAFMC (TA), EUROPA

MILLS fired the last ten rounds in his magazine at full automatic. "YEE-HAW, GET SOME!" Gunnery Sergeant Hin walked up behind Mills at his firing position in the underground range, and reviewed his score. "Quite extraordinary Midshipman Mills you fired with ninety-eight percent proficiency!

"YEE-HAW, did you see that? Y'all don't mess with Texas!"

There were by comments from the other positions like, "Asshole!" and, "Did you think you were shooting your Mama?" Mills unperturbed by the comments continued. "It's just that you limp-dick shitheads don't know that nobody can out shoot a Texan." Gunnery Sergeant Hin broke in with, "Alright knock it off. Lock and load one more magazine at three hundred meters. Mills, the Commandant wants to see you, so turn in your weapon at the armory, and report."

Mills responded pausing to ensure his weapon was empty. "Yes, Gunnery Sergeant Hin," and then added for everyone in the line, "She probably wants to give me a commendation or something. Obviously, **she** knows talent!" That was followed by, "In your dreams!" and "Sure, sheep dip!" as he strutted away.

Mills literally sat on the edge of his chair at attention, as was the prescribed method for the Midshipmen at the Academy. He stared straight ahead, as also was the prescribed manner, and waited. The Sergeant Major at the desk across from him paid him no more attention than if the chair he occupied was empty. The nameplate in the middle of the desk read, "Sergeant Major Logan EGAFMC." Mills sat there for what seemed like hours, but there was no asking, "How long would it be?" The Sergeant Major would not answer him anyway. Finally, there was a buzz on the Sergeant Major's desk. The Sergeant Major looked up at him, and said one word. "Proceed."

Mills stood to attention made a crisp right face and marched into the Commandant's office. He marched within exactly one pace of the middle of the Commandant's desk stood at attention and stated. "Midshipman Mills reporting as ordered, ma'am!"

The Commandant continued reading whatever was on the screen on the right side of her desk and ignored Mills. Mills stood at attention in the prescribed manner with eyes straight ahead focused on the large Marine Corps emblem on the wall behind the Commandant's deck. The emblem is between the two flags standing in holders in front of the bulkhead, each one exactly parallel to the sides of the Commandant's desk.

The flag over the Commandant's right shoulder is the standard of the Earth/Giann Alliance. The flag over the left is the Earth/ Giann Alliance Fleet Marine Corps standard. The Marine Corps Emblem still used the ancient globe with the eagle perched on a diagonal fouled anchor. The old American and British Marines used the emblem for centuries. The only change that had come with the Giann alliance was the addition of the cross lateral depiction of the Milky Way behind the globe. The banner across the bottom still carried the ancient motto, "Semper Fidelis," always faithful. The banner demonstrates that the Corps values and traditions have not changed in more than a thousand solar cycles. It is widely known. "When things turn nasty, the Fleet turns to the Marines."

Colonel Juliet Kellogg, EGAFMC, depressed a key on the operating pad of the computer and looked up at Mills. Colonel Kellogg has been in the Corps almost thirty solar cycles. The scar running down the left side of her face and her short cut graying hair give her an appearance of a woman much older. Juliet has been a Marine since she left home as a teen. Civilian women would have had the scar disappear with surgery and hair treated to keep the color, but vanity was not a vice for the Commandant. She earned the premier assignment as the Commandant of the Academy after losing her left leg rescuing malibdium miners on a small planet in the Spiegel system. Although the Alliance has not yet come into contact with a violent sentient species, there are a few planets that have been explored that have had very dangerous flora or fauna.

In this case, the miners were extracting the ore on a frozen planet. They broke into a chamber containing rather lethal reptilian like creatures. The creatures managed to kill over half of the miners before they even knew what hit them. The remaining miners managed to hold them back with mining lasers while they walled themselves up in a dead end tunnel and called for help. The then, "Captain Kellogg", volunteered to go into the tunnels leading two squads of Marines on a rescue mission. In the citation of her EGA Medal of Valor, it describes how Kellogg and her Marines fought their way down to the miners. Then extracted them, and in a running battle brought all of the surviving miners to the surface.

Kellogg and two other Marines then fought a delaying action inside the mine entrance until engineers could rig charges to seal the opening. In pulling her last wounded man out before the explosion, teeth and claws badly mauled Kellogg slashing the left side of her body. Kellogg earned the EGAMV, (Earth / Giann Alliance Medal of Valor), a promotion, a new prosthetic leg, and the assignment at the Academy.

The Commandant studied Mills with a hard look that seemed to weigh his soul. She then reached into a basket on the left side of her desk and removed an information disk with the name Mills, Charles P. labeled across the top. Kellogg placed the disk in a loading slot and reviewed the contents on her monitor for a few moments then spoke.

"Mills, I wanted to see you personally, to see if I could find a Marine inside that uniform that is worth salvaging. Let us review shall we? You have five demerits for rude behavior, ten demerits for arguing with other Midshipmen. Five demerits for tardiness and let's not forget, ten days extra duty for sneaking into Gunnery Sergeant Hin's quarters and removing the volume control from her translator." Kellogg gave Mills an icy stare. "When are you going to grow up son?"

Mills started to open his mouth, "But . . ." Kellogg cut him off right there. "MIDSHIPMAN DID I GIVE YOU PERMISSION TO SPEAK?" Mills closed his mouth so fast he bit his tongue. Kellogg looked back at the contents of the file and began quietly.

"You have qualified as an expert on the weapons range with the classes' highest score. You hold the record time for the confidence course and first in your class in martial arts." Kellogg gave Mills a hard glance. "Now for grades, **last** in your class for military history, tactics, small unit leadership, ship propulsion, astronomy, physics, biochemistry, and last but not least, **failing** astral navigation." Kellogg gave Mills a disgusted look. "How in the hell do you expect to **lead** Marines if you don't even know where you are?"

Mills once again started to open his mouth but thought better of it and just sucked on his painful tongue. He could feel sweat rolling down his spine to the middle of his back. The room felt like the hot prairie of the Texas panhandle in August. Mills then realized his mouth was so dry he probably could not talk now if he had to. Kellogg stared at Mills and watched him sweat. She just stared at him for a few more moments to help ensure Mills was getting the full benefit of the silence.

Then, she finally spoke. "Midshipman Mills, You must realize, graduation for your class is not very far off. Between now and graduation you **will** get no more demerits. You **will** get along with the other Midshipmen. Lastly you **will** pass astral navigation!" The Commandant pushed back her chair and stood. To Mills it seemed like she loomed over him like the specter of death. "DO YOU HEAR ME MIDSHIPMAN?"

"MA'AM, YES MA'AM!"

"Midshipman, you are dismissed." Mills made an immediate about face and marched briskly out of the office. It took all of his self-control not to run!

Immediately after Mills exited the office Sergeant Major Logan walked into the doorway knocked twice on the frame and walked into the room. Logan chuckled as he walked in. He was sure glad the Old Lady was not giving him an ass chewing. He knew the Old Lady very well. The Sergeant Major admired and respected her immensely. Logan had been with the Old Lady ever since she was a new Second Lieutenant. Corporal Logan was the last wounded man that Kellogg had pulled from that mineshaft on Spiegel 2.

Logan walked over to the Commandant's desk and set down a data disk containing the daily reports for her review. Kellogg still stood seemingly lost in thought. Logan waited for a moment then queried. "Well Skipper, do you think it will do any good?" She continued that thousand kilometer stare. "I don't know Sergeant Major, I just don't know."

Kellogg sat down picked up the data disk and put it into the computer slot. As Logan turned to leave, he heard her sigh, then mumble. "**Kids**, what's the Corps going to do with these kids!" Logan chuckled again on his way out.

Chapter 6

LEADERSHIP

GUNNERY Sergeant Hin found Maryann alone at the weapons practice range. The long indoor range has individual firing cubicles where all types of weapons are used. Automatic targets up to three hundred meters away keep track of the shooters score. Ten meters behind the firing cubicles are several weapons cleaning and maintenance tables. Hall is the last one to complete cleaning her weapon after the afternoon of target practice. When she saw Hin, Maryann rose to attention and awaited the Gunny's instruction. Hin walked over sat down on an empty ammunition box and looked at hall. "Be as you were, Midshipman Hall."

Maryann returned to polishing the remaining spots of cleaning fluid from her weapon. Hin watched her for a while then spoke. "Midshipman Hall, may I have your opinion of Midshipman Mills?" Maryann turned to Hin with a sour facial expression.

"I'm sure Midshipman Mills is an able Officer Candidate, Gunnery Sergeant Hin."

Hin studied Hall without expression as Maryann polished an already immaculate weapon. "Humans have a wonderful expression; I believe its cut the bull!"

"What do you want me to say?"

"How about telling me the truth?" Maryann looked down at the cleaning rag she still had in her hands. "Ok, I think he's a jerk! He's a loud mouthed egotistical chauvinist with the opinion that he's the Creator's gift to the universe!"

"That sounds like a truthful opinion. What if all the bluster, and over confidence you see is just hiding a lonely man that is constantly looking for acceptance?" Maryann stared at Hin for a moment in disbelief and then doubled over in laughter. It took a moment but she finally composed herself. "Gunnery Sergeant Hin! You've got to be kidding!" Hin gave her a blank stare. "Have you found that I have a propensity for humor?"

The smile fell from her face and Maryann neatly folded the cleaning rag in her lap. "No, Gunnery Sergeant Hin, I guess not. But why tell me?"

"Midshipman Mills is failing Astral Navigation." Gunny Hin let that sink in for a moment. "Final exams are coming up in just a few planetary cycles. It will be the last chance for Midshipman Mills to pull up his marks and graduate from the Academy." Hin paused ensuring she had Maryann's full attention.

"The Mission of the Academy is not just to train Marine Officers. It also gives us the core values that guide us. Some of those values are Leadership, Loyalty and Teamwork. Many have thought that the motto of the Corps, (Semper Fidelis), means loyalty to a government or a planet. However, what (Always Faithful), **really** means is faithful to the Corps, faithful to each other. If you ever have the bad luck to be stuck in a hot landing zone on some Creator forgotten planet taking fire from all sides, you will realize that the Marines at your back are the most important beings in the universe. You **will** be faithful to them and they **will** be faithful to you. No Marine ever goes it alone. This Corps of brothers will carry on that tradition as long as there are Marines!"

Gunnery Sergeant Hin rose from her seat on the box. "Those in your Squad that don't have duty this weekend have forty eight hours of liberty. I highly recommend you take some time to relax, enjoy and think. You are dismissed." Maryann came to her feet and slowly walked towards the exit hatch. Just as she reached it, she heard.

"Oh there is one more thing."

Maryann paused and turned allowing Hin to continue. "You are Midshipman Mills' Squad Leader. When I was speaking of leadership, I meant **yours** not **his**. Midshipman Hall I do believe Midshipman Mills **will** pass Astral Navigation!" Maryann slowly turned then stepped through the hatch.

Returning to the Squad's compartment Maryann found almost everyone getting into his or her dress uniforms preparing for liberty. Maryann found John Phillips sitting on his rack dressed in duty utilities. "You have the duty tonight Sailor Boy?"

"Yeah Pug, Tommy Chin and I will keep the Academy information deck safe tonight from all sorts of dangerous riff-raff!"

Midshipman Thomas Chin from the State of East Asia grimaced as he worked to pin collar devices denoting him as a Midshipman, on his duty utilities. Chin responded as he looked in a mirror and struggled with the pins. "Such a treat, I get to sit and answer communicators all night next to Phillips!" Having finally gotten the last device in the right spot he turned to Maryann. "I don't understand. Why can't they just have the main computer answer them?"

Yolanda Pierce who was one bunk over paused for a moment while dressing. "I think it's just to keep all those **hot** Asian men off the streets!" Tommy made a surprised face and John chuckled. Unbuttoning her dirty utilities and placing her boots below her rack for future polishing Maryann stood up and then looked around. "Hey, has anyone seen Mills?"

Shaking her head Pierce turned to Hall. "He hasn't come back here after his meeting with the Commandant; perhaps he went straight out on liberty. What about you Hall, what are you going to do?" Maryann stood there with a thoughtful look undecided. Yolanda walked over fastening the last two buttons of her tunic. She gestured at Phillips and Chin. "They have duty tonight. Jim Bower is going with Tan to watch some vintage historic videos. How about you and I go to the Mine Shaft and have a cool beverage or two? Mills hangs out there perhaps we will see him. That is if you're **really** interested in seeing him."

The Mine Shaft is a bar not far from the Academy in the vast underground complex. As the name suggests many of the civilian miners that work on Europa frequent the place. Maryann gave Yolanda a doubtful look so Pierce gave her a playful slap on the shoulder. "Oh come on it will be fun!" As Maryann went to shower and change, she thought. *Those are famous last words!*

Jim Bower grew up as a farmer. His father was a farmer, as was his father. Farming went back in Jim's family as far as the great Oklahoma land rush. He grew up in what used to be Oklahoma in the middle of the old United States. The consolidation of countries into Continental States had been important for equal representation in the Earth/Giann Alliance Council and for trade. It also stopped the nationalist bickering that used up resources and had held Earth back in developing star exploration. The old countries of the United States, Canada and Mexico were now the State of North America. The British Common Wealth is no longer composed of independent countries. It is the State of Great Briton.

Jim, like many people where he grew up had never met a Giann. His first interaction was with his Squad member Tan. As Jim and Tan became friends, he enjoyed learning more about the Giann and their culture. Jim found Tan open and informative on all aspects of Giann society. As they left the Squad Bay, for the theatre Jim could not resist asking more questions. "Tan, you and your twin are male. Do you guys go out on dates with female sets of twins?"

"Not exactly James. Giann do not mate physically nor do we have male/female social or marriage bonds. When male sets of twins are of the correct maturity, they find an appropriate female twin set. The two sets then form a mating relationship. They then excrete genetic bonding fluids that are mixed and incubated. Another twin set is produced that could be either male or female. There are no mixed twin sets where one is male and the other female. In Giann culture, there is no differentiation of work for males or females. The large females are formidable warriors as are the males. In addition, they and are just as capable and efficient doing heavy labor. This is the same for the smaller sets of twins and their professions.

Jim gave Tan a look of mild embarrassment. "That is a little more information than I needed but it's nice to know. What about who gets to be in charge. How do you pick your leaders?"

"All the Giann work together as equal associates. The only distinction for leadership comes from experience. The most experienced Giann always lead the less experienced follow. That is why the Giann Planetary Council, the leaders of our society, is the Council of Elders. Each set of twin's works in the society at the same experience level. James you appear to be a little perplexed."

"Tan, you're a large Giann and so is Gunny Hin. However, without your uniforms I would not be able to tell you apart."

"There are very subtle differences, but a human may not notice. Of course, through telepathy all Giann instantly know if they are communicating with a male or female. As you know for the accommodation of Human society, the male Giann wear silver translators that have a Human male sounding voice. The female Giann wear a gold translator that has a Human female sounding voice. It was felt that these changes were important for the working relationship of Giann and Humans. The Giann in the military services also wear their service insignia on the left side of their translator."

Arriving at the theatre the conversation stopped. After putting the proper amount of credits in the entrance kiosk, Jim reflected. "Boy there's a lot about the Giann I didn't know. It seems the more I learn, the more questions I have!"

"We all learn daily James. I will enjoy watching the recordings of these ancient Humans with you and perhaps learn something more."

"You bet Tan. It just doesn't get better than the Three Stooges. You're in for a treat."

Chapter 7

EGAS INQUISITIVE

THE Wardroom changed from stunned silence to a blur of motion. Michael ran to Angela, gently lifted her from her chair, and cradled her head as he set her on the table. Commander Moore the ship's Surgeon and Dr. Sen the Lead Expedition Surgeon rushed to Angela's side. Phillips picked up his communicator and ordered. "Medical Team to the Wardroom, bring along a Ship's Gurney!"

Dr. Chase almost knocked Phillips over coming around the conference table to Angela's side. Dr. Moore shouted, "GIVE US SOME ROOM!" Dr. Sen went to where Mike Stil was holding Angela's head with his arm. "Excuse me Commander if I may have her head please."

Dr. Sen gently reached his long hands under Angela's head. He straightened her spine, which opened her airway. "We need to turn her slowly on her left side. Commander Stil, please you will need to back away a little bit so we can turn her your way."

Mike Stil appeared in shock and moved his mouth wordlessly. Henry Chase had come up behind Stil and with his hands under Mike's arms slowly pulled him backwards to make room. Captain Phillips glanced at all the staff that was still in the room. "CLEAR THIS COMPARTMENT **NOW!**"

Those staff members that had frozen in their seats quickly followed the others out of the Wardroom. Angela moaned with both hands grasping her stomach. Dr. Moore felt for her pulse and noted the small pool of blood on the table as they had turned Angela. Dr. Sen at Angela's head quietly instructed her. "Dr. Stil, slow deep breaths please, slow deep breaths." Shortly after the exodus of the staff, the Medical Team entered with the Ship's Gurney and an Emergency Trauma pack.

The Ship's Gurney is a floating padded stretcher. The bottom of the stretcher has an adjustable field projector that can nullify the ship's artificial gravity so the stretcher can float at whatever height desired. A Hospital Corpsman pushed the decrease arrow on the operation pad and the gurney gently settled to table height next to Angela for the ease of moving her. Dr. Moore took command of the Medical Team at once.

"Give her oxygen at 12 liters per minute. Start two IV's, make one ringers lactate the other normal saline. Put her on the portable fetal monitor, the portable cardiac monitor and the oxygen monitor. We'll transport her down to Sickbay on her left side." Michael kneeled next to Angela as close to her as possible gently taking her hand. Angela moaned and opened her eyes. "Michael!"

"I'm right here babe." He gently squeezed her hand.

Chapter 8

THE MINE SHAFT

(Europa)

CHUCK Mills sat at a corner table by himself staring at the fourth, double whisky on the rocks. The Mine Shaft is a small hole in the wall bar in the commercial civilian sector of the Europa complex. It has a long plastic and synthetic wood bar. The bar, chipped and scarred from years of abuse from intoxicated patrons runs along one wall near the door. The rough metal floor slants slightly towards a central drain screen so the owner can hose down the floor every night after closing. Plastic imitation wood tables crowd the rest of the room filled with off duty workers.

The plasticrete walls of the room, once painted with scenic palm trees now covered with unfunny graffiti and dirt. At intervals along the walls are coin operated monitors, which display scantily clad women dancing to old favorites. Mills paid no attention to the crowd of off shift miners and other civilians determined to get drunk in the early evening. Mills spoke to the glass leaving wet rings on the seldom-cleaned table. "Well it looks like I blew it again."

Mills thought back to when he was a child. He remembered when he was a little boy in the area still called Texas. He loved to spend time with the person he most admired in the entire world his dad. He didn't see his dad too often because he was gone a lot. However, when he came home Charlie's dad would take him fishing or camping and tell him about all the wonderful places he had seen. Charlie's dad was a Marine. He would tell Charlie about the strange planets, amazing plants and animals he encountered. He would explain how he and his buddies in the Squad helped each other through exciting adventures. Charlie always knew what he wanted to be when he grew up. Charlie wanted to be a Marine, just like his dad.

Charlie was about eleven the last time his dad left. Charlie remembered that as he packed his gear his dad said that he probably would not be gone too long this time. He said where they were going was not too far away and they were only going to help some miners that were stuck in a tunnel. Charlie remembered seeing his dad in uniform waving as he left. "I'll be back in two shakes, take care of your mom; I'll see you then sport!"

A lunar cycle later, Charlie came home from school and found his mother in the living room crying. There were three strangers in the room with her a Marine Chaplin, Marine Captain and a Marine Sergeant Major. The Marine Chaplin attempted to offer some comfort. "He gave his life in the bravest tradition of the Corps." Charlie slowly went back outside, sat down on the front steps, and cried. He had lost his best friend in the whole world.

As Chuck grew up his mom did her best to raise him but he just seemed to get himself in trouble. One of the few things that helped him to stay out of trouble was his talent for sports. When Chuck received a sport, scholarship to college his mom was overjoyed. Although he did well in sports, Chuck didn't have many friends and got through college with almost minimal grades. After graduation, Chuck's mom cried when he said he was going to apply to the Marine Corps Academy. Never less,

Chuck was determined to go so she gave him a hug and wished him well. Chuck knew selection for the Academy with the low marks he had in college was going to take a lot of luck. However, he had figured he should be able to get by just as he had in college.

What Chuck didn't know was when he applied to the Academy his mother wrote a letter to her husband's old Squad Leader, Don Logan. She wrote of the difficulties she had raising Charles, the difficulties he had in school. She also wrote about the fears she had of Charles' selection to the Academy due to his low marks in College. Sergeant Major Logan wrote Mary Lou Mills and explained what he could do to help. He said he would submit the proper paperwork on Chuck's behalf for the son of a Marine that had died heroically in the line of duty. Logan did however add that he felt it would be best for the boy if he didn't know they had communicated. Chuck was the last one selected for entrance in the Academy that solar cycle.

As Mills wallowed in his current state of depression, he noticed Hall and Pierce come in the door. Mills ducked down a little but with all the people standing in the crowed bar he doubted they could see him. He thought. *Great, just what I need they probably heard that I'm about to be sacked and they can't pass up the opportunity to give me crap about it.*

When the rotund server with a sour expression returned, Mills ordered another drink. *Well, screw them; I know that I can be a better Marine than any of them are. They don't like me anyway. I don't care. I don't need anybody.* Mills tossed back his fifth drink and sat studying the fingerprint-clouded glass.

Hall and Pierce walked up to the one small space at the bar that was open. The large obese bartender, red faced and sweating profusely finished giving a round to a group of drunken miners. He eyed the women, frowned at their uniforms and grunted. "What'll it be?" Pierce held up two fingers, "Two beers." Maryann glanced around and shook her head, "Geese, what a garden spot. If you put all these guys together you just might come up with one set of teeth."

"Give it a chance the place will grow on you."

"I just hope they have medication for that."

Pierce chuckled as the beer arrived. The fat bartender slammed the containers on the bar spilling some of the contents. He used a dirty rag he kept thrown across his shoulder to wipe up the spill. "That'll be four credits."

As Pierce dug in her pocket for the credit chips, the bartender wiped the sweat off his face with the dirty rag on his shoulder. Without a pause, he picked up a beer glass and started polishing it with the same rag. Pierce pushed over the credits raising an eyebrow at the dirty rag. The bartender ignored the look and asked. "Do you want a glass with that?"

"No, I think we'll pass."

The bartender gave them one more disapproving look then left to appease another group clamoring for service. Maryann had just finished her first sip of beer when she heard behind her a loud drunken voice. "Hey Al, I just love women in uniform how about you?"

"Yeah Red, they remind me of Girl Scouts."

Maryann looked over at Yolanda who just rolled her eyes and frowned. The voice grew louder and more insistent. "Hey baby, I said I just love women in uniform. Let me buy you a drink!" Pierce replied over her shoulder. "No thanks buddy we're fine."

"I'm not talking to you. I'm talking to your little friend here."

Maryann felt a large hand on her shoulder. She turned to brush the hand away and stared at one of the biggest men she had ever seen. The guy had to be even a head taller than Yolanda! He had broken brown teeth; dark blood shot eyes and a grin that looked like a predator stalking a meal. The guy smelled as if he hadn't showered in cycles and with the black grime on his coveralls looked like he had just come from the mines. Maryann attempted to push the hand from her shoulder. "As my friend said, no thank you we're fine."

The grip tightened as rock like fingers and thumb dug into her tunic. "Now don't be like that, me and my friends just want to have a friendly drink with ya!" Maryann looked past his shoulder at the three equally filthy grinning men behind him. Maryann tried to ignore the pain in her shoulder as his grip tightened. "Please remove your hand. We're not looking for any trouble here." The miner glared down at her and snarled. "What's the matter? Are you bitches too good for us?"

The bar grew quiet as everyone began to notice the drama unfolding. Maryann glanced to her side and saw two of the miners begin to close in around the other side of Pierce. Yolanda looked back and forth between them like a mongoose between two cobras. Hall turned her attention back to Brown Teeth. "If you don't want any trouble then all you have to do is be friendly!" Hall stared at his alcohol-dulled eyes and considered the chances of a blow to the Adams apple when she heard a voice to her right.

"She said take the hand off of her, shit for brains!"

The miner released the hold on Hall as he turned to face this new threat. Maryann saw Mills standing to her right not quite a pace away. He appeared relaxed with his arms to his side and his body at a slight angle to the miner. Maryann noted the knees slightly bent and weight distributed evenly on the balls of his feet. Maryann thought, *classic defensive stance*, as she slowly slipped her hands behind her back gripping the edge of the bar. Brown Teeth clenched his fists and snarled menacingly. "This ain't any of your business boy!" Chuck gave a slow smile. "Ah, but your wrong again shit for brains. That's **my**, Squad Leader you're bothering!"

The miner bellowed and launched himself at Mills grabbing for Chuck's tunic with both hands. Chuck stepped in between the miner's outstretched arms grabbing the man's coveralls with both hands. As the two of them collided Mills slammed his forehead into Brown Teeth's nose breaking it with a resounding crack. At the same time, Mills took his back leg and jammed his knee into the miner's groin. The big man kept coming forward from the inertia of his charge. Chuck dropped and rolled backwards pushing up with the knee in the miners groin flipping the man over him to land flat on his back.

Hall and Pierce didn't wait for an invitation. Pierce took the bottle in her hand and smashed it over the head of the miner nearest her. The man crumpled like an imploding soufflé. His buddy threw a right arm punch at Yolanda's head. She ducked under the blow slipped an arm up under his armpit and behind his neck slamming his face down on the bar. He slipped to the floor like clothes from a wringer. Hall had grabbed the edge of the bar with both hands, swinging her legs up and kicked the forth miner straight in the face. The kick sent him flying backwards over a crowded table tangling him up with surprised customers, spilling pitchers of cheap beer and shattering glasses.

The bar was suddenly still, the only sound coming from the tinny speakers of the monitors on the walls. Chuck stood up and looked at Brown Teeth lying on his back bleeding from his broken nose, holding his testicles moaning. The two men at Yolanda's feet didn't move. The last miner sent flying over the table by Maryann sat up looking groggy spitting out teeth. Maryann looked around the room and saw that the shock of the quick encounter was beginning to wear off. Some of the other miners were beginning to mumble between themselves and group together. Hall made a quick decision. "LET'S GO!"

Hall, Pierce and Mills headed out the door in a sprint! Outside the bar, still running down the passageway back towards the Academy, Maryann grabbed a hand of Pierce and Mills who were running on each side of her. Continuing down the passageway past closed storefronts with both of them in tow Maryann laughed. Chuck gave her a confused look and shouted. "WHERE ARE WE GOING?"

"WE'VE GOT ASTRAL NAVIGATION TO STUDY!"

Chapter 9

EGAS INQUISITIVE

To the cry of, "Captain on the Bridge!" Phillips entered from his Ready Room. He walked over to the communications console where the last night's Officer of the Deck, Lieutenant (Junior Grade) Purcell was reviewing the night's communiqués. He came to attention at Phillips' approach. "Good morning Captain."

"Good morning Mr. Purcell, report please."

Purcell gave a brief summary of the night Bridge Watch including the status of the ship any and all problems encountered during the Watch and then a recap of the projected Orders for this morning. "Sir currently in preparation for the missions scheduled for today is shuttles 1 through 3. Shuttles 1 and 2 will be carrying Dr. Chase an advance party of his scientific personnel and Major Pel with two Squads of Marines to the surface of the planet.

Purcell handed Phillips a copy of the mission's manifests. "These are the manifests of personnel on each shuttle. Shuttle 3 will carry Dr. Stil's assistant Ms. Holmes and two able seamen Petty Officer Kipp and Seaman Arnald. They will do the examination of the satellite. All three shuttles are scheduled for launch at 0800."

"Very well, and what is the status of Dr. Stil?"

Purcell quickly reviewed his notes. "The Ship's Surgeon reports that Dr. Stil is in stable condition. Uh, let's see, her fetal heart rate is fine and further decisions will follow this morning. In addition, Lieutenant Commander Stil is with his wife in Sickbay and Lieutenant Rin will be assuming his duties on the Bridge today."

"Very well Mr. Purcell, when you are relieved by Lieutenant Rin please inform her I will be in Sickbay."

"Aye sir, will do."

Phillips turned and exited the Bridge heading amidships and down three levels to the Sickbay. Arriving at the Sickbay, Phillips found Dr's Moore and Sen talking with Mike Stil in the Physician's office. Stil appeared disheveled and exhausted. It was obvious that he had spent the night at Angela's side. Through the observation window, Phillips could see Angela in bed with IV lines and several different types of monitors attached. Commander Moore stopped talking when Phillips approached. "Good morning Gentlemen. I just stopped in to get an update on how Dr. Stil is doing and ask your plan of action."

Dr. Moore took the lead. "Morning sir, Dr. Sen is far more experienced in these matters and has taken over the primary care of Angela. Dr. Sen?"

"Captain, Dr. Stil currently is resting quietly. We have been monitoring her for fetal distress and treating her for shock. Dr. Stil has both previa and partial abruption of the placenta."

Phillips raised an eyebrow in a questioning look so Dr. Sen continued with a more basic explanation. "Previa is a condition where the placenta has developed over the uterine entrance. Abruption is a condition where part or the entire placenta has pulled away from the uterine wall. Vaginal delivery is not possible if the placenta is blocking the entrance of the uterus. Since the abruption is only partial, the fetus is still receiving nutrients and we have been monitoring the fetal heart rate closely for signs of distress. Signs of distress would signal that the abruption is getting worse."

"Yesterday Dr. Stil began having contractions, which initiated the abruption. We have been giving her intravenous magnesium sulfate to suppress her contractions and we have been treating her for shock. We are currently preparing her for delivery by caesarian section."

"Is Dr. Stil in any danger?"

"I do not believe so. Her vital signs have stabilized and the fetus is doing well so our plans are to take her to surgery this morning." Dr. Sen nodded to Mike Stil. "As we were just saying, now that both mother and child are stabilized the prognosis is very good." Phillips looked out at Angela again. "When will you take her in for surgery?"

"As soon as her preparations are complete, about 0800."

Phillips turned to Michael Stil. "Mike you look beat. You have a couple hours before the surgery, how about a quick shower and some rest?" Stil looked at Phillips with puffy blood shot eyes filled with worry. "Thanks for your concern Captain, however with the Doctor's permission I'll shower here." Commander Moore nodded at the request. "Certainly Mike and I'll have the Corpsman pick you up some chow and coffee."

Mike Stil nodded in thanks and went back out to sit by Angela. Phillips turned to Moore and Sen. "Very well Gentlemen, please keep me apprised of any developments I'll be on the Bridge."

Chapter 10

DOWN TO ROMEO

CAPTAIN Pel felt the small bump as the shuttle landed in the large clearing about half a kilometer from the nearest dome. Captain Pel had one Squad of Marines and half of the Scientific Team in shuttle 1. In his briefing before leaving the Inquisitive, Pell instructed the Science Team to wait aboard the shuttles as the Marines deployed outside. As a precaution, the Marines wore their armored environmental suits and the Science Team pressure suits. Even though the atmosphere cleared the science probes, regulations required the precaution when landing on an unknown planet.

The back ramp of the shuttle went down and his Squad scrambled out dividing right and left. Leaving one Marine in the shuttle barely restraining the eager scientists Pel stepped on the new world. Stepping to the side of the shuttle Pel could see Gunnery Sergeant Bin with her Squad already deployed around the other shuttle. Gunny Bin nodded her helmet and Pel raised his arm and made a circle motion with his arm and one finger up. One Fire Team from each Squad headed out from the landing area sweeping to the left. As the two Fire Teams swept around the area, the rest of the Marines kneeled in a rough circle around the landing zone with weapons at the ready.

Waiting for the safety sweep to conclude, Captain Pell took the opportunity to look around at the unfamiliar landscape.

Pell knew from the orbit mapping images that the plain where they landed was actually the middle of an enormous flat ancient crater. The soil appeared reddish brown with small spindly bushes growing haphazardly across the landscape. Looking across the distance with the enhanced optics of his helmet Pel could see occasional stunted appearing trees. Walking over to the nearest bush Pel looked at the small oblong leaves moving in a lazy breeze. The leaves are a grey brown with green colored veins traveling out of the stems. Seeing the green color Pel thought perhaps there is some chlorophyll here after all.

As Pel examined the bush, his communicator earpiece came to life. "Captain Pel, this is Corporal Mason we have swept out to one thousand meters no sign of threats, animal or plant."

"Ok Corporal, return to the perimeter." Tuning to the shuttle frequency Pel advised the crews that the scientists could safely leave the shuttles. Of course, Chase was the first off the shuttle trying to look at everything at once. The scientists set up their equipment and retested the air and soil as per the landing protocols. Once given the all clear, everyone was glad to remove the suits. The shuttle crews continued to monitor sensors giving telemetry to the Inquisitive and monitoring for any threats up to a thousand kilometers around the site.

The scientists broke up into three groups. Chase wanted to take a team immediately up to the nearby dome leaving a group by the shuttles to investigate the soil and weather. The third group is to go to the ancient rim of the crater and procurer samples for later analysis by Angela Stil. Pel sent Gunny Bin and one Squad with Chase and Corporal Mason with two Fire Teams of Marines with the group going to the rim. Captain Pel and the remaining Marines stayed with the group at the shuttles.

Chapter 11

EGAS INQUISITIVE

(Bridge, 0830)

CAPTAIN Phillips sat in his chair gingerly sipping hot black coffee as he watched the progress of shuttle 3 on the monitor. It was matching velocity with the satellite. Ensign Vicof was maneuvering the shuttle in close so Holmes and her accompanying crewmen wouldn't have far to go for their examination of the object. Phillips watched in calm admiration. *Damn that kid is good! I told him one hundred meters off and I bet he's within a few centimeters of that!*

After the launch of shuttle 3, Phillips had taken the Inquisitive into a higher orbit a little more than one thousand kilometers away. It was a minor precaution but Phillips was always a cautious man. Chief Bin interrupted his thoughts. "Captain you have an incoming communication from Major Pel on the surface of the planet."

"Put him on Chief."

On his monitor, the image of shuttle 3 disappeared and the face of Major Pel at the communications console of shuttle 1 replaced it. Major Pel was brief. "Captain both shuttles are down safe. I have set a perimeter and Dr. Chase and his party are beginning their exploration of the dome approximately five hundred meters away."

"Very well Major Pel, carry on."

"Thank you, sir, Pel out."

Phillips switched the screen back to Shuttle 3 and the people who were now floating toward the object. He then switched his view to the external monitors of Shuttle 3. Phillips watched as first Holmes and the crewmen recorded the surface of the satellite with their suit cams from all angles. Curious, Phillips adjusted his monitor to pick up the audio recording that Holmes was making of her examination.

"The object has the appearance of stone with the marbling consistent with igneous type rock. The color appears a brownish black and the surface smooth. The surface is odd however, it lacks the normal pitting or weathering expected of a mineral or metallic object in space. Upon closer examination 'let me pan in on this', what appeared to be marbling at a distance appear to be curved lines etched into the surface kind of like a drawing. I'm moving closer to examine these markings."

Phillips watched as Holmes moved to within a meter of the object. The lines took on the appearance of a face. "It's approximately a meter high and a meter across. It has the appearance of a representation of a misshapen humanoid face with long up turned ears or perhaps bone like structures or horns. The representations of the eyes stare straight. The broad flattened area that could be a nose is slightly off center in the face and what could be a lipless mouth filled with long irregular teeth appears in a fierce grimace."

As Phillips looked at the distorted face, Chief Bin interrupted again. "Captain, I have audio for you from Major Pel."

"Very well Chief, put it on."

The picture from Holmes' helmet cam stayed on the screen as Pel's voice came through the speaker. As Phillips watched, Holmes moved closer and her hand was gesturing toward the face as if explaining the formation of the mouth.

"Captain, while Dr. Chase is examining the dome some of his team has been examining the nearest crater." Phillips continued watching Holmes as she slowly approached the surface of the object. "Yes Major Pel?"

"The team at the crater has confirmed although it is very old the crater was not caused by meteorite impact or other natural phenomena."

Phillips continued watching Holmes as she swept her hand in front of the mouth continuing her monolog. "Go on Major Pel."

"Captain the team has verified that it is a bomb crater!"

Phillips continued to watch Holmes on the screen and repeated to himself. "It's a bomb crater?"

Then Phillips sat up in his chair with a start! "CHIEF, OFF AUDIO WITH PEL, PUT ME THROUGH TO SHUTTLE 3 NOW!"

To Phillips everything seemed to be moving in slow motion. He watched as Holmes made another sweeping motion with her arm and pointed to a corner of the face. He heard Chief Bin say, "Captain, I have Ensign Vicof in Shuttle 3." Phillips stared in horror and shouted, as Holmes' hand got closer to the object. "VICOF, CANCEL THE MISSION, GET THOSE PEOPLE OUT OF . . ." With the last sweep of her hand, Holmes touched the object.

Chapter 12

EGAFMC (TA), EUROPA

Cₕᵤᴄᴋ Mills frowned in the mirror as he fastened the last few buttons on his dress tunic. "I hate these dog and pony shows." Yolanda Pierce glided up next to him adjusting her uniform. "Hey, don't hog the mirror. I would think you of all people would be glad to see graduation!"

Mills still didn't look any brighter, "Yeah, yeah, yeah."

Maryann sat down next to John on his rack. John was struggling with a perfectly polished new pair of dress boots. "Well Sailor Boy, what kind of assignment would you like to get with your first set of Orders?" Phillips finally secured the boots and looked up. "You know I really haven't thought much about where I would like to be assigned. I have given some thought to where I know I wouldn't like to be assigned." Maryann cocked her head and looked at him. "And that is?"

"I wouldn't like to be assigned to an on planet garrison or training base. I would rather be out with the Fleet. I want to see a little bit of this galaxy not sit behind a desk or lead some type of ceremonial guard."

"So you long for action and adventure, fighting desperate battles on unknown planets against terrible foes!"

John felt his cheeks warming and chuckled. "Gee I guess you've got me there! No, I believe I would rather just be out where things are interesting." Hall stood up and looked down at him.

53

"You know Tommy Chin told me that there is this ancient Asian curse. It went, (May you live in interesting times.)" As Maryann turned and headed towards the hatch, she added. "I just hope it doesn't get too interesting for you Sailor Boy!"

At the hatch, Maryann stopped and turned around. "All right people lets fall out to the Main Hanger Bay. We've got less than ten minutes before we graduate and get sent out to protect the galaxy!"

The Main Hanger Bay is a large cavernous room with a sealed retractable roof. It's the launching and storage hanger for the Academy's shuttles. It is also great for large ceremonies such as Academy Graduations with its field size floor. When Colonel Kellogg entered the Main Hanger Bay, Sergeant Major Logan was waiting patiently to the right of the hatch. As she entered, he hollered. "ATTENTION ON DECK!"

The graduating Platoon with the rest of the Midshipmen Corps came to attention with the thunder of heels snapping together. There was one change to the proscribed uniform of the Platoon that was graduating. On the left breast of their tunic tunics instead of the Academy insignia, they now wore the Alliance Fleet Marine Corps insignia. The Sergeant Major strode to in front of the Midshipman Platoon Leader. He stopped at attention and the Platoon Leader saluted. "Alpha Platoon and Midshipman Corps all present and/or accounted for **Sir!**"

Sergeant Major Logan returned the salute did an about face and saluted Colonel Kellogg. "Alpha Platoon and Midshipman Corps all present and/or accounted for **Ma'am!**" Colonel Kellogg returned the salute and stepped up to the podium flanked by the EGAF and the EGAFMC Standards.

"Midshipmen, staff and guests, we are here today for the graduation and commissioning of Alpha Platoon. They are this solar cycles graduating class of the EGAFMC Academy.

These Midshipmen have worked hard over the last four solar cycles to complete the Academy's rigorous requirements. They have learned the basics of the Corp's leadership qualities and principles. I say the 'basics', because the learning doesn't end here, it is only the beginning."

"We live in a universe that is constantly changing and is full of unknown hazards. As the Alliance Fleet explores further out in our galaxy there will be more unknown challenges every cycle. The mission of these new Officers will be to continue to learn, adapt and overcome the challenges that they will encounter at whatever assignment awaits them. There is no doubt in my mind that these Officers will embrace this mission in the best traditions of the Corps. The Adjutant will now swear in the new Officers."

The Adjutant commanded the entire graduating Platoon to raise their right hand and repeat the oath of Allegiance, Loyalty and Fidelity. At the completion of the oath, Colonel Kellogg snapped her right fist to the Corps insignia on the left pocket of her tunic! "SEMPER FI!" The new Officers and every other Marine in the hanger bay pounded the insignia on the left pocket of their uniform with their right fist! **"SEMPER FI!"**

After the sound died away, Colonel Kellogg continued. "Sergeant Major Logan will now commence with the replacement of the Officer's insignia of rank, and distribute their first set of Orders."

Gunnery Sergeant Hin rolled a table in front of the graduating Platoon. On the table were a stack of orders and a new set of Second Lieutenant's bars for each new Officer. As she called each Officer's name, they would march to the spot in front of the Sergeant Major. The Sergeant Major and Gunny Hin would each pin one bar to the end of the Officer's tunic epaulets. At the completion of the pinning, the Sergeant Major would hand a set of Orders to the Officer. Both Logan and Hin would then come to attention, salute and then add, "Congratulations, Sir or Ma'am."

This continued until the entire Platoon was standing back at attention with their new devices of rank and Orders in their left hand. Gunny Hin rolled the table back out of the way and Logan returned to his position behind Colonel Kellogg. Kellogg stood there for a moment looking at the expectant faces then smiled. "Congratulations Marines and good luck," then added, **"DISMISSED!"**

As the Staff and the Academy Midshipmen left the Hanger Bay, the members of the graduating Platoon walked around and congratulated each other. Maryann ran over and gave Phillips a big hug. "Well Sailor Boy, where are you assigned?" John glanced at his orders. "First Platoon assigned to the new Marine Landing Ship EGAS Starfury. How about you Pug?"

"Third Platoon on the Starfury isn't it great? Yolanda Pierce will go to the Second Platoon and Mills to the Fourth!"

As they walked, back to the Squad's quarters John informed Maryann. "I hear the Starfury has the new combat shuttles. Each one can carry a full Platoon of Marines. The shuttles have combat armor and twin energy cannons one set in the nose and one set in a top turret. They are specially built to handle hot landing zones."

"That's comforting, but I hope we will never have to go into a hot LZ."

Hall and Phillips returned to the Squad Bay and found everyone already packing their gear. Pierce stopped carefully placing uniform parts in her Sea Bag as they entered. "Well we have fourteen planetary cycles Leave time before we report to the Starfury. What are you guys going to do?"

Maryann opened her locker. "I'm taking Leave on Earth. I'm going to spend some time with the family and eat all the non-processed fruit and vegetables I can get my hands on!" John sat on his bunk and unrolled his Sea Bag as he spoke. "I guess I'll visit my mother for a while. My father has been out with the Inquisitive since before I joined the Academy. It may take another two or three solar cycles for him to return. I just hope the Starfury is still in port when he returns."

Chuck Mills is across the compartment stuffing gear and clothes in his bag. "After I drop off the dirty laundry at home there's this great little bar just outside of Old El Paso. It has a stool with my name on it. The place has aged whisky and young fillies. Just wait til' they get a load of a real Marine!"

Pierce stopped and turned to Mills. "Geeze, Mills it's obvious you're going to take the valuable time and expand your . . . mind! Me, I am going to visit relatives and stop at the old museums in Washington D.C. They actually have stuff there from before there was space flight!"

Tommy Chin and Tan came through the compartment with bags on their shoulders. Hearing the conversation Tommy thought he would explain. "Tan and his twin have invited me to Giann for a tour of some of their temples. The Giann religion in many aspects is similar to Buddhism. I will be the first of my family to visit the Giann home world. It's a great honor."

Maryann emptied her locker and started packing her gear. "Well it's been fun I'll miss you guys, have a good Leave." Maryann watched Pierce and Mills shoulder their bags, and then added. "Remember that ancient saying. Eat, drink and be merry for tomorrow we serve!" Leaving the compartment first, Mills couldn't resist. "Yeah, yeah, but don't call me Mary!"

Chapter 13

EGAS INQUISITIVE

ONE moment Phillips was looking at the monitor and the next, was flying from his chair into darkness! Phillips landed hitting hard against what he thought might be a console. He was feeling his way along the deck for the way back to his chair when the small red emergency lights blinked on and the collision claxon started. Shaken and struggling to his feet he yelled to Lieutenant Rin rising behind the operations console. "WHAT IN THE CREATOR'S NAME WAS THAT?"

Lieutenant Rin depressing controls on the panel shouted above the blare of the claxon. "IT WAS A MASSIVE ELECTRA-MECHANICAL DISCHARGE! MAIN POWER DOWN, GENERATORS DOWN, WE'RE ON ONE QUARTER BATTERY POWER!"

"DO WE HAVE COMMUNICATIONS? WHAT ABOUT SHUTTLE 3?"

"ALL COMMUNICATIONS ARE DOWN. WE HAVE EMERGENCY POWER TO THE BRIDGE PASSAGEWAYS AND SICKBAY ONLY! I WILL PUT PRIORITY TO THE RE-ESTABLISHMENT OF COMMUNICATIONS BUT IT WILL TAKE TIME TO TRACE THE FUSED CIRCUITS."

Phillips glanced at the board. "WHAT ABOUT SICKBAY?"

"AT ONE QUARTER BATTERY POWER WE ONLY HAVE EMERGENCY POWER FOR THE BRIDGE THE PASSAGEWAYS AND SICKBAY!"

"GIVE PRIORITY TO ESTABLISHING FULL POWER TO SICKBAY, THEN TO COMMUNICATIONS. AND TURN OFF THAT DAMN ALARM!"

Phillips started for the communications console and on the way there, the claxon went silent. Chief Bin was sitting in front of the console trying to coax a response out of the powerless unit. Phillips reached Bin's side and placed a hand on her shoulder. "Chief with communications out I need you to run down to Sickbay. Find out how Dr. Stil is doing. Let Commander Moore know we will have full power to the Sickbay just as soon as we can!"

"Aye, Captain."

Chief Bin left the confusion of the Bridge in a lopping Giann stride.

Chapter 14

SICKBAY

Dr. Sen had just removed the child from the uterus when the Sickbay went black. He was thrown across Angela anesthetized on the table. He curled his long fingers around the slippery child behind the head, neck and the buttocks. Hearing a cough from the baby he turned the child in the dark so the airway was open and the mouth down to facilitate the drainage of fluids. The emergency lights blinked on and Dr. Sen saw the Nurse and the Corpsman scrub technician getting to their feet. He yelled! "TAKE THE CHILD!"

The Nurse grabbed a towel and slipped it over her hands. Dr. Sen gently placed the baby into the towel. The Nurse quickly swaddled the baby in the towel then cradled the child in her arm so she could use a bulb suction to ensure the mouth and nose was clear of fluid.

Dr. Sen gingerly removed his weight from Angela then clamped and cut the umbilical cord. He noticed a lot of blood coming from where the placenta had ripped away from the uterine wall. The tear had left a large gaping hole. Sen grabbed a pile of sponges and pressed them into the hole to stop the bleeding. Holding pressure on the sponges, he turned to Dr. Moore administering anesthesia at the head of the table. "How are her vital signs?"

"All my monitors are out. I'm ventilating her manually. All I have now is a racing pulse; I'll have a manual blood pressure in just a moment. Obviously she's in shock!"

Continuing to hold pressure to the packing Dr. Sen gave instructions to the Circulating Nurse. "Hang one unit compatible whole human blood. Open both IV's full and I need a battery powered cautery laser NOW!"

The Corpsman darted for the exit doors heading for the sterile supply room. At the doors, he ran full into Mike Stil entering the room with a look of horror on his face. They both tumbled back out the doors just as Chief Bin arrived in the Sickbay. The Corpsman picked himself up and continued to the supply room for the laser. Chief Bin helped Stil to his feet. "Commander, you should know better. There is nothing you can do in there but get in the way."

"But I have to know if she's all right. What happened to the ship and the power? If anything happens to Angela, I don't know what I'll do!"

Chief Bin guided Stil by his arm back to a chair in the Surgeon's Office. "Commander the Captain sent me with a message for Dr. Moore. I will be right back and I will tell you how your wife is doing. But you must stay right here!" Mike gave her a vacant look, nodded then put his head in his hands. Chief Bin turned and went back to the operating room's doors. She cracked the door and spoke while the Corpsman handed Dr. Sen the cautery laser. "Commander Moore, the Captain states he is giving full priority to the restoration of the Sickbay power. He also asks the condition of Dr. Stil."

Dr. Moore readjusted the IV's and continued the manual ventilation at the head of the table. "Thank you Chief. We have stabilized Dr. Stil but she has lost a lot of blood. There is too much damage to her uterus so Dr. Sen will have to remove it. You may tell the Captain I believe her prognosis will be good, and the healthy baby boy is doing just fine."

Nodding her understanding, Chief Bin quietly closed the door. She returned to the Surgeon's Office to find Stil in the same position she had left him. She sat down in a chair, which she turned to face him. "Commander Moore states that he believes your wife will be all right. They had some complications but they have her stabilized and the surgery will take just a little longer. Dr Moore also mentioned you have a healthy baby boy!"

Stil looked up at Chief Bin with tears streaming down his face. "I just didn't know what to do. I was out of my mind with worry, but she's going to be ok?" Bin nodded and took his hands in her long fingers. "Commander I understand it's difficult when you have a loved one that is in danger and you are powerless to help. However, Angela's in good hands and I believe Dr. Moore when he said she would do well. Now, I have to return to the Bridge but before I go let's take a peek in the room that they are using for the nursery and see that little boy of yours!"

Mike took a towel and wiped off his face. Standing up, a slow smile began to span his face. "It's a boy huh?" Mike Stil grinned all the way to the nursery.

Chapter 15

DWS CONQUEROR

(D'mon War Ship)

HARRAK sits in the Command Throne on the Bridge of his ship. The massive chair designed to fit his body has high long armrests to support his four-meter frame. His war helmet with the D'mon insignia of the "Horned Warrior," hangs on a hook attached to the side of the throne. On the right breast of his armor are the four red slashes of a Prime War Leader. The D'mon crew addresses him as "Prime". His gauntlets and boots have slots to leave claws free for use in battle. To the D'mon the claw kill is the most prestigious act a warrior can accomplish. The D'mon that do not have natural claws, have metal claws attached to hands and feet for this purpose. Many one on one disputes end in a claw kills. On many occasions, the wining warrior will eat pieces of the adversaries' eviscerated organs to demonstrate their ferocity and viciousness. Traits admired in all renowned warriors.

The D'mon warriors, through their genetic mix, have many different physical forms depending on the breeding species. Harrak has armored scales and slanted eyes with nictitating membranes set slightly back on his scaled head. He also has the natural claws, which come from his reptilian ancestry. Korab his First Officer or "Sub Prime," has a boney horn protuberance on the top of his forehead and thick black fir covering his body. He lacks the natural claws on his six fingered hands and wears the metal substitutes. He displays the three red slashes of a Sub Prime on his armor and his helm is custom fitted to accommodate his horn. One trait is common among the D'mon is the quickness of development. This gives the D'mon overwhelming numbers for expansion but also requires a nomadic existence, which must expand their Empire.

After birth, a D'mon reaches adulthood in only two growth cycles, which is the D'mon equivalent to two solar cycles. A lunar cycle is a partial growth or a "partial," and a planetary cycle is a "grow." The D'mon all train to be warriors once they reach adulthood. The female D'mon battle just as fiercely as the males. The D'mon Doctors artificially impregnate genetic compatible conquered females to carry the young. Since the young develop so quickly, many of the females die in childbirth. This would be a waste of the female D'mon warriors. Therefore, a desired spoil of the D'mon Fleet is a genetic compatible species.

The young that survive their first battle are welcomed as warriors. They earn the "Horned Warrior," insignia. The new D'mon if killed, are expendable. They were not yet blooded warriors. The warriors join a "Claw." A Claw has fifty members. Each Claw commanded by a Sub Prime. The more Claws a Prime Warrior commands the more power and prestige they carry.

Harrak spat when he read the Orders sent to him from the Elevated Prime. (Fleet Commander) His ship has been on patrol at the edge of the Empire for almost two growth cycles. His crew was already restless and now this! He pressed the communications slot on his armrest with a sharpened claw. Every warrior on the ship knew his rasping growl. "All Sub Prime Leaders prepare your warriors. We go to the Planet of Shame!"

Korab made a sign against evil with his hands and spat. The other warriors on the Bridge made similar gestures and looked at one another anxiously. Korab spoke what the others dared not mention. "Prime, a D'mon ship hasn't been to the Planet of Shame for several thousand growth cycles. Everyone knows the legend of the unspeakable golden warriors that slaughtered thousands in that miserable battle!" Korab made another sign against evil then continued.

"It took what was left of the whole War Fleet just to sterilize the Planet of Shame from orbit. There was no gain what so ever. Tens of thousands of warriors massacred for nothing. War Fleet Command swore to never return to that cursed place!"

Harrak turned to Korab his eyes thinning to mere slits. He answered his Sub Prime in a voice that hissed. "What are you, warriors or superstitious younglings? The golden warriors have been dead for thousands of growth cycles! When the Fleet left the Planet of Shame so long ago, they left a beacon that would notify us of contact with a new breed able species. That beacon activated a short time ago. Our Orders are to probe this new species take any technology we find and bring back any breed able females. Half of our ship's crew contains untried younglings not yet full warriors. It will take us almost a full growth cycle to reach the Planet of Shame. By then we will have even more younglings. A battle will train them. We will be the War Leaders that conquered the Planet of Shame! We will be famous! This action may even gain you your own ship and me a place at War Fleet Command!"

As Harrak finished Korab was already salivating through his twisted fangs. Harrak knew that what he had said would slowly spread from the Bridge warriors through the rest of the ship. Harrak slipped his forked tongue up around his eyes in satisfaction. *Let them dream of gain and glory, as long as they fight for me!*

Chapter 16

EGA GRAND COUNCIL CHAMBER

(Earth)

THE Council Chamber is a large round room with the EGA Seal placed in the center of the marble floor. The Earth / Giann Alliance Seal also contains a large holographic projector that displays star maps and items of interest to the Alliance Council Members. The Head of the Council elected by the members currently is a human. Alexander Rivera has been the Council Head for almost thirty solar cycles. His long white mutton chop whiskers and big toothy grin give him a comical appearance, which belies the many cycles of experience he has haggling and controlling the sometimes unruly Council. His tall desk is at the open end of the horseshoe shaped Council Members gallery. The gallery starts from the floor up in tiers so each member can see over the member in from of them anyone speaking on the floor. The most senior of members sit in the tiers near the floor while the junior members are up in the "Nosebleed" sections.

The human members of the Council represent the States that sent them or in the case of the Giann the Island or Province. The planet Giann has the majority of its population around the equator. There are many beautiful tropical Islands, which circle the equator. The majority of the Giann members come from these. There are also two larger continents north and south of the equator. The political sectioning of these continents resulted in the Giann Provinces.

As a senior member of the Council, Wingate Toath was present in his seat near the floor when the Fleet Officer briefed the Council about the accident that occurred in the Romeo system. With lackluster attention, Toath shook his head in feigned interest at the personnel lost or injured in the accident. The only information that Toath really cares about are the items that will help expand his own ambitions or that of his corporation, Toath Enterprises. Therefore, it wasn't the Officer's sad report of the accident that piqued his interest, but the data report from the Inquisitive that caught his eye.

Toath Enterprises has many subsidiaries including a major defense contractor called PTS Corporation. The initials PTS stand for Peace through Strength. Wingate Toath for many solar cycles has privately been lobbying for the expansion of the military side of the Fleet, due mostly to his mistrust of the Giann, and the many lucrative contracts he had been able to funnel to the subsidiaries of his corporation. With the success of the lobbying there followed many lucrative contracts for PTS Corp. Unknown by many, PTS is a veritable "Cash Cow", for Toath Enterprises.

Publically Toath is also the elected head of the "Galaxy Peace Party", which touts the disarming of Fleet ships and peaceful exploration in unarmed vessels. The GPP also advocates isolationism and withdrawal from the alliance with Giann. Many members of the GPP believe the "Baldies" as they call the Giann, are secretly working to destabilize the Earth States and take all the space-mining resources for themselves. The GPP has talk communication shows that blame most all of Earth's problems on the Alliance with the Baldies. Some of the placards posted in the poorer parts of the Earth cities say things like, "Humans are the top of the food chain." or "We don't need Baldy rule." In many instances, the people that support and advocate the GPP have never even met a Giann.

The item that caught Toath's attention in the Inquisitive data report is the crystal like element, which seems to block all types of energy. A major part of PTS Inc. works on developing the military's stealth technologies such as the new space fighter they have under development. While sitting with the sad expression Toath thought. *Let's see, how can I best exploit this little bit of information.*

Chapter 17

EGAS DAUNTLESS

S ECOND Lieutenants' Chin and Tan stood at attention before the ship's Marine contingent Officer in Charge, Captain Lin. The tall gray Giann turned from a communication screen to apprise the new Officers. "Please have a seat gentleman. Welcome aboard." He rose from behind his desk and handed each of them a training package with their names already embossed upon them. Captain Lin sat on the corner of his desk as they checked the contents. Then he began their briefing.

"As you may already know the Dauntless is the first Fleet, Medium Space Fighter Carrier. There has been a lot of resistance on both Earth and Giann to the building of star ships with a purely military purpose. There was both ethical and economical resistance to expanding the military in space. I'm sure you're familiar with the ethical arguments. Many beings on both worlds say we have peaceful cultures and should explore the galaxy in a peaceful non-threatening way. These beings say the introduction of military ships demonstrates expansionist tendencies and us to be aggressive. They also argue that there has been no contact with a violent star faring species and the capital used to build ships like the Dauntless is wasted. Another argument is that the resources used should to build more mining and research vessels or the development of peaceful colonies."

"The Alliance Council weighed these and many other arguments including the fact the Marines have already been used on several occasions to rescue or defend miners and colonists from non-sentient violent life forms. Historically both of our species have learned that colonization and trade eventually needs some type of protection. The security forces in the corporate world do not have the training nor have the assets to protect free trade and travel among the stars. So here we are, men, the Dauntless' Mission is to protect that travel and trade. The Dauntless, armed with eight batteries of energy cannon has fore and aft missile torpedo launchers. The ship will carry two Squadrons of single pilot space fighters."

"Lieutenant Tan you will lead First Platoon assigned to shuttle number three and Lieutenant Chin you will have Second Platoon assigned to shuttle number four. You will have to work closely with the fighters for close air support during hostile landing training." Tommy Chin raised a hand indicating a question. "Pardon me sir; is the Marine contingent aboard the Dauntless really large enough to make hostile landings?"

"Good question Lieutenant; actually our primary mission is security of the Carrier itself. Any hostile landings would be in the form of rescue or extraction missions. The training with the fighters in close air support will primarily hone their skills for them to work with the combat shuttles from the Starfury. Once we get enough of the new space fighters, you will also train to pilot them. The Space Fighter Carrier's primary mission is aerial assault and fighter combat operations. Are there any further questions?"

"No sir!"

"Very well, then. You both have a lot to do. Report to your Platoons. We shall institute the training schedule in two planetary cycles. That's all for now you are dismissed." Without further questions, Tan and Chin left the compartment excited about their new future aboard the Dauntless.

Chapter 18

EGAS STARFURY

For Second Lieutenant, Maryann Hall, life aboard the Marine Landing Ship was both intriguing and exhausting. Besides the landing assault training in the new shuttles, there was security duty on the Bridge and Platoon physical training in and out of environmental suits. There was also General Quarters and Collision drills at all unexpected hours.

The absolute worst Hall thought was when there was a General Quarters drill right in the middle of her five-minute shower allotment! At the sound of the claxon the shower automatically cut off and Maryann had to struggle into uniform and then full combat armor still covered in soap. At their battle station, John Phillips noted the wet and soapy hair under her helmet. He leaned forward and made a sniffing sound. "Ah, you smell so fresh like a wild Irish spring!" Maryann jammed an elbow in his stomach and stomped on one of his toes. This knocked the wind out of him and caused him to yelp in pain. Maryann gave him a hard look. "How's that for a wild Irish spring Sailor Boy?"

In addition, all new Officers were required to continue their education of historical tactics and develop a working knowledge of all the ship's systems. By working with their Platoons, they also expanded their leadership and management skills.

At the Academy, Maryann learned the rudiments of leading Marines. At her first command, she learned management and leadership were a mixed bag of family type relationships. A Platoon Leader is responsible for not only leading and training but also responsible for the welfare and morale of their Marines. Maryann found the greatest resource for handling this new relationship was her Platoon Sergeant, Gunnery Sergeant Müller. Müller is a career Non-Commissioned Officer from the State of Western Europe. He is a tall muscular man with tightly cropped graying blonde hair. His serious Teutonic demeanor is broken at times with a broad toothy grin given freely when one of his Marines performs especially well. At these times, Müller will nod his head and state with a pronounced Germanic accent. "That's very goot, very goot." All the other senior NCOs on board the ship have the highest for respect for Gunny Müller. In addition, every Marine in his Platoon would gladly trade an Alliance Council Commendation for a "Very goot," from Gunny Müller.

Müller taught Hall how a leader actually takes care of their Marines. He taught her the day had not finished until after a walk through the Squad Bays. He taught her to speak with the Marines listen to their concerns and develop that parental bond that shows the Marines that the Platoon Leader cares about them as individuals. She learned every Marine had concerns and day-to-day problems that were beyond their military duties and shipboard life. There were financial difficulties, families far away and of course the occasional disciplinary problems. Maryann learned that by helping to alleviate many of these minor stressors and demonstrating genuine concern she had developed the mutual respect needed for a team training to go in harm's way.

Maryann's first eighteen lunar cycles on the Starfury seemed to go quickly. With excellent evaluations hard work and the Commanding Officers recommendation, she achieved promotion to First Lieutenant along with the other new Officers. Maryann saw little of Phillips, Mills or Pierce except for the occasional times in the Officer's Mess or the joint Platoon training exercises. The group of them gathered in the Wardroom at the same time to celebrate their new promotions early one Sunday morning. Sunday was the day that the Mess Specialists would make individual omelets or waffles to order and everyone called it Sunday brunch. The group got a big laugh when the Mess Specialist brought Maryann an exquisite looking handmade omelet. As the omelet was set in front of her Hall's response was, "Very goot, very goot!"

Maryann asked John about his father and the progress of the Inquisitive. John said the small research colony is established and there had been no further problems after the satellite explosion. He informed them the Inquisitive lost a shuttle, the shuttle crew and the satellite exploration team. Fortunately, there was only minor damage to the Inquisitive and only minor injuries to the crew. Pierce finished her breakfast, placed her napkin on the table then asked. "Have they figured out what caused the explosion?"

"Their best guess is that the satellite may have been some type of left over bomb related to the ordnance that created the craters on Romeo." Chuck Mills asked for a second stack of pancakes and turned to Phillips. "Have they found anything else?"

"Not much besides the dome like bunkers. They have spent most of the last solar cycle trying to figure out what they are. They still haven't figured out how to open one, or if they even, have an entrance. Of course, they have been very careful with the examination of the domes. They don't want a repeat of what happened with the satellite."

Maryann placed her fork down and nodded. "Since the research colony is established, will the Inquisitive be returning soon for resupply and refit?"

"My father in his last communication home stated the Inquisitive should be breaking orbit in the next few lunar cycles."

Mills pushed back his second empty plate and loosened his belt. "I bet you'll be glad to see the Old Man."

"If I get a chance to see him at all, with the Board of Inquiry, I'm sure will convene."

With a tone of concern, Pierce inquired. "What do you mean, Board of Inquiry?"

"The Captain of a vessel is responsible for the welfare and safety of their ship and all aboard. There were five crewmen and a civilian scientist killed when the satellite exploded. In addition, let's not forget the destroyed shuttle and the damage to the Inquisitive. I'm certain there will be a Board of Inquiry to look into the events of the mishap. I just hope they don't start pointing fingers of blame." Maryann frowned with a sigh. "I'm sure your father did all he could under the circumstances. I don't believe he will have to worry about blame."

"Oh I'm sure everything will come out ok. It's just that with the inquiry, my father won't be able to spend a lot of time with my mom."

The meal finished up on that somewhat somber note. Each Officer shook hands and then returned to their duties. On the way out Maryann caught up to John and put a hand on his shoulder. "It'll work out John; at least he'll be back."

"Yeah I guess you're right. See you later Pug."

Phillips took her hand from his shoulder and gave it a little squeeze. Maryann watched him turn and head for his Platoon area. She could not help but feel the quiet sadness trailing behind him.

Chapter 19

THE PLANET CALLED ROMEO

(535.6 AC)

Lieutenant Commander, Michael Stil watched his son make a mess of his breakfast. Mikey is almost two solar cycles old and showing all the energy for his age. It seems he takes great relish in smearing his warm cereal all over his little table and his face. Angela walked into the kitchen, part of their planetary prefab home and frowned. "Michael Stil, just look at what your son is doing! I leave the room for five minutes and Mikey is a mess!" Stil unsuccessfully tried to hold back a chuckle. "Like father, like son I guess."

Angela grabbed a towel wet it at the sink and started wiping the toddler's face. "Mikey don't you listen to your father. You're a big boy and big boys don't play with their food! Michael Stil, you should be ashamed of yourself. You just encourage him!" Stil saw the look on his wife's face so he stopped smiling and decided to change the subject as he finishes his breakfast. "I'll be working over at the new job at the Science Center today. Since Captain Phillips, approved my transfer to the settlement's military support, Major Pel has been kind enough to give me an office."

"So what will you do there?

"I'm the new Logistics Officer for the security contingent." Angela looked at Mike and her eyes softened. "Mike, are you going to miss the Inquisitive? You're giving up a lot to stay here with Mikey and I." Mike shook his head and smiled again. "Nope, I really didn't have to think about it. Starship life is interesting but I couldn't spend all the time away from my family like a lot of the crew do. I guess my father was right our family just isn't suited for starship life." Angela finished wiping up the table and picked the baby up out of the chair. "When your tour is up will you resign your commission?

"I don't know yet. I just don't know."

Angela sat down in a chair placing Mikey in her lap. She turned him towards her and started to help him into his little parka. "You know these little clothes that the crew members made for Mikey are just adorable!"

"Yeah it must be tuff on the kid to have several hundred God Parents!"

Mike had noticed many of the crew and research people stopped in just to see and play with Mikey, especially the Giann. Many of the Giann had never seen human children and they loved to interact with the toddler. Even the normally stoic Major Pel would make excuses to stop over and then end up playing blocks with Mikey. The Giann found him delightful. Michael thought about that for a moment watching Mikey chew on one of the parka hood strings.

"The Giann seem to like him a lot. Even the large ones with all their strength are always so gentle with him. It's almost if when they are playing with him they are the same age and enjoy the games like he does." Angela finished dressing the toddler and looked over at Mike.

"It's like they have the ability to really become their inner child. They play with Mikey as if they were the same age. There is a lot we still have to learn from the Giann. They're an amazing species."

Mike left the table and put his dinnerware in the washer. He pressed the wash button turned and leaned against the counter. "So what are you and Mikey going to do today?"

"Dr. Chase and a group of mineralogists are still working on the nearest dome trying to figure out what it is for. This mineral they have found in the soil seems to be highly concentrated in the structure of the dome. They haven't even found a break in the surface. For all we know it may not have an opening. The dome may just be the top of a deeply buried structure.

Today they are going to start excavating around the base to try to see how deep it goes. I'm going to take Mikey with me and we're going to analyze the geological samples from the excavation. Gunnery Sergeant Bin, Chief Bin's sister twin is going with us. She said she would be happy to help look after Mikey." Mike laughed! "I bet you within five minutes they're both digging in the dirt and having the best time!" Angela picked up Mikey and paused in the doorway. "Like you said, like father, like son!"

Angela and Mikey walked over to the Science Center and found Gunny Bin waiting. She was sitting in one of the small land vehicles. The six wheeled rovers are used to move supplies and as local transportation. It wasn't far to the dome but they also had additional equipment to transport. The small rover took them there in just a few minutes. As Gunny Bin started unloading the equipment, Angela picked up Mikey and straddled him on her hip. "Let's go and see what Uncle Henry is up to, ok Mikey?" Mikey smiled and pointed at the group of people by the dome in that way that all toddlers do.

Dr. Henry Chase was looking down into the ten by fifteen meter excavation. The excavation goes right up to the curved side of the dome. He turned as Angela and Mikey approached breaking out in a big smile. "Good morning Angela, I see you brought the boss out with you!" Mikey put out his arms and Chase picked him up whirling him around in a circle making him laugh with glee. Angela placed her fists on her hips and pouted. "Dr. Chase, if you make that baby throw up his breakfast, I hope it goes all over you!"

Chase laughed and gave Mikey a hug then returned him to Angela. "That big guy is the only true spaceman among us. A little flying will never hurt him." Angela harrumphed and peered at the excavation. "Have you found anything interesting yet?"

"No nothing yet, just the same unbroken smooth surface. We don't even know if it's hollow. Our sensors can't penetrate the stuff. It appears to be made of the same materials as the planetary rock but with a lot more of the crystalline substance in it. We can't cut it, scrape it, burn it, and it doesn't appear to have eroded over time like the natural planetary rock."

Angela, still holding Mikey, walked around the excavation to the untouched area around the dome. She looked closely at the beautiful golden-brown crystalline color of the surface. She then put a hand to the surface to feel the texture.

Chase was examining some of the rocks from the excavation when he heard Angela scream! Everyone dropped what they were doing and ran to the other side of the dome. Angela was sitting on the ground about three meters from the dome. She was holding Mikey across the middle of her chest pointing at the dome. The group of scientists ran to Angela's side and Gunny Bin picked up Mikey from her arms. Then everyone seemed to notice where Angela was pointing. It's an open doorway in the dome! A couple of the scientists took a step towards the door and Chase shouted, "STOP! No one goes near it!"

Everyone froze. Turning to the scientists, Chase commanded. "Get recorders and scan everything from about ten meters away!

Gunny Bin, go with Angela and take Mikey back to the rover and stay there for now!" Pulling his communicator from his belt, Chase continued, "Major Pel, this is Chase. We have a door open to the dome."

"I'm on my way Doctor."

"Please inform the Inquisitive of our find and bring along Lieutenant Commander Stil. This seemed to involve Angela."

"Will do sir, anything else?"

"No that will do for now Major, Chase out."

Attaching the communicator back on his belt Chase turned to one of his assistants. "Baker, take the other rover back to the Science Center. Pick up Dr. Pel, and bring him up to date on what we found. Also, bring a camera-bot from the lab. After what happened with the satellite, I believe we'll be a lot more careful with the dome." Baker left at a trot and Chase was already directing the rest of the team to fence in a ten-meter area around the doorway.

Mike Stil sat at his desk in what he would describe as his "closet". It was the small room given to him in the Center's admin section. He looked up as Major Pel rushed in wearing full combat armor and weapons. "Come with me Commander!"

Mike grabbed his hat and ran to catch up to the Giann leaving the building in a fast long legged stride. Out front, Mike was surprised to see Pel heading to one of the larger rovers. In the back of the vehicle, there was a security team of Marines in full combat gear. Mike jumped in the passenger side and the rover started with a lurch and quick burst of speed. Mike buckled his safety belt then hung on to an overhead strap. Mike yelled, squinting to see with the wind in his face. "WHAT DO YOU HAVE, MAJOR PEL?"

"I received a communication from Dr. Chase. He stated that they have opened a door in the dome and that Dr. Stil was involved.

"Mikey is with Angela today! Are they all right?"

"I have no reports of any injuries. Dr. Chase requested I bring you along."

As they neared the dome, Mike could see Angela sitting in the small rover with Mikey in her lap. Gunny Bin is standing next to them looking very much like a lioness guarding cubs. They pulled up in a cloud of dust and Mike jumped out and ran over to Angela and Mikey. Pel and his Marines jogged straight to the dome with the security team breaking up to two fire-teams one to either side of the dome. By now there was a crowd of people and equipment around the tapped off area where Angela found the door.

"Are you and Mikey alright? What happened?" Mikey gave a big smile at seeing his dad and reached out with his arms. Mike picked him up gave him a kiss and held Mikey while Angela told him about all the excitement. "Henry and his team were excavating next to the dome attempting to find an entrance. I walked up with Mikey spoke with Henry for a moment and then walked around the dome a little ways. I was looking at the texture of the dome and when I touched it, a door popped open. I guess it opened so quickly it surprised me and I stumbled backwards. I landed on my bottom with Mikey in my lap. That's all, honest! Henry secured an area around the door and called for a mobile camera-bot, You, Dr., and Major Pel. Henry had Gunny Bin bring us back to the rover and now I can't see what's going on!"

"Honey, please just stay right here a little longer. I'll go over and see what Henry has found. I'm sure Henry just wanted to make sure that you and Mikey were safe. This surprise probably gave everyone a scare."

Handing the boy back to Angela, Mike walked up the hill toward the dome. He found Chase in conversation with Dr. Pel. Major Pel stood silently behind them as if awaiting urgent orders. Mike looked at the section of dome enclosed in the caution tape circle with a fire team to each side. The camera-bot sat facing the dome and the excavation team stood together outside the tape quietly talking. Mike walked up to the middle of Chase's animated conversation with Dr. Pel.

"It was open approximately ten minutes. We didn't time it because we didn't expect it to close. We took some initial pictures of the door and as we were positioning the camera-bot, it closed. We've gone all over the door location area but nothing we've tried has opened it again."

"Have you duplicated the events that initiated the first opening?"

"Of course we did! We touched every single centimeter of area where Angela made contact, with no results.

"You said, we?"

"Yeah, my team and I tried."

"I suggest you duplicate the events of the opening exactly as they happened."

"Of course, Angela, perhaps there's a reason it opened for her!"

Mike made a small cough in the back of his throat before interrupting the conversation. "Ah, mm Gentlemen, have you considered any risks that may be involved if Angela touches the dome again?" Dr. Pel turned to Stil at the interruption. "I believe the risks would be minimal since there was no consequence other than the door opening the last time she touched the dome."

Mike not sure, if he was satisfied with the answer, looked back and forth at the expectant faces of Chase and Pel. Finally, with a raise of his eyebrows and a shrug of his shoulders Mike decided. "Well, let's ask her."

Angela slapped the side of the dome in anger and frustration. It has been more than an hour and there have been no new results. The Marines sat in the dust their weapons up, sipping water in the dry heat. They have that abject look of boredom that comes with time served in the military with less than exiting assignments. The scientists keep dusting and re-dusting equipment sitting on the ground. Down by the small rover Gunny Bin draws circles in the dust with Mikey in the shade of the vehicle.

"I know I touched it right here! Now I'm touching it all over the place and nothing happens. What's with this?" Mike sat on an equipment box outside of the taped area. He tossed pebbles in the dust and watched Gunny Bin play with Mikey. Finding another pebble to toss, he could hear their frustration.

"Let's go through it again. After talking to me, you walked to this area here. Are you completely duplicating all your movements before you touched the dome?" Angela crinkled her forehead in concentration then nodded. "I think so. I came from the excavation this way with Mikey on my hip. I turned to the left facing the dome and traced the marbling in the stone with my finger. One moment I was touching the dome and the next, pop! The door was open!"

"You had your arm around Mikey on your hip, like this?" Chase simulated a woman with a small child with his arm crooked around as if holding the child close to his body on his hip.

"That's about it."

Chase reached down and picked up a padded canvas camera case. He judged it to be about Mikey's size and handed the bag to Angela. "Try this." Angela put her left arm around the case balanced it on her hip and touched the dome again, "Nothing!"

Angela and Chase stared at the unbroken side of the dome. Chase absently scratched his beard in dismay. Dr Pel looked at Chase and Stil then glanced toward Mikey playing by the rover. "There is one aspect of Angela's story that you have not duplicated."

Both Angela and Chase slowly turned to look at Mikey quietly playing a counting game in Gunny Bin's lap. Mike Stil saw the speculative looks and jumped to his feet. "Oh no, Chase. I know what you're thinking but this is alien technology and I'm not going to let your experiments include Mikey!" Chase turned to Stil with a look of irritation.

"Dr. Pel is correct. We must totally duplicate the actions that opened the dome if we are to be successful. Neither Angela nor Mikey incurred an injury when the door opened. Angela said herself she only fell backward because she was surprised at the sudden opening!"

Angela stepped up to Mike and tenderly reached up with her hands placing her fingers lightly on his temples. Looking into his eyes, she spoke quietly. "Michael he's right. We have to find out. Sweetheart you know I won't let anything happen to Mikey. I have a feeling. It's as if, I just know it won't hurt us. I'll have Gunny Bin right beside us and Major Pel and his Marines are here. The technicians said there was no radiation or dangerous gasses detected. I feel it will be alright, trust me!" Stil looked deeply into his wife's eyes and knew there was no changing Angela's mind. As Michael looked up Gunny Bin was already rising and bringing Mikey over to Angela.

Chapter 20

EGAS SEARCHER

(Scout, Mapping and Exploration Vessel)
(Four solar light cycles outbound from the Romeo system)

LIEUTENANT Elton Singh was in the small cramped sonic shower when the alarm sounded. He cut the power to the shower unit. Threw on his pants, struggled with his tunic and hit his head twice in the low gravity, heading to the Bridge. To conserve power the SME's only produced 1/6th of Earth's gravity, which made them a challenge to traverse through with any speed. With a crew of only four, the SME's were all engine, mapping and sensor equipment. They cover a lot of space quickly, map the assigned sectors and return to known space in a short time. The crew's comforts were not a high priority in the design of the ships. However, the upside is the SME crews fly for four lunar cycles and then have the next eight off. Arriving on the Bridge, Singh was still buttoning his tunic. "What is it Mr. Maple?"

Ensign Henry Maple, the SME's Navigation and Communications' Officer looked up from his console. "A ship sir, she's a big one too! It's coming toward us from the galactic rim not from known space!"

"Any chance it's a Giann vessel?"

"I don't think so sir. I've never seen anything like it and there's no match in the computer database. Besides, it's coming from the wrong direction. We should have it on visual in just a moment."

Lieutenant Singh buckled himself into his command chair. "Ok Mr. Maple put it on the forward view screen." Singh looked at the vessel and adjusted the controls on the arm of his chair for closer magnification. "Geeze, it looks like a flying junk yard!"

The vessel was large rectangular and appeared to have a hodgepodge of boxes pipes cylinders and miscellaneous chunks of metal attached all over the surface. As they watched, four long cylinders with stubby wings disengaged themselves from the side of the ship and headed straight for them.

"Steer a course to keep out of their way Mr. Maple. Petty Officer Willis, fire up the comm. and see if we can talk with them. Seaman French, secure all doors and prepare for high speed maneuvering. If we can't talk with them we'll run."

Singh watched as the four small vessels separated with two coming straight for them and two heading on an intercepting course the direction the SME had turned.

"Sir, I have no reply to repeated hails."

"Very well Willis. Mr. Maple, change course again to a 180 heading."

Maple quickly imputed the new course and the quick turn pulled them against their safety harnesses. "What are those things?"

As Singh watched, an energy beam shot from the lead vessel and there was a loud explosion and a responding concussion from aft of the ship. "Those Mr. Maple are space fighters! Evasive action full power let's get out of here! Willis broadcast a Mayday. We are under attack by unknown vessels. We are attempting evasion maneuvers!"

Maple plotted a new course and watched as the ship turned into an incoming missile from one of the fighters that had flanked their course. Lieutenant Singh watched the screen in horror and had just enough time to mutter, "Geeze."

"Auuooo," Korab howled with the thrill of the kill! Flying one of the Swift Claw Fighters, he had watched the pathetic little ship turn right into his trap. He spoke to the fighter on his wing. "This species is weak! They turn to run and fear to fight! The Prime is right we will be famous. We will capture a whole new breed able species of slaves!"

Parek, a youngling and not yet a full warrior was relieved at surviving his first sortie as the Sub Prime's wing partner. Although his claws still shook, he would never admit he had felt fear. Turning back to the ship behind the Sub Prime, he glanced at the spreading debris field. "Yes Sub Prime, it will be glorious!"

Parek would never mention that it looked like the vessel was an unarmed scout ship. Upon return, he would brag about the fierce battle and his great deeds.

Chapter 21

EGAS INQUISITIVE

CHIEF Bin contacted Phillips directly at his Command Chair. Seeing the urgent flash of incoming communication from Chief Bin, Phillips set aside his log work and switched his console to the communications screen. "Yes chief, what is it?"

"Captain we just had an incoming emergency message from the EGAS Searcher. It seems they are under attack." Phillips body tightened in his chair.

"What is the status of the Searcher now?"

"It is unknown sir. We received video from the Searcher showing the approach of a large vessel. Then what appeared to be space fighters detached from the vessel and attacked the Searcher. The video shows the Searcher taking evasive action then the video ends."

With an icy calm belying his concern, Phillips ordered. "Chief put the video through to my console. Have Lieutenant Rin report to the Bridge to take the con. I would then like Officers Call in the Wardroom in one hour."

"Aye sir, you'll have Officers Call in the Wardroom in one hour."

"Now get me EGAFC on the comm."

After speaking with Fleet Command, Phillips watched the short recording four times before handing control of the Bridge to Lieutenant Rin, so he could proceed to the Wardroom. He took a hot cup of coffee with him to the briefing but it didn't warm the cold feeling he had in the pit of his stomach. Entering the Wardroom Phillips is greeted by, "Attention on Deck!" He walks briskly to his chair declaring, "As you were." When everyone again sat, Phillips began.

"Ladies and Gentlemen we may have a problem. A little over an hour ago, we received an emergency message from the EGAS Searcher. The Searcher is a scout and mapping vessel that was mapping systems about twelve parsecs or four solar light cycles from here."

Phillips activated a switch on his chair, which controlled the holographic projector in the middle of the conference table. The projector displayed the local star map of the area indicating the location of Romeo, the Inquisitive and the last known location of the Searcher. "I have watched the video communication from the Searcher several times. With no further communications from the Searcher, I believe an unknown assailant has destroyed the Searcher. We'll take a moment and review the emergency communication."

Phillips looked around the table and noticed the varied emotions of his Officers as they watched the short communication and digested the information. The emotions appeared to range from anger shock and disbelief of the humans, to the calm inquisitive thoughtful look of the Giann.

"I have forwarded the information to EGAFC and I believe we have two possible scenarios to consider. The first is the aliens that destroyed the Searcher may have no idea we are here and may not head our way. The second is they know we are in the area and are on the way here. After reviewing the broadcast from the Searcher, I have noted that the Searcher attempted to communicate with these beings with no response. The aliens then attacked the Searcher out of hand. I conclude and EGAFC agrees that if this ship is coming here, it may be hostile towards us too. With the nearest friendly military ship, at least a solar cycle away EGAFC has given us three recommendations. Negotiate, fight or get as many of the colonists off Romeo as we can and run."

Lieutenant Graham, the Officer in Charge of Shuttle Flight Operations indicated he had a question. Phillips nodded at Graham indicating he should speak. "Excuse me sir. It took us lunar cycles to get all of the colonists down to the planet and since then we've lost one shuttle in the satellite explosion. How much time would we have to evacuate?"

Phillips looked to Lieutenant Commander Din. The Giann served as the ships Astral Navigation Officer. "Commander Din?"

"Captain since the alien vessels are unknown I can only speculate about their speed. By watching the initial approach the mother ship made to the EGAS Searcher, they are fast in comparison to the Inquisitive. Since the alien ship popped into space close to the Searcher then slowed, I speculate faster than light speed somewhat of the order of our newest military ships. Perhaps even two parsecs a planetary cycle."

To Phillips' annoyance, in his excitement Lieutenant Graham interjected. "Six planetary cycles, Captain, we'll have a hard time getting everyone off in that amount of time, and even if we did, then what? The Inquisitive is a little more than light speed research and exploration vessel. They could run us down easily! Plus if we empty the shuttles of defensive firepower and ordinance to carry passengers we cut our defensive capability in half."

Phillips rose from the conference table and stared out the view port. He chewed on his inner lip as he weighed his alternatives. Romeo appeared to hang above the port but the beauty of the planet was far from his thoughts. Finally, Phillips turned with his decision. "Well it appears we're too slow to run even if we could get everyone off the planet. Therefore, we are down to two options, negotiating or defend. We will try to negotiate if given the opportunity but we will plan to defend. Chief Bin?"

"Yes sir?"

"Chief, contact Major Pel and his Marines. Have them start on defenses for the settlement. Lieutenant Graham, I want you to arm your shuttles, and then start patrolling the edge of the system. By the Creator, the Inquisitive may not be a ship of war, but if they want a fight maybe we can give them a bloody nose!"

Chapter 22

EGAS DAUNTLESS

"I REALLY envy you guys," stated Lieutenant John Phillips. He passed the salad bowl to his left and sampled his lunch in the Dauntless Wardroom. Tommy Chin and Tan had invited their old Academy friends to a tour of the new ship and have lunch in the Officer's Mess.

"Yeah," Mills interjected between mouthfuls of chicken and rice. "Here we're training in the dirt with the Grunts and you guys are getting to train with the new space fighters." Nodding, Tommy Chin agreed. "It is great, but we'll be stuck here around Europa for who knows how long training and retraining. You guys are shipping out soon to see the stars."

Between sips of her ice tea, Maryann looked to Tan. "How many fighters will the Dauntless carry?"

"The Dauntless will carry two Squadrons of twelve fighters. Tommy and I go to Beta Squadron when our training is complete. The Dauntless has now only received two fighters, so we spend a lot of time training in simulators. Unofficial word is, when our training is complete the Dauntless will link up with the Starfury to train in close air support with the ground troops."

"Well I can't think of two better guys to be flying high cover when we're down in the dirt."

Maryann raised her glass of Oolong tea and pronounced. "Let's have a toast to the new Squadron!"

With the raise of the glasses, Pierce added. "And may you always kick butt!"

Just as the toast was finished, a communications Petty Officer hurried up to their table. She spoke to Lieutenant Chin first quietly, and then addressed the visiting Officers.

"The Duty Officer has directed me to inform you the Dauntless has received a message from EGAFC. A mapping vessel has been destroyed by forces unknown a few parsecs away from the planet being explored by the Inquisitive. The Inquisitive anticipates that an attack on the ship and the settlement may be imminent. EGAFC is sending the Starfury to support the Inquisitive at best possible speed. All officers and crew of the Starfury are to return at once to prepare to get underway."

There was a short moment of stunned silence then everyone was moving. Tommy shook John's hand. "Good luck guys, I wish we were going with you."

"You guys just get this new Squadron on line. I have a feeling we're going to need you." Tommy pounded the emblem on his chest with his fist. "Semper Fi." John responded the same with, "Semper Fi," then turned and hurried to catch up to the others.

On the Shuttle back to the Starfury, everyone seemed to be discussing the possibility of seeing action. Maryann noticed John was very quiet. "What's bothering you Sailor Boy?"

John looked down towards his boots. "It's the Inquisitive Pug. She has some defensive capabilities but she's not a war ship."

"I know you're worried about your father, but look at it this way. He's one of the best Captains in the Fleet. If anyone can hold out until we get there, it will be Captain John Phillips. What we have to do now is get our Marines ready to go into action. We have our own job to get done." John looked up and nodded. "You're right. I have a job to do and worrying isn't going to help any. It's just that it's going to take us so long to get there!"

Maryann nodded in agreement and took John's hand. She gave his hand a little squeeze and they both looked out a view port across from them at all the increased activity around the Starfury as their shuttle slowly approached.

After their friends had left, Tommy Chin and Tan hurried down to the Dauntless Hanger Deck to watch the arrival of the rest of the Squadron of space fighters. They are designated SF-4, being the fourth in the series after three prototypes. The sleek arrow designs with curved retractable wings give the SF-4 the ability to maneuver in both space and atmosphere. The ion thruster drive uses the breakup of water molecules into hydrogen and oxygen giving them the most powerful space engines yet devised for such a small craft. Multiple horizontal vertical and lateral exhaust ports give it excellent maneuverability. Additionally the SF-4 can refuel at any water bearing planet or outpost. Offensively the SF-4 has dual forward energy cannons that fire alternately so one is firing as the other is charging. Additionally there are ten hard points, five to each side to carry space and/or planetary use missiles.

Defensively the fighter has the new Giann developed energy shielding which absorbs and vents energy back to space. The SF-4 has a last resort rear defense for use in escaping attack from behind. Officially, it is the M-101 Object Dispersal Launcher. The defense ejector carries thousands of tiny metal balls which when ejected while in a full power burn leaves a metallic cloud in the path of a sub light speed pursuer. The M-101 Object Dispersal Launcher has been affectionately nicknamed "Junk in the Trunk," by the new space fighter pilots.

Chin, Tan and the other new pilots finally started training in tactics and mock air battles above Europa, the second lunar cycle after qualifying in both simulator and fighter. They trained in the classic four finger formations with four fighters breaking into fighting pairs of lead and wing man.

While not actually logging hours in the fighters, the pilots trained in the simulators reenacting famous air battles from every century of flight. These air battles went all the way back to that ancient Earth war, World War I. By the end of six lunar cycles of intense training, the Squadrons are finally ready for deployment aboard the Dauntless.

After a great deal of debate at the EGAFC, the Fleet Command finally decided to call the new SF-4 space fighter the SF-4 Banshee. The name suggested by the scream the fighter makes cutting into the atmosphere helping to increase the fear factor of the formidable fighter.

Chapter 23

THE ROMEO SYSTEM

"Look! Their ship lumbers out of orbit!"

"Shut up Parek!"

Korab was annoyed that Parek broke communication silence. Korab glanced right and left at his attack wing of fighters. He could feel the joy and anticipation of the upcoming battle and the assured victory. Upon entering the system their scanners displayed the large transport orbiting the planet and the three, armed shuttles hidden behind one of the moons. Obviously, the shuttles thought they could surprise the fighters on their way into the system but they were far too slow and weakly armed to do much damage. The warriors destroyed them with little more than a fly through. As Korab watched the armed transport raising out of orbit to meet them he had little concern as to the outcome. Now that the enemy was rising to meet them, there was no reason for stealth. Korab gave the last briefing to his warriors.

"To all warriors, remember to target only the energy cannons and engines. We want the ship intact. It may carry breed able females and useful technologies."

Chapter 24

EGAS INQUISITIVE

"Sound General Quarters and then ahead full Mister Nomarie." Captain Phillips stated as he buckled himself into his Command Chair. Just seconds after Ensign Nomarie's, "Aye sir," the claxon started to sound. Phillips watched the double "V" formation of space fighters divide and decided they would attack both sides of the ship at once. "Lieutenant Rin, prepare all weapons."

"All weapons manned and ready sir!"

Phillips watched the craft come into range then calmly stated. "Fire at will Lieutenant Rin, fire at will."

As the forward weapons opened fire, the attacking ships dodged and bounced back and forth working hard to avoid the energy pulses aimed their way. Phillips noted at least three brilliant flashes, which were the destruction of attacking craft. As the attacking craft split to each side of the Inquisitive Phillips shouted! "NOW, Lieutenant Rin, close in missile defense, give it to them, NOW!"

Korab timed the release of his first missile so it was away speeding toward the forward cannon turret before he made the cut to the left. The plan was to fly both sides of the transport at once taking out the defensive batteries on the way. There was a bright flash of destruction as his fighter danced away avoiding the dwindling pulses of the few remaining guns. As Korab flew lead, down the side of the large ship, he saw the ports of the Launch Bays open and space suited figures operating portable multiple missile launchers.

Korab shouted, "PULL UP! PULL UP!" Hundreds of tiny flashes betrayed the launching of the small missiles. Korab looked quickly over his shoulder as his fighter climbed up and over the transport. He caught a glimpse as fighter after fighter that was not agile or lucky enough to avoid the missiles flew into destruction. Korab spat with anger and frustration. "All fighters, target those Launch Bays before they can close the doors and rearm those launchers!" Korab with the remainder of his fighters and the fighters of Parek's group broke off turned and launched their missiles into the open doors of the Launch Bays.

Chapter 25

ROMEO

M ICHAEL Stil, Major Pel and Gunny Bin were walking the ground defenses of the settlement when both Pel and Bin stopped and looked skyward. Stil stopped and looked at Gunny Bin. "What's wrong?"

"My twin and the other Giann crew members are dead."

Mike looked quickly upward and saw a bright light in the sky. The light expanded and then winked out. He turned to Major Pel who still gazed skyward. "Was that the Inquisitive?"

"Yes, their battle is over and now ours begins."

"Is there anything else we can do to prepare?"

"We have done what we can. This settlement is not a military outpost so our defenses are weak at best. We do not know the objective or plans of our enemy only that they do not appear to negotiate. Perhaps the Inquisitive was a threat to them and we are not. Whatever is the case, we shall know soon."

Angela was with Mikey and sat holding him in the middle of the living room as the first sonic booms began. Michael had told her that aircraft making military tactical landings come in so fast they create a sonic boom. Each boom increased her feelings of fear and Mikey sensing his mother's distress began to cry. Michael told Angela to stay in the middle of the house away from the windows. She began to hear explosions and the pop of projectile weapons. Then there was the whoosh and the resulting explosions from mortars. The concussions were getting closer and closer. Finally, a shell landed toward the front of the house blowing in the windows. Angela covered Mikey from the debris that flew in the house and crawled under the kitchen table.

Angela turned in fear as the front door came crashing open. Michael came running in followed by Gunny Bin both carrying projectile rifles their uniforms dirty and torn. As Angela rose from under the table, Michael picked up the baby. "You've got to go!"

"Go where?"

"Gunny Bin is going to take you and Mikey up to the dome on the hill. You can open it and remain safe inside. These creatures attacking us are over running Pel's Marines and we don't have much time!" Angela was crying as she stood and took Mikey from Michael's arms.

"What about you? Aren't you coming?"

Michael stepped close and held both Angela and Mikey. He looked down at both of them tenderly. "I've got to go to the Science Center and help Henry destroy the records there before they are captured by the aliens. There is just too much information there about our cultures that can fall into enemy hands." Michael nodded over Angela's shoulder at Gunny Bin. Gunny Bin stepped forward. "Angela we must go NOW!"

Michael stepped back and Angela turned and glanced one last time around their home. Through the door to their bedroom Angela spotted Michael's identification tags still on their chain lying on the dresser. With Mikey in her arms, she ran in and grabbed the tags. Coming back in the room, she nodded at Gunny Bin. "I'm ready!"

Michael rushed over gave Angela and Mikey a kiss then ran back out the front door. Gunny Bin stepped forward. "The back door, we'll use the back door." Gunny Bin went through the door first and looked both ways. "Go now hurry! I'll be right behind you!"

Angela ran out the door and up the road toward the dome. She glanced back over her shoulder toward the settlement. It was all smoke and chaos with figures running between the buildings exchanging weapons fire. Angela stopped and looked toward the Science Center just as part of the building exploded! The blast knocked Angela over like an invisible fist. Angela curled around Mikey on the ground as debris began to fall from the sky. She felt the heavy weight of Gunny Bin as she lay over them protecting her and Mikey. As pieces of the building fell all around them, Angela heard Gunny Bin grunt as if she lost all her air. When it stopped raining debris Gunny Bin rolled off them. "Get up quickly, run!"

Angela picked up Mikey and Gunny Bin picked up her weapon and turned to face figures that were beginning to follow them. Angela saw flashes from the weapons of the figures as they moved. As Gunny Bin turned to face the threat, Angela saw the piece of bloody metal stuck in Gunny Bin's back. "No, you need help, your hurt!"

Gunny Bin sat forward brought her weapon up and began firing at the figures below. In her mind, Angela heard Gunny Bin say loudly. *"TAKE MIKEY TO THE DOME, NOW!"*

With Mikey in her arms, Angela ran to the dome. She could still hear Gunny Bin firing behind her as she pressed her hand to the dome and the door opened.

Inside it was quiet and in the gentle light of the dome, Angela could see the small couch. She thought of how much it reminded her of a cradle as she laid Mikey down. Angela looked down and noticed she still had Michael's identification tags in her hand. She gently put the chain around Mikey's neck and gave him a kiss on the forehead. Mikey looked up at her and smiled. It was as if all fear had left him. "Now, Mikey, you be a good boy. I will be right back. I have to help Aunty Bin. We'll all be safe in here!"

Angela gave Mikey another kiss then rose and ran back out the door. The door closed and in the soft light Mikey felt warm and sleepy. As he closed his eyes, Mikey didn't notice the curved crystal cover that came up and over the cradle. Once the lid had closed, the cradle slowly sank into the floor of the dome.

Chapter 26

DWS CONQUEROR

Korab stood stone still under the fury that burned in the Prime War Leader's eyes. "KORAB, YOU USELESS WORM! I SPECIFICALLY TOLD YOU I WANTED THAT SHIP INTACT!

"Bu-but Prime, they were shooting at us with mobile missile launchers from the Launch Bays! How was I to know they had many other munitions stored in the Bays! I thought . . ."

Harrak came to full height above the quivering Sub-Prime and spat. "YOU THOUGHT! YOU THOUGHT!" Then Harrak relaxed a little and slowly turned away from the obviously relieved second in command. In a terse almost quiet whisper, Harrak proclaimed. "You don't think. You OBEY!"

To the terrified Bridge crew his speed was blurring. Harrak spun fully around his left hand claws extended tearing through the neck of Korab so fast that Korab was dead before he could register surprise at the Claw Kill. The lifeless body collapsed upon itself. Ignoring the blood pooling on the deck, Harrak walked before Parek. "Do you have anything to say?"

"No Prime!"

"Do you have any idea how many breed able females and how much usable equipment was lost today?"

"No Prime!"

"IT IS TOO MUCH!"

Harrak stalked to the navigation console picked up a rag and absently wiped the blood off his claws. His gaze directed to the planet out the view port Harrak stated. "Parek, you will be the new Sub-Prime." Parek pulled himself up to his full height with obvious pleasure. "Thank you Prime, you will not regret this!" Harrak turned and grinned at Parek displaying his lower fangs. "If I ever do, you will quickly join Korab. Now tell me what you found on the surface of the planet."

"After the ship was . . . gone. We divided into two groups and flew in before the landing shuttles carrying the warriors. Since there was, only the one settlement down there it wasn't too difficult to identify. As the shuttles set down, we flew over the settlement taking out defensive positions of opportunity. Since there were but a few heavy weapons, after we neutralized them we landed and went in with the warriors. There were two different species down there. One, called Giann, the other called Human. The Giann are thinner with oval heads and large eyes. They come in large and small varieties. The large Giann both male and females appeared to be warriors. The bulk of our losses came from these warriors. Our scientists tell me that the female Giann are not compatible for our breeding. The humans appear smaller weaker and slower than the Giann warriors do. I have no idea why some of the Giann warriors seemed to be taking orders from a human. Few of the humans appeared to be warriors and those that weren't ran and died like D'mon cattle. The human females though are breeding compatible and we captured almost twenty of them."

Harrak put up his hand. "Stop, what do you mean ALMOST?"

"The scientists say one of the human females captured had her reproductive organs removed!"

"And they let her live after that? What's the use?"

"We brought her along because the younger females seemed to quiet when she was with them. Perhaps she is a Lead Female?"

"Let her take care of the breed able ones until they produce. The fewer the problems with transporting the females, the better it will be. However, if she causes trouble, kill her in front of the others as an example. Put monitors on the surface of the planet to let us know if either species returns. Do it quickly. Tomorrow we will leave to rejoin the Fleet. If they come back in numbers we will need more ships to support us!"

"Yes, Prime, as you command." Parek left the Bridge quickly stopping only to tear the Sub-Prime insignia off Korab's body.

As the deck crew removed the body and cleaned the blood off the Bridge, Harrak sat and watched the planet below. He wondered about the warnings about the golden warriors. If there were any, there certainly weren't any here now. He chuckled to himself. The whole legend was probably just an old story to scare the younglings. Why then was there the old written prohibition on coming to this system? Bah! The claws of his warriors went through these species like through cattle. *Let them come.* He thought. *Let them come. They will make me rich and powerful. Perhaps I will even some day lead the Fleet!*

Chapter 27

PLANET ROMEO

Deep beneath the dome 535.6 AC (18 Lunar Cycles Later)

AWAKEN Defender.

That voice. No, that thought, penetrated the man's deep sleep like sunlight through mist.

Awaken Defender.

At first, it appeared hazy, but then to total clarity. The man opened his eyes. Above him, he saw the gentle curve of the tan ceiling melting into the walls, which suggested a round room. As he looked around he asked, "Where am I?"

You are at . . . home.

The voice/thought had paused as though searching for the word that would best fit the man's description of his environment.

The man thought for a moment then said. "You said, Defender, are there others?"

No.

"I can hear you but I cannot see you."

That is because I am within you. I speak to you in your mind.

"Why are you within me?"

I am Teacher. I shall guide you and to prepare you for your future battles. All the information that is available in the storage libraries has been recorded your mind as you slept. You have all the historical data of this planet and the beings that dwelt here. That information includes all the species they had met and studied. This past data you will remember when it is required. I am here to help you after you awoke, to learn new things. Many questions you may have about this place, this planet, or the people that designed me, you can access by just concentrating.

The man closed his eyes concentrated and remembered. Most species that knew them just called them, "The Old Ones." They have many names by many species and many cultures but there were no records of them ever labeling themselves. They were an old star-traveling race of beings. Though some legends said, they traveled everywhere throughout the galaxy, there were no records of them colonizing or branching out from their own planet. The Old Ones had advanced technologies but they neither helped nor hindered the development of the beings they met until the arrival of, The Evil Ones.

The legends don't say where they came from; some say another galaxy, some said a long lost corner of our own galaxy. The only fact agreed upon is they were nomadic, traveling from system to system. They called themselves, "D'mon." The Old Ones in their pragmatic way just referred to them as, "The Evil Ones." They were vicious warriors and annihilated or enslaved any that opposed them. They absorbed any species they could breed with to expand their fleets and enslaved the rest. Their young developed so quickly often the females would die because of their body deteriorating in the development of the young. Subsequently, the desired spoils of the D'mon were technologies to expand their fleets and the subjugation of a breed able species.

The Old Ones knew of their coming long before they began to attack systems anywhere near them. Prior to the coming of the D'mon, the Old Ones had no need of a military defense. After all, they had lived for eons in peace. To counter the threat they began to prepare by creating warriors called, "Defenders." The developing Defenders ingested food and fluids, which contained a substance, which the Old Ones referred to only as the, "Element."

The Element was a substance found only on the Old Ones' planet, and was their most closely guarded secret. The Old Ones had found that the Element had unusual and beneficial properties. The Old Ones used biochemical-accelerated growth to develop a Defender, but the Element still needed to grow with the body. As a result, the growth and training of a Defender still took time.

Only the first few Defenders were ready when the Evil Ones arrived. The Old Ones sent the Defenders with the combined might of the neighboring species against the Evil Ones. Due to the Element, the Old Ones could track the position and the progress of the Defenders throughout the battle. The Defenders fought bravely and killed thousands of the Evil Ones, but one by one, the Old Ones saw the Defenders Elemental markers cease to exist. Once the Evil Ones arrived at the Old Ones' planet, they held such a fear and loathing of the Defenders they didn't even attempt to conquer the planet. They launched every major missile weapon on their ships and totally sterilized the planet.

For some reason that is unknown, the Evil Ones stopped their advance at this system. Why did they stop? There is only speculation for the records are long gone. The planets and cultures were defeated and stripped of technology. They then reverted to barbaric survival. History reverted to myth and legend. The last thing the man remembered was the true name of the Old Ones. The other species called them Anjiils. "Yes, I remember the war, the Evil Ones and why the Defenders were created!"

Good, for now it is time to begin your training.

The Defender sat up in his bed and saw he was in the middle of the room. To his right he saw a table with a central hollow space, which protruded out of the wall. Above the table was a reflective surface in which he saw his own image. The Defender remembered these were a sink and mirror. As he swung his feet over the side of the bed he looked around and "remembered" what the other furniture or items where. A table, an eating alcove, a food and water dispenser an alcove with toilet and shower and of course there is the bed and door. Coming to his feet, the Defender felt a shiver since there was nothing covering his body.

Lesson one, clothes. Defender you have the ability to create your own body covering. The clothes come from the molecules of the Element, which has combined with your body. The clothes can be as soft as silk pajamas or as hard as full Elemental body armor. Your subconscious default body covering will always be full Elemental body armor. This is so if taken by surprise while sleeping or ill, you will have protection. So first, think and remember a type of clothing you would like.

The Defender chose a tan sweat suit with tan socks and soft canvas shoes. The instant he recognized the thought he was wearing a tan sweat suit with socks and canvas shoes.

Now think full body armor.

The sweat suit changed to golden body armor complete with a slightly wavering Elemental field somewhat like a helmet around his head. The Defender noticed that the force field helmet appeared invisible but by looking in the mirror, from the outside it had a faint golden glow. With the Elemental field type helmet in place, he had a full field of vision. To the right of his eyes was a numerical readout. It gave in meters the distance to what he was looking at that moment.

The armor is either impermeable or partially permeable depending on your environment. In an environment such as the surface of this planet, the armor will allow an exchange of clean breathable gasses filtering only dust and contaminates. In space, under water, or in a non-breathable atmosphere the armor produces the air you need. Remember, when your armor produces something, it uses your body's store of the Element. After prolonged use, you will feel hungry and thirsty. You must ingest food or fluids, which contain with the Element to replace the Element that your body used. Now that your body has grown in combination with the Element, you require the Element to survive. You are no longer exactly like the species of your origin.

As the Defender changed his armor back to his sweat suit, the Defender asked, "Teacher what is the species of my origin?"

They called themselves "Human".

"Have they gone?"

No the remains of most of the humans that came here are still on the surface of the planet.

"What happened to them?"

The Evil Ones eliminated most of them. They took a few female humans with them when they left.

"Am I to battle the Evil Ones?"

Yes.

The Defender thought about the idea for a moment then accepted the conclusion as a fact. "I will avenge those humans." The Defender walked over to the sink counter and found two rounded metal rectangles on a metal chain. He picked them up and examined them carefully. "Teacher what are these?"

I believe they are identity disks. The human female that brought you to the dome put them around your neck before she left.

"What does the writing say?"

I do not know. The translator, implanted in your brain, can translate over one thousand verbal languages and eight hundred written. However, except for those disks I have no other sample of the human written language.

The Defender looked at the disks in his hand then took them by the chain and put them around his neck. "I shall keep the disks that were given to me."

Then we start. Exit your quarters and follow the passageway to the training center. From here on, everywhere you go you will run!

The Defender ran to the door and followed the twisting turning passageway. With sweat blurring his vision and his legs feeling stiff and heavy, the Defender slowed then stopped. "Teacher, how far is it?"

It is only ten kilometers, in time you will make this run in minutes.

Finally, the Defender came to what appeared to be the surface of the planet. Standing at the entrance of the passage, he saw lush green vegetation with wide sandy paths that went straight, right and left from him. On either side of the passage entrance are large basins on pillars at about waist high. Clear water splashed into the basins. It dropped from outlets in the rock, about a meter above each basin. Next to the basins were hooks with soft towels.

These are water stations. They are throughout the training complex. Remember to refresh yourself between each segment of training. You must always remember be it battle or training during a pause you must refresh yourself with food or water that replaces the Element that your body uses. You will understand this well when your body produces your weapons and armor. You will feel the need to replace the Element as you weaken.

He went to the basin washed the sweat from his eyes and drank deeply from the cool sweet water. Refreshed, he walked to the intersection of the paths. Looking up at the clear blue sky the Defender asked. "Is this the surface of the planet?"

No, this is the vast training chamber. It is in the shape of an oval. As you will now run the perimeter, you will notice that you will pass other passageways into the rock on your right side. These are tunnels to other Defender quarters.

"So eventually I will return here. How will I know which passage leads to my quarters?"

Look behind you Defender.

He turned and blinked his eyes in astonishment! Above the entrance etched into the rock was his likeness.

The Element in the rock produced your likeness as you first left the passageway. The likeness will remain as long as you use the quarters.

The Defender turned and again looked at the vastness of the chamber.

The light in the chamber as in your quarters are the correct spectrum with the correct amount of heat to mimic your species requirements. You require certain wavelengths of light to develop properly. The foliage, which is native to this planet, never less produces oxygen in a similar concentration for your physiological requirements. The vast space, the light and foliage will also help your psychological requirements since your species has not fully adapted to living underground. You are currently several kilometers beneath the surface of the planet.

The path, which leads straight out of the passageway, leads to the arena. In the arena, you will learn to develop and use your weapons, your armor, and offensive and defensive techniques. Now run the perimeter course and pay attention to what you see.

The Defender started down the path to his right. As he ran, he noticed obstacles along the path large square stones, trellises of wood squares, round pits four and five meters deep, walls ten meters high and ladders crossing high poles at different heights. As he ran, Teacher explained each obstacle, some you climb, some you jump up upon, some you crawl under, some you jump over, some you swing over, and some you will break through.

On the run this afternoon, you will start on this course. In due time, you will also complete this training course in minutes.

Returning to the original passage tired and out of breath, the man stopped and leaned over with his hands on his knees.

Refresh yourself Defender. Always remember to refresh yourself.

He placed his face in the cold clear water and drank greedily. The water in the basin tasted wonderful! Amazed at how quickly his fatigue faded, the Defender ran to the arena. All the paths from the tunnels ended at a large path that circled the arena. On the outside of the circular path were multiple water stations. Each water station had its own complement of towels. On the inside of the ring was a flat sandy area about one hundred meters across. Separating the outside path from the sand of the arena was a one half meter golden ring of metal.

Defender, stand inside the ring.

The Defender crossed the golden ring and walked about ten meters toward the center of the arena. A wall of blinding sand flew out of nowhere! The Defender felt the push of the gale force winds but didn't feel the sand hitting him. Holding his gloved hand up he realized he was already in full body armor. Looking straight, he could see the sand part just before his face where it was striking the helmet like, Elemental field.

Your armor is now a reflex. When you are in danger, your armor will form by reflex.

The Defender looked down at his gloved hand. He turned it over and felt a few grains of sand between his fingers. When he desired, he could feel the individual grains just as if they were in his fingers. He could feel through his armor, and he formed his armor! "Formed? Formed from what?"

It formed from your skin. The Element in your skin lets you form another epidermis that contains the Element. When the threat is over and you require your regular garments, the Elemental armor is absorbed and the clothing made.

As quickly as the sand storm started, it stopped. All was again still in the arena.

As you train, you will fight in all known environments. This is possible within the arena. Always remember, in a non-breathable environment such as space, underwater or in toxic gasses, your armor will use more of your bodies Element. You will fatigue faster and have to stop and refresh sooner. At the beginning of your training, I will direct you to refresh as you fatigue. As you progress in your training and become skilled, you must choose the time to refresh yourself. In the great battle with the Evil Ones, many of the Defenders had no experience. They became fatigued and over whelmed before they could refresh. Now, stay in full armor and proceed to the center of the arena.

The Defender walked to the center of the arena and awaited further instruction.

Now clear your mind and think Saber.

The Defender thought, "Saber" and stood expectantly, nothing happened.

Defender you are right hand dominant, reach back over your right shoulder by your neck.

Doing as instructed, he felt a hilt of a sword just over his right shoulder. Turning his head as far as he could, on the edge of his vision he could see a rough white hilt with golden cord wound tightly around the grip. He grasped the hilt and the saber easily slipped out of the scabbard now attached diagonally to the back of his armor.

The blade is made of a beautiful crystal. The hilt a non slip white knurled ceramic with the gold gilded cord wound tightly around it at one centimeter increments. The golden hand guard resembled the type used on the ancient katana. He grasped the saber next to the guard and when he opened his hand palm up the weapon has perfect balance. He looked closely at the curved crystal blade. "The blade looks nice and hard but won't it break or shatter?"

Try the Blade Defender.

Before him appeared a three-meter high wooden post about fifteen centimeters thick. Next to the post was a granite pillar, flat on top one meter high and about fifty centimeters thick. Last, there was a three-meter steel "I" beam. The Defender put both hands on the hilt of the saber and sliced right through the wooden post. Next, he came straight down on the flat top of the granite pillar and cleaved the pillar in two halves. Finally, he sliced at the steel beam and the blade penetrated about five centimeters and stuck. He jerked on the hilt and the saber pulled free.

Now, try the steel again but think, "Heat".

The Defender thought "heat", as he swung at the steel. The saber glowed brightly and cut smoothly through the steel leaving melted edges on the two halves he created.

You will use the heat to cut through enemy armor and steel.

He closely examined the saber and was surprised to find no nicks or scratches on the blade. When he raised the blade to sheath it, he was amazed when it seemed to jump back into the scabbard.

Draw your saber Defender.

As instructed, he drew the weapon and held it before him.

Now, throw the saber Defender.

He drew back his arm and threw the saber as far as he could. He watched, as it flipped over in the air hit the ground with a loud clang and skidded to a halt about thirty meters away.

Defender, concentrate on a slow return.

Following the instructions, he thought slow return. The Defender watched the blade turn on the ground until the hilt faced him, then it started a slow slide towards him. Before the saber reached him, he knelt and opened his hand. The saber slid right into his open palm.

The Elemental Saber comes from the Element that has combined with your body. As with polarized molecules, it returns to your body. I suggested slow return, since the thought "return" will give it speed. The saber will appear to fly into your hand. Now when you think return you will expect the speed at which it will come. Now think "Dagger".

With the thought of "Dagger", a dagger in a sheath appeared on the inside of his left forearm with the hilt just above his hand. The Teacher explained that the dagger had the same properties as the saber and when thrown can return to the hand or sheath in the same manner.

Remember Defender, your weapons return to the Element in your body. As the Element in your body depletes there is less attraction for your weapons, so less chance of retrieval. Take the time to refresh and rejuvenate the Element in your body. Defender, now imagine your Spear.

With the thought of spear, on the outside of his right calf there appeared a cylinder five centimeters thick and ten centimeters long. It is snaps into two golden retainer clips on his armor. As he bent to unclip the cylinder, he felt a small latch right where his thumb would naturally rest on the cylinder. Once the cylinder was in his hand, he pushed the latch. The cylinder telescoped out to a two-meter spear with ten-centimeter flat pointed spearheads on each end. He found the spear could either stab or slice as needed in either direction. He found the only difference in how the spear worked was when the spear returned it contracted back down as a cylinder before returning. This action prepares the spear to clip on for storage and negates the chance of a returning spear point causing injury.

Teacher directed the Defender through the daily training activities. Each day started the same with quick nourishment then the run down to the arena. Each challenge on the circular training course grew easier as each day the speed of the Defender increased. In the arena, the Defender fought all sorts of opponents and learned their tactics, strengths and weaknesses. The training in the arena had also started at a slow pace but after each opponent, the next opponent's speed increased. The Defender developed speed and accuracy with his weapons and no longer had to think of each weapon. Faster and faster, as he needed a weapon it jumped into his hand. At first single, then multiple opponents faced the Defender. As his speed increased, so did the number of challengers.

Chapter 28

EGAS STARFURY

A-OOGA! A-OOGA! Maryann awoke to the scream of the claxon. She jumped down from her rack and maneuvered around all the other Officers in various states of dress, to her locker for her gear.

"ALL CREW, MAN YOUR BATTLE STATIONS. ALL MARINES, REPORT TO YOUR LANDING SHUTTLES. THE STARFURY HAS JUST ENTERED THE ROMEO SYSTEM!"

With that announcement, Maryann climbed into her combat uniform and body armor. Maryann trotted along with everyone else from the Marine Squad Bays to the Shuttle Launch Bays. At the hatch of the Launch Bay the Marine Armorer was handing out weapons, ammunition and neutron grenades. Strapping on her weapons and grenades as she walked, Maryann proceeded to the end of the Bay where Gunny Müller was getting the platoon organized.

"Effery Marine, check the gear of the Marine next to them. Ensure all veapons are loaded but der safeties are set. Nothing jingles on your armor ant check all communication links."

Gunny Müller seeing Maryann arrive snapped to attention and saluted. Maryann returned the salute. "Stand easy Gunny, what's the situation?"

"Der Platoon is all present and accounted for Ma'am. Effery
Marine has five hundred rounds for personal veapons und fifty
rounds for pistol ant four grenades. Ve also haf von Squad off
Marines from der Heavy Veapons Platoon assigned to us. They
are two neutron mortar crews' und two heavy automatic weapons.
Ve carry enough food und vauter for three days."

"Very well Gunny, get the Marines mounted up and into the
shuttle. The Bridge says there are no space threats so we should
be going down to Romeo within the hour. Captain Gin the new
Company CO, is holding Officers Call at the other end of the
Launch Bay. I'll leave my gear by the ramp. I should be back
shortly with anything new." The Gunny responded, "Aye ma'am",
and turned to move the Platoon into the Shuttle. Maryann jogged
over to the meeting at the end of the Bay. She arrived between
Phillips and Pierce just as Captain Gin began speaking.

"As you already know, the Bridge has stated that sensors find
no other ships in the system. They have located what appear to be
debris of one ship and a couple of shuttles out by one of Romeo's
moons. There are no communications coming from Romeo.
The Starfury will examine the space debris after we go down
to the planet to search for survivors. The shuttles will go down
in diamond formation and will land about a click away from the
settlement. After landing Second Platoon will form center point
with First Platoon, right and Third Platoon left. HQ Platoon
will be drag and reserve. Fourth Platoon will dig in and form
security for the shuttles. Heavy weapons will stay with Fourth
Platoon by the shuttles."

"With some luck, the hostiles overlooked the small settlement
and only went after the Inquisitive. If they have, the people in
the settlement are keeping communications silent. Just in case,
give the orders to your Marines to open fire, only if attacked.
I don't want a survivor shot by a jumpy Marine. Are there any

questions?" Captain Gin looked into the faces of his Officers and saw no questions. "Good luck, see you on the ground!"

Maryann walked with John back to the shuttles. "You watch your back over there on the right Sailor Boy."

"Same to you Pug. Good luck."

Maryann gave him a parting salute as she turned up the ramp of the Third Platoon's shuttle. Gunny Müller handed Maryann her weapon and gear as she came up the ramp. Her Platoon was already strapped in with personal weapons strapped in a storage boot by their right foot. Maryann looked around at the expectant faces, as she took her seat and strapped in across from the Gunny. They sat in the last two seats next to the ramp. "I'm the first one out folks; if anyone is going to trip it'll probably be me!" That produced a small nervous laugh. Maryann knew that for almost all of her Marines, this is their first combat landing.

"Now, when the ramp goes down we break left, diamond formation. First Squad point, Second Squad left flank, Third Squad right flank and Fourth Squad on drag. Heavy Weapons will break off and form with Fourth Platoon for security for the Shuttles. Mortars dig in with Fourth Platoon to provide fire missions as needed. Lead Corpsman will be in the center with me. Gunny Müller picks his spot."

"I vill be wit der First Squad on point."

Maryann felt the lightness of space as the shuttle left the artificial gravity of the Starfury. Shouting over the roar of the engines, Maryann directed. "OK PEOPLE, LOCK AND LOAD!"

Maryann's command directed the Marines on the shuttle to pull their weapons from the storage boots. Rings on the weapons clip to a crisscross harness across the front of their body armor. Holding the weapons diagonally across their chests with barrel up, they pulled their slides and ammunition fed into their weapons. The Platoon was ready. After landing, all the Marines had to do was push their weapons forward and the weapon rings would release.

"Now remember, we're looking for friendlies down there, so listen to your helmet comm., no firing without authorization. Return fire if attacked otherwise listen for Gunny or me on the headsets. Are there any questions?" There were a few scattered no's. "I CAN'T HEAR YOU PEOPLE!"

A resounding, "NO MA'AM", followed that!

"Very well", replied Maryann as she turned rechecked her own gear and left the Platoon to their thoughts.

Chapter 29

DWS PREDATOR

(D'mon Fleet Flagship, of the Elevated Prime)

"WHY should we believe you Harrak?" snarled the Elevated Prime. Harrak looked around the long table at the mostly hostile faces of the other Prime Warriors. "You have brought back no new technology only a few females that you could have picked up anywhere! You say you were at the Planet of the Shame, but there were no Golden Warriors there! Odd story I would say."

As he looked around Harrak saw far too many heads nodding in agreement. Harrak replied as his anger began to build! "I would have captured a new ship if that fool Korab hadn't been so incompetent!" The Prime across from Harrak spat. "It seems convenient to blame it on a dead underling."

"What about the alarm signal? You all must have gotten the signal that a breed able species returned there", Shouted Harrak with spittle flying from his fangs!

"Yes we all got the signal but that still doesn't prove **you** went there! The Council has no proof you had a message ordering you to go there! It appears your arrogance and ambition has finally pushed you over the edge!" Harrak threw back his chair and jumped to his feet. Saliva dripped from his fangs and his claws were exposed!

WHAM! Harrak jumped back as the energy bolt blasted a deep hole in the wall just past his head. He could smell the ozone from the bolt and the stink of melted metal. He knew one more aggressive move and he would be dead. The Elevated Prime with the smoking weapon still in his hand hissed. "This is a Council of Primes! It is not a blood challenge for new warriors! My next shot won't miss, now sit down!" Harrak looked around and saw he was the last one standing. With a look across the table that could melt steel, he finally grabbed his seat and sat. He turned his attention to the Elevated Prime.

"Look. I'm not asking the whole Fleet to go back. The sensors I left on the planet have signaled a return of the same two species as before. All I ask is for a couple of ships to volunteer to come with me. I will equally share what technology and females we find. It makes sense that they would send a better-armed vessel to find out what happened to their ship."

Harrak dramatically slammed his fist on the table. "I just want to be able to crush any opposition easily and quickly. Who is with me?"

Harrak looked from one face to the next all the way around the table. Most were shaking their heads, some were looking elsewhere, and some examined their claws. Then his eyes fell on Old Skmor. The scarred old warrior is the Prime of the D'mon ship Decimator. Harrak saw the cold calculation in his eyes then slowly a nod. "The Decimator will follow." With that Skmor's oldest son, Pilak added. "The Warrior's Revenge will follow too!"

Harrak stood. Skmor and Pilak stood also. The three of them looked to the Elevated Prime. The Elevated Prime looked down the table and brooded. Finally, he gave a nod. "Go, I lift the ban on the old planet. But . . ." He said as he lifted one clawed finger in warning. "If you find trouble, there will be no help from the Fleet. And . . ." He said with an evil grin. "If you are successful, fifty percent of your spoils go to the Fleet! Take it or leave it!" The room was deadly quiet as Harrak glanced first at Pilak then Old Skmor. A smile cracked the old scarred face of Skmor then a small nod. Harrak turned to the Elevated Prime and slammed his fist on the table. "WE'LL TAKE IT!"

Chapter 30

ROMEO

AFTER a fast tactical landing, the Marine Company spread out, slowly sweeping through the old defensive positions, and finally approached the settlement itself. Maryann signaled a halt while once again taking the identification tags off a mutilated skeletal torso with limbs and head missing. Maryann handed the tags to Müller. "Gunny, you ever seen anything like this before?"

Müller placed the tags in a bag with the others found on the remains at the fighting positions. "No, but this must haf been some very violent battle. The remains that vern't blown apart appear to be ripped and cut to pieces. Ve can't tell how many the defenders killed the attackers must have taken their dead with them. Veapons and ammunition are all gone only torn up bodies remain. Very bad this, this is very bad."

Maryann nodded in agreement, as she watched one of her Marines stumble over to a rust colored bush bend over and vomit. She noted even the normally stoic Giann looked uneasy. Her comm. earpiece on the Company channel came to life and Maryann received a message from Captain Gin. After replying to the message, Maryann turned to Müller. "Gunny, Captain Gin is having Officers Call up at the building labeled Science Center. Rotate the Squads bagging the bodies and keep two Squads on security at all times. Have the heavy weapon crews dig in just in case. Put the mortars twenty-five meters behind, and one automatic weapon on each end of the perimeter."

"Aye ma'am," Müller replied returning to the grisly task.

Captain Gin appeared even more somber than usual for a Giann as Maryann jogged up to the group in front of the damaged building labeled "Science Center". Captain Gin nodded acknowledgment of her arrival. "Overall, what the Company has found is this; an unknown number of an unknown enemy easily over ran the hastily prepared defensive positions. After over running the perimeter it appears they took or destroyed everything mechanical or electrical they could carry. There are no remains of any human females although they killed all Giann females both military and civilian. The attackers were extremely violent and barbaric. The bodies are in pieces. It appears the attackers were only interested in taking the equipment. Some of the scientist's journals and notes are still scattered around the Science Center."

"The last entries in Dr. Chase's journal have to do with the opening of the dome up the road on the hill. Lieutenant Commander Stil from the Inquisitive, had a child that is missing, as is his wife. They may have been lost with the Inquisitive. There are remains in the Science Center with a Naval Officer's uniform on the parts but the identification tags are missing. Until the medical people can check the DNA of the remains, we can't be sure who is who. The missing equipment includes such mundane items as electric shavers and food processors."

"The Starfury notified me that when we landed we set off a couple of electronic proximity sensors. These are the kind usually tied to remote weapons systems. Obviously, these sensors didn't control weapons but a communication signal. The Comm. Center on the Starfury confirmed that when we landed a flash message went off world. My guess is and the

Captain of the Starfury concurs it probably went to the species that destroyed the Inquisitive and the settlement. We have too many questions here and not enough answers but one thing stands out. I believe that whoever did this are probably on their way back. The Starfury has been in contact with EGAFC, and Fleet Command has decided we're to stand our ground. There is something here that they think is very important and they do not want to give it up."

"The Starfury is a warship with a whole lot more firepower than the Inquisitive. Our Company of Marines can deal out a hell of a lot more hurt than the small Marine contingent from the Inquisitive could. The forty-millimeter energy rail guns on the landing shuttles will be our antiaircraft coverage. I want each shuttle set around the perimeter in a rectangle with over lapping fields of fire. Up the hill behind us is one of the golden domes and behind that the country is too rough to land aircraft. Therefore, we will have a curved perimeter facing west where we landed which is the best LZ."

"Start digging in Marines. At the bottom of the perimeter curve, I want Lieutenant Phillips and First Platoon. To the right will be Mills and Fourth Platoon. To the left I want Pierce and Second Platoon. Lieutenant Hall, I want your Platoon divided. Two Squads to the north in a back up position one-hundred meters behind the right side of the perimeter as a fast reaction force and two Squads to the south to reinforce the perimeter there. Combine mortar teams One and Two to dig in north of the dome. Teams Three and Four dig in south of the dome. I want automatic weapons placed every twenty meters along the perimeter. The Starfury will go out of system and hit the mother ship from behind. We are also expecting the Dauntless with her space fighters at any time. If the Dauntless can show up before the bad guys get here, her fighters and the Starfury may be able to take them out, and we may not get involved." Captain Gin looked at the faces of his Officers and added. "Are there any questions? The Command Post along with Medical will be here at the Science Center. Good Luck."

Phillips, Pierce and Mills started the walk back down the hill to their individual Platoons. Maryann decided she would walk a way down with them. After about twenty-five meters, John stopped and looked at the others. He noticed a worried expression on Chucks face. "Well what do you think?"

"I've got a bad feeling about this. I think if the Dauntless doesn't make it here in time we just might be in a world of hurt."

John looked at Pierce. Yolanda shook her head and smiled. "With or without the Dauntless, I just want to give some payback. You all saw what these pieces of crap did to Pel and his Marines let alone the unarmed civilians. Phillips turned to Maryann. "Well Pug?"

"Don't worry guys Third Platoon will be there for ya. We have a hell of a lot more firepower than Pel had. I think Yolanda's right; it's time for some payback!"

Gunny Müller approached up the slight hill, Maryann watched her friends continue down to their Platoons. Maryann realized she actually didn't feel as confident as she sounded. She felt a little sliver of fear tickling the back of her neck. When Müller arrived, she briefed him on where their back up positions would be located. She tried to keep her face an unreadable mask but Gunny Müller had seen it all before. When she finished the brief, Müller slapped her on the shoulder. "Don't vorry. Ve will do goot, very goot!" Maryann chuckled and shook her head as they walked together to brief the Squad Leaders.

Chapter 31

DWS CONQUEROR

"WE are in the system Prime but there is no evidence of any ships," announced Parek from the sensor display. "It looks like the species that were here before have been rebuilding. It also looks like they have added some new fortifications."

Harrah's eyes narrowed in suspicion. "Send a message to Decimator and Warrior's Revenge. Have them swing wide through the system especially around the moons where those other foolish ships tried to hide."

"Certainly, as you wish, Prime."

Harrak glared at the view screen enhancing the magnification to look at the new defensive positions. "They have more warriors there this time. However, to leave them without off world ship support is foolish. Our warriors will over run them as easily as last time. How much time until we reach orbit of the planet?"

"As we slow for orbit it will be at least one grow, Prime."

"Good! Alert the warriors! Next grow, after we gain orbit, the landing ships will descend!"

Chapter 32

ROMEO

THIRD Platoon had just finished their two back up positions about one hundred meters behind the front curved outer perimeter. Maryann took her place with First and Second Squads to the north and Gunny Müller was with the Third and Fourth Squads in the southern position. Their two positions were smaller curved trenches mimicking the outer perimeter. Like the outer perimeter, they had escape ramps dug at intervals for a tactical retreat. The Platoons on the outer perimeter had been busy placing antipersonnel mines three hundred meters to the front. They also placed range stakes starting at two thousand meters in towards the perimeter for the mortars and automatic weapons to set up fire zones. Maryann stopped her work as her communication earpiece came to life.

"Platoon Leaders this is Captain Gin. I have received word from the Starfury. They have left the system. Long-range sensors have identified three large ships coming into the system. At the speed they are decelerating, they should reach orbit tomorrow. The Starfury will attack if they start to drop landing craft. One to three is not very good odds but if the enemy is involved with landings, they may catch them unawares which will give the Starfury an edge. If the bogies reach orbit by tomorrow morning, I anticipate they will be landing straight away. This will put the sun in our eyes as they land. Make sure all your Marines have their darkest visors on their helmets pulled down at sunrise. Get some rest tonight; they can't land within a thousand kilometers without us knowing about the landing. Gin out."

Third Platoon slept at their defensive positions same as everyone else in the Marine Company. It seemed to Maryann that the amount of sleep the Marines got was relative to the rank of the Marine. Maryann noticed that the Marine Privates seemed to sleep all night. The Corporals slept about three quarters of the night, Sergeants about half and Maryann very little. She was willing to bet the CO didn't sleep at all. The grey of dawn was just pushing away the night when her earpiece came to life.

"Look alive, people! Boats are coming down. The Starfury is swinging in to engage. Good luck Marines! Gin out."

Maryann shouted to her Marines just as she could hear all the other Platoon Leaders shouting to theirs. There was no reason to stay quiet this wasn't going to be a very quiet day.

"ALL RIGHT MARINES DARK VISORS DOWN, LOCK AND LOAD. THE BALLOON JUST WENT UP AND WE GOT VISITORS COME TO DANCE!"

Maryann could see silver flashes coming through the dusty looking clouds. Then she saw the contrails of the hot gasses following the boats down through the atmosphere. As Maryann watched the contrails descend, and heard the following sonic booms, Private Fletcher next to her said just about what everyone must be thinking.

"Crap, there sure is a lot of 'em."

Chapter 33

DWS CONQUEROR

"PRIME, a ship has just entered the system behind us!"

"I KNEW IT!" roared Harrak! "Have all our landing shuttles left?"

"Yes Prime."

"Then launch all space fighters. Half of them will go with us to destroy this ship and half to support the ground warriors."

"Prime, the Decimator and Warrior's Revenge have just started to launch landing shuttles. Their space fighters won't be available until all landing craft have left their Launch Bays."

"I know that you idiot! Launch our group and the others will just have to catch up when they can. Now get this ship out of orbit and face the oncoming enemy NOW!"

Chapter 34

EGAS STARFURY

"Full ahead, Mr. Koffroth." Captain Jason Taft, Commanding Officer EGAS Starfury stated as he buckled himself into his Command Chair.

"Aye Captain, full ahead," responded Koffroth.

Taft heard the beeping of an alarm from the sensor and fire control station. Ensign Parrish at the station calmly turned off the alarm and noted the threat. "Captain one of the ships has already off loaded landing craft and is leaving orbit. It will be between us and the other ships shortly."

"Very well, Mr. Parrish I see them." "Lieutenant Koffroth, hold course for ten seconds then come to course zero two zero. That will put us off their starboard side on the pass. We will volley missiles at their starboard Launch Bays and the starboard engines. Once past we will continue and use the nearest moon's gravity well to turn us around for another pass."

"Aye Captain, on course zero two zero."

Taft felt the small tug of the directional change then patiently waited while Ensign Parrish stared at the fire control monitor. "Captain, we will have a firing solution for missile launch coming in; five, four, three, two, one. We have a solution!"

"Fire Mr. Parrish, Fire!"

"Captain, all missiles are away!"

Chapter 35

DWS CONQUEROR

"AIEEE," screamed Parek! "Prime, the ship is traveling full speed just out of range of our energy cannon! They aren't going to slow and fight. They mean to fly right by us. At that speed, the space fighters won't catch them. PRIME, they just launched missiles!"

"Hard left, full speed," Harrak commanded, as he watched the monitor screen with growing concern.

"But Prime, we're still launching space fighters!"

"Screw the fighters! Do you want to lose the whole ship? Have the energy cannon target those missiles, fast!"

Parek could feel the "Whap, whap, whap," of the energy cannons firing along with the close in projectile systems. He watched in disbelief as the last two unfortunate fighters that hadn't gotten away in time smashed and exploded on the side of the ship as it turned. Parek was about to inform the Prime when the impact of multiple explosions threw him over the console shattering his shoulder on the back of the Prime's throne. Harrak thrown from his throne flew into the back of the warrior bent over the fire control console. His impact shoved the warriors head through the screen of the console killing him instantly. Harrak picked himself up ignoring the dead warrior. "How bad was it?"

Holding the useless arm across his chest Parek limped over to the damage assessment control. "It looks like the energy cannons took out seven out of ten missiles. The remaining missiles took out the right side engine and Launch Bays number two and four. We have one-half power and the warriors are venting the Launch Bays to space to extinguish the fires. We can only recover fighters or landing craft in the left side Bays."

"Ok." Spat Harrak. "They got us once but that trick won't work again. Check with the other ships and see if they have off loaded all of their landing craft. If so, then tell them to send a few of their fighters to the planet for ground support. Then take the rest with them and, KILL THAT SHIP!"

Chapter 36

ROMEO

THROUGH the enhanced vision of his helmet, John watched the craft in the distance land and release streams of warriors. He keyed his Platoon channel to calm his Marines. "Steady folks they will come in range of the mortars in another couple of minutes." He heard the "Bam, Bam, Bam," of the automatic sensor controlled forty-millimeter guns before he saw the fighters streaking down through the clouds. "EVERYBODY GET DOWN! WE'VE GOT INCOMING!"

John tasted the bitter light brown alkali soil in his mouth as his face slammed into the bottom of the trench. Explosions rocked the ground all around the huddled Marines sending shrapnel dirt and debris everywhere. Each person tried to make themselves as small as possible in the trenches as the destruction rolled over them.

As quickly as it started, the explosions stopped. John heard the "Whomp, Whomp," of outgoing mortars and took a quick glance out of the trench. Through the dust and smoke, he could see that three out of four of the forty-millimeter guns are out of action and that only two mortars were firing. He looked up and down the trench and saw there were a few empty spaces where the Marines assigned didn't get up. The Corpsman traveling down the trench would just stop and shake his head. High explosives and energy cannon didn't leave much to fix.

"OK MARINES SPREAD OUT AND FILL IN THE EMPTY SPOTS. KEEP YOUR LINES OF FIRE. WE'LL OPEN UP AFTER THEY HIT THE MINES AT TWO HUNDRED METERS!"

Maryann was startled as someone came sliding into the trench next to her. Captain Gin spoke quietly. "I brought my Headquarters group with me. I left the Doc and his assistants with a Squad for security at the Science Center. If they break the perimeter, there will not be much left to command."

Just as he finished speaking two more fighters flew over the defenses strafing both the perimeter and the backup position with energy cannon. With his face in the dirt not far from Maryann's Captain Gin still had to yell. "WE SURE COULD USE SOME AIR SUPPORT! I HOPE THE DAUNTLESS MAKES IT HERE IN TIME! With that attack, the last forty-millimeter gun erupted in flame and debris.

As the enemy approached the minefields at a steady lope, John could see the remaining mortars couldn't walk their fire in fast enough to make much of a difference in the large number of advancing warriors. Seeing the enemy for the first time clearly through the smoke and dust, Sergeant Barney of Third Squad proclaimed. "The Good Lord Creator, protect us for they surely look like Demons!"

The Demons as John now thought of them, slowed as the mines and the withering fire from the perimeter took its toll. John jammed magazine after magazine into his weapon. However, after the minefields the mass of warriors began to gain speed again. As John fired, he noticed that the enemy to his front and left were thinning as more and more of them raced to his right. Keying his helmet mike, John warned Mills. "Chuck the majority of them seem to be coming in on your side!"

Phillips could hear Mills speaking over the loud staccato of an automatic weapon. "We've burned through over half of our ammunition already and I've got a quarter of my people down!"

Captain Gin broke in on the communication. "Lieutenant Mills, help is on the way keep up the fire, the reaction team will bring more ammunition."

Gin turned to Maryann. "Take three Squads with you every third Marine to carry extra ammunition. We can't let Fourth Platoon get overrun!" Maryann gave him a quick "Aye sir!" then keyed Müller. "Gunny, bring Third Squad with you. Mills is having trouble on the right. Leave Fourth Squad with Captain Gin and the HQ group. Every third Marine is to carry extra ammo. It's about time we got to dance!"

"I am on my vey!"

The automatic weapon that Chuck was using jammed from the heat of sustained firing. Cursing, Mills dropped the firing handle and pulled his rifle to his shoulder. Twenty-five meters from the antipersonnel wire strung before the trenches the Demons pulled small shiny silver balls attached to ceramic handles from loops on their belts. Lobbing them overhand they dove for the ground as the balls over ended into the wire. Chuck yelled a warning then dove for cover. "GRENADES, EVERYBODY GET DOWN!"

There were hundreds of explosions all along the wire in front of the perimeter. Maryann and the reaction team sprinted for the perimeter in two lines. The first line fired over the heads of the Fourth Platoon defenders into the advancing enemy. The second ran behind with weapons strapped to their back as they brought all the ammunition they could carry. The enemy was up and charging again, although the smoke from the explosions that flattened the wire hadn't even cleared the air. The Marines from the reaction team slid into the empty spots in the trench and poured fire into the horrific figures that advanced to within ten meters of the trench.

With grotesque bodies beginning to pile up just outside the perimeter, the charge began to slow. At first individually then in small groups the enemy began to back away. They fired weapons and threw spears, knives and grenades as they backed away. Nevertheless, after a few minutes there were only dead or twitching bodies just outside the perimeter.

Chapter 37

EGAS STARFURY

"Mr. Koffroth, start the deceleration process. We will bleed off some speed to make the gravity loop around the moon."

"Aye, sir, deceleration is starting now."

"Captain, sensors show two of the ships leaving the planets orbit accompanied by space fighters."

"As expected Mr. Parrish, Lieutenant Koffroth, the little trip around the moon will take the rest of the day. We'll meet them head on tomorrow morning when we've finished our loop. Right now secure from General Quarters let the crew get some food and rest. I do believe we'll have an interesting day tomorrow."

Chapter 38

ROMEO

M ILLS watched as the monsters retreated far out of range and added. "That was a close one. I hope they've had enough for today." Maryann slowly looked around at all the bodies and devastation then groaned, "Oh, Gunny!"

Five meters away stood Gunny Müller. The spear through his chest had him pinned against the trench wall. As tears began to form in Maryann's eyes, his right hand still holding the strap of an ammunition box slowly relaxed and opened allowing the box to slide to the floor of the trench.

Rushing to his side Maryann yelled, "CORPSMAN!" However, she knew it was too late. The Corpsman ran up and crouched next to the Gunny putting two fingers at the side of his neck to check for a pulse. With the sadness of a man, that has seen too much death; the Corpsman gently shook his head then closed the Gunny's sightless eyes. Chuck slowly came up and put an arm around her shoulder. He then slowly drew her away down the trench. "You know the first thing old Müller would have wanted you to do was take care of his Marines. We've got a lot of wounded and those Marines still able to fight need food, water, ammunition and rest."

The Corpsman saw her back straighten and then the two Officers left around a bend in the trench. Before moving on to check for any other wounded he noticed the trail of wet spots where her tears had fallen into the rust colored alkali dirt of the trench.

Captain Gin slowly walked along the perimeter. It has been more than four hours since the Demons had retreated. The Platoon Leaders and the Company Sergeant Major were with him on the perimeter inspection. Every fourth healthy Marine was on the perimeter locked and loaded. All the wounded had been taken to the Science Center where the Surgeon and the Corpsmen were busy. The dead Marines are in a back room of the Center covered with plastic tarps.

Captain Gin stopped and looked through his helmet optics at the landing boats in the distance. Since the retreat, the sentries have not seen one of the "Demons", as everyone was now calling them. When they retreated, they didn't take a single wounded one with them. An outer perimeter patrol lead by Pierce dispatched any that didn't die from their wounds. John Phillips wounded in the right shoulder by shrapnel when the wire blew, had the arm slung to his chest. Captain Gin spoke as he watched the silent landing craft in the distance.

"We lost a third of the Company today. All four, air defense weapons are gone. Two mortars destroyed and no ammunition left for the other two. The mortar teams now have other weapons and are with the decimated Fourth Platoon. The outside wire is down and we have no more mines to use. Are there any suggestions people?" Mills just couldn't resist. "Yes sir. We could ask them to surrender!"

As everyone else just groaned and shook their heads, Captain Gin responded. "That is an option Lieutenant Mills. An option with very little chance of success, but it is an option."

Phillips stepped forward. "What about the Starfury sir?"

"The Starfury is currently out of communications range heading around one of this planet's moons. In her attack this morning, she damaged one of the ships but now the other two are heading out to meet the Starfury in the morning. I believe the Starfury will have her hands full when that time comes."

Captain Gin nodded to Sergeant Barney, cleaning an automatic weapon in First Platoon's sector. He stepped down from the perimeter wall and brought the group with him. Captain Gin stopped between the perimeter and the backup position and faced the group. "I believe that tomorrow morning they will come again. I also believe we'll not be able to hold this perimeter, Sergeant Major."

"Sir?"

"You will take command of First Platoon." John Phillips began, "But sir!"

"Can it Phillips, your right arm is in a sling. You can't shoot a rifle, you can barely shoot your sidearm with your left hand and you're on medication for the pain. You will be at the back up position with me. Lieutenant Hall your Third Platoon will take the position on the right. When the perimeter can no longer hold, I will order you to retreat to the backup position. The Headquarters group and the remnants of Fourth Platoon will furnish cover fire as you fall back. I have Marines now sandbagging the Science Center. It will be our final position.

When the Marines from the perimeter are falling back, I will take the HQ group back to the Science Center with me. If we can't hold the fallback position, you will retreat to the Science Center. The HQ Group and the security Marines at the Science Center will once again give covering fire. Anyone have any questions?"

No one cared to ask about what would happen after the final retreat to the Center. Even Mills was strangely quiet. "Then get your people fed. Distribute all the ammunition and grenades we have left and get some rest. Hopefully, tomorrow will be a long day."

Chapter 39

DWS CONQUER

"**W**HAT DO YOU MEAN THEY RETREATED?" howled Harrak!

With his head down in submission, Parek stammered. "But prime, almost half of the warriors were killed or injured!"

"So? They were just at the point of victory!"

"I guarantee you Prime. Tomorrow our warriors will sweep over these creatures like waves over sand." Harrak brooded as he thought his claws slowly extending and retracting. "You guarantee do you? Well then, take a shuttle down to the planet. You lead them!"

"But Prime! I am injured!"

"Would you rather lead injured, or die right here?"

"As you wish, Prime," with a small bow of the head, Parek quickly left the Bridge for the next shuttle to the planet's surface. Harrak once again watched the slow turning of the planet below. Nightfall was coming to the area where the battle raged today.

Patience, he thought. *Tomorrow the Decimator and the Warrior's Revenge will capture the ship circling the moon and the warriors will finally overwhelm the resistance on the planet. Tomorrow will be a very fine day indeed! I will return to the Fleet in glory and then take revenge on those old shriveled warriors that were so fearful of the Planet of Shame! I will indeed then lead the Fleet!*

Chapter 40

ROMEO

Standing in the trench at the center of what was left of her Platoon, Maryann placed her four grenades in the dirt on the ledge before her. The morning air smelled of smoke, ozone, blood, feces and fear. Maryann glanced to the right, and left at the dirty tired faces. She lifted her visor and raised her voice so the whole Platoon could hear.

"Every other Marine is to have grenades ready on the ledge of the trench. At three-hundred meters, we'll open fire. At seventy-five meters I will order, "Grenades out." At the speed these things run, I believe they will run into the grenades just as they start going off. Throw them just as fast as you can." Maryann pulled down the visor on her helmet and could see the line of Demons lopping towards them in the distance. "Ok Marines, fix bayonets!"

Maryann knew the forty-centimeter blades of the bayonets decreased the accuracy of the weapons but since the Demons attacked in mass, it wasn't much of an issue. The Marines would need the bayonets to keep the Demons from getting too close with knives, spears and claws.

Maryann looked through the scope of her weapon and saw a figure on a hill just outside of weapons range. The figure had one arm strapped to its body and seemed to be directing the mass of horrific beings on their way. Maryann thought. *Oh, if I just had a*

snipers rifle you bastard. I'd put a round right between your ugly eyes!
At three-hundred meters, the earpiece in Maryann's helmet came
alive. Captain Gin said, "FIRE!"

As one, the whole perimeter opened up. Through the smoke
and dust, Maryann could see Demons falling but more just kept
coming. Maryann keyed her comm. set and picked up a grenade.
She yelled, "GRENADES!" Then waited until the first of the
Demons passed the seventy-five meter marker then shouted,
"OUT!" She threw the grenade as far as she could and followed it
quickly with the other three.

The explosions slowed and killed more Demons but as they
slowed, they began to return fire with all sorts of weapons. One
by one, Marine weapons began to fall silent. The Corporal at
an automatic weapon next to Maryann received an energy bolt
to the head. For a moment, the hand of a headless torso kept
the weapon clattering until the body fell over. When the beasts
were moments from gaining the trenches, Maryann heard the
command. "Fall back, head for the fallback position!"

Maryann glanced right and left to make sure that the few
Marines in the perimeter near her started up the ramps out of
the trench to the fallback position. Switching her weapon to full
automatic she hosed down Demons dropping into the trench as
she backed up. At the ramp out, she made sure she was the last
one out and put her last magazine in the weapon. One more time
she emptied her magazine both ways in the trench then ran as
fast as she could for the sand bags marking the fallback position.

Maryann felt like she was in slow motion. The smoke laden
air burned her lungs as she ran as fast as she could. She could
see the Marines at the back up position alternately firing past
her at the enemy behind and cheering her on as she ran. She
could see the pock marks in the dust around her as projectiles
hit everywhere near her. The run for the sandbags seemed to

take forever. Then she was there and she jumped! Diving over the sandbags Maryann felt a stab of pain as a projectile hit her left knee! She somersaulted into the trench holding her weapon across her chest and hit the bottom hard. Maryann almost lost consciousness as the torn knee hit the trench wall at the end of her roll.

Chuck Mills grabbed one of the Marines that had arrived before her and handed off the automatic weapon he was firing. He rushed over to where Maryann lay against the trench holding the bleeding knee in both hands. Chuck fired a pain medication cassette into her thigh then bound the knee with a battle dressing. John Phillips came over from the far side of the position with his hand weapon in his left hand. "Can she move?"

"I think so, if you can give her a hand. Pierce and I with the rest of Marines here should be able to hold at least until you get her back to the Center. But you better move fast!"

John holstered his weapon then bent and grasped the back of Maryann's utility belt with his good left hand. Pulling her up, Maryann gasped in pain. John then asked Chuck to put her arm around his neck and he told her to hold on. Maryann nodded that she understood. Before leaving, John glanced out a firing slit and could see the Demons boiling out of the ramps that come from the perimeter. "Buy us a couple of minutes Chuck. You won't be able to hold here for long. As soon as we're at the Center, start retreating with your Marines. The Captain is standing by to give you guys covering fire."

"You bet buddy, now take off and leave these bad boys to me!"

Phillips with Hall in tow began hobbling his way up to the Science Center. Chuck Mills tapped the Marine at the automatic weapon on the shoulder. Giving him a thumb back signal indicating he should head back to the Center, Chuck once again started firing the weapon in short controlled bursts. Pierce saw

Phillips and Hall leave the trench. Pulling an empty magazine from her weapon and inserting a new one, she stepped up next to Mills to begin firing again. Pierce had to yell over the weapons fire. "WE CAN'T HOLD HERE FOR LONG. I ONLY HAVE TWO MAGAZINES LEFT AND THE OTHER MARINES DON'T HAVE VERY MUCH MORE!

"YOU START THE MARINES WE'VE GOT LEFT, BACK TO THE CENTER ONE BY ONE. I HAVE ONE MORE CAN OF AMMO FOR THIS WEAPON. AFTER YOU LEAVE, I'LL BE RIGHT BEHIND YA!"

Chapter 41

ROMEO

(Beneath the Dome)

DEFENDER it is time.

"Teacher, am I ready?"

Yes Defender, you are ready. On the surface of this planet, the Humans and the Giann fight a desperate battle against the Evil Ones. They need your help.

"Teacher, I feel fear!"

Yes, I know Defender. All sane beings feel fear. You have worked hard and trained well. You are ready.

"Will you be with me Teacher?"

I will always be with you Defender.

"Then I am ready. I will go."

Chapter 42

ROMEO

(The last position)

ONE by one, Peirce had the remaining Marines fall back. The fit carried or assisted the wounded there just weren't enough people left to take the dead. Mills continued firing in short bursts but as the fire from the position slackened the Demons became bolder and slowly moved forward. Pierce fired the last round from her rifle dropped the weapon and pulled out her pistol. She pulled the slide chambered a round and moved next to Mills. "EVERYBODY ELSE IS GONE. ARE YOU COMING?"

"I'M RIGHT BEHIND YA, NOW GET OUT OF HERE!"

Pierce holding her weapon in both hands stood up to the top of the trench and fired her entire magazine at the advancing Demons. She then turned up the ramp leading out of the back of the trench and zig-sagged her way to the Science Center. Diving over the sandbags in front of the Center, Pierce rolled and came up in a squat released the empty magazine from her weapon and jammed in a full one. Captain Gin slid over next to her taking careful aim and fired slow single shots from his weapon. Gin inquired, "Where's Mills?"

With her arms resting across the sandbags firing slowly, Pierce replied. "He was supposed to be right behind me!" The automatic weapon at the last position kept up its scattered fire but Pierce and Gin could see that it would only be a matter of moments before the Demons overran the trench.

Suddenly to their left racing down the hill from the dome, the embattled Marines saw what looked like a golden figure. As the figure ran, a double bladed spear appeared in its hand. The golden figure smashed into the Demon line just as it was about to swallow up the trench.

The Marines watched in amazement as the figure leapt, turned and jumped all the while the double bladed spear tore through the Demons as a scythe through grain. Pierce noticed that energy weapons had no effect on the figure and projectiles bounced off. The figure appeared to have no covering on his head but a slightly wavering golden luminescence. The energy field around the head seemed to stop or deflect all weapon fire or blades a few centimeters from contact.

Two Demons carried a large tubular looking weapon to the top of the outer perimeter and aimed it at the sandbagged Center. The golden figure threw the spear impaling both Demons driving the bodies back over the perimeter. A crystal sword appeared in the figure's hands and glowed with fire as it cleaved through metal armor and helmets. As more Demons charged the golden warrior, more Demons died. Atop the outer perimeter, a Demon with one arm strapped to its side waved a pistol and drove the mass of Demons towards the single threat trying to overwhelm the figure.

Over the top of the outer perimeter, Captain Gin could see three Demon fighters streaking down from the clouds heading in on a strafing run. "EVERYBODY GET DOWN, INCOMING AIR ATTACK!"

Seeing the Demons retreating, Chuck stopped firing. He was letting the barrel of the weapon cool. He saw the fighters coming and elevated the barrel of the weapon. He would attempt to take one of them out with the last of his ammunition. As they came in low, he could see the flashes of their energy cannon as they opened fire. Jamming down on the trigger, Mills screamed. "COME ON YOU BASTARDS, LET'S DANCE!" As he fired, Chuck could see the deadly explosions walking in what seemed like slow motion directly towards his position.

Chapter 43

EGAS STARFURY

THE fighters attacked the Starfury relentlessly, like angry bees swarming around an intruding bear. Taft could feel the concussions of the energy bolts as they battered the scared armor of the Starfury. The anti-air batteries fired continuously at the fast elusive foes. There were scattered cheers on the Bridge as the occasional fighter exploded with small pieces being scattered to the void of space. Ensign Parrish watched the sensors carefully. "Captain, both ships have gone to flank speed. The ship on the right has taken a hard port turn. It will pass to our starboard. We are too close to turn and outflank her Sir!"

With the armored doors closed on the forward view ports, Taft peered at the small view screen attached to his chair console. "Well it looks like they sacrificed these fighters to slow us down. Take us from full ahead to flank speed Mr. Koffroth. Open all missile launcher doors. It looks like we're going to have to run the gauntlet!" Taft felt no sensation of the increased speed but on his monitor, the fighters fell behind.

With all three ships traveling at maximum speed, the distance closed very rapidly. Ensign Parrish said a quick prayer to the Great Creator and watched the range close. "Captain we will be in range in five, four, three, two, one NOW!"

"FIRE, MR. PARRISH, FIRE! LAUNCH ALL MISSILES!"

Suddenly Taft felt an aura of calm knowing he had done what he could. He watched the dancing pulses of their cannon as they reached out hungrily at the two ships. He watched as the cannon of the other ships reached for his. He saw the trails of the missiles as they raced to certain oblivion and the trails of the enemy missiles coming towards him.

WHAM! WHAM! WHAM! The concussions threw any crewmen that weren't strapped in to their deaths. Taft felt his own straps tearing into his shoulders and waist. The Bridge smelt of fried electronics, smoke, blood and vomit. Lieutenant Koffroth strapped in at his console, jerked side to side like a piece of rope in the mouth of an agitated dog. The pounding continued, alarms sounded everywhere, automated hull sealant hissed out of emergency hoses all over the ship. Then suddenly it stopped! Feeling sick and dry mouthed Taft croaked. "Damage report Mr. Koffroth."

Lieutenant Koffroth wiped blood from his mouth on the sleeve of his tunic. His face had hit the console during the exchange. "Starboard engine is down. Three cannon batteries left, one on port, two on starboard. All starboard launchers damaged, three left on port side. Multiple hull breaches, the automated system is repairing the small holes. We have six compartments open to space, their airtight doors currently holding. Muster of killed and/or missing crewmen not yet completed sir."

Taft shook off the slight dizziness he felt. "We took a beating Mr. Koffroth. Bring her around to starboard. Arm the port launchers we still have operational. What's the status of our playmates out there?"

"Captain, one is dead in space and burning. The other ship is turning our way and appears to have moderate damage. The space fighters are catching up and will be on us in minutes."

"Well Mr. Koffroth I fear we won't be able to put up much of a fight this time. Three guns won't keep the fighters at bay. Even the fighters can breach our open compartments. Put the launchers and cannon on automatic slaved to my control. Then sound abandon ship. Get as many of the crew as are left into the Life Pods, you included Mr. Koffroth. I shall attempt to hold them off long enough for the Pods to get away. Get away from the ship and head towards the planet's surface just as soon as you can."

Lieutenant Koffroth struggled out of the straps on his chair and hit the emergency claxon. The claxon started and an automated voice repeated the order to abandon ship and proceed to the nearest Life Pod. "Captain, you've got to leave too. If you don't leave with us you will never get off!"

"I'm sure you are aware Mr. Koffroth the automatic system will fire the launchers and guns, but in the condition the ship is in it won't reload them. I need to tie up those fighters or the Pods will be sitting ducks out there. Now it was a pleasure serving with you Mr. Koffroth but you had better leave. We don't have much time."

Koffroth came to attention and gave Taft a crisp salute. "Aye, sir, I'm proud to have served you. Good Luck." Koffroth turned and was the last of the Bridge crew to leave. Taft returned the quick salute and stated softly, "And good luck to you Mr. Koffroth."

With Parrish's sensor station empty, Taft opened the armored doors uncovering the view ports. He wanted to see firsthand what was going on outside. He watched as the Life Pods launched. They quickly turned away from the oncoming Demons and flew behind the Starfury out of his field of vision. Taft could see the remaining fighters and the enemy ship slowly approaching. If Koffroth saw through, his thin lie about the weapons not reloading, Taft didn't see it in his face before he left. However, he knew how loyal the Lieutenant was and figured he wouldn't leave without a good enough reason.

Taft took a key from a chain around his neck and unlocked the metal covered panel on the side of his chair. Inside the panel are six square buttons. The labels read, one through six. They had a label right above the buttons, which read, "Self Destruct." As he punched in his code, Taft swore. "We just might have a surprise left for the bastards. We just might."

Chapter 44

ROMEO

P IERCE peeked over the sandbags just in time to see the explosions roll over Mills' position and continue towards the Center. Before the explosions could reach the sandbags of the Center, the last fighter in the line of three exploded! Then the second fighter lost a wing, somersaulted to the left, and crashed in a ball of fire! The lead fighter stopped firing and quickly pulled up trying to get away from the two small curved-wing fighters that were on his tail!

"Oh no, you don't!" Tommy Chin stated as he walked energy rounds up the tail of the enemy fighter until it exploded. The small fighter pair made a long turn and as they flew back over the settlement, the pair did a victory roll above the Marines. Pierce quickly changed her helmet comm. channel from intercompany to ship communications. "Tommy Chin is that you?"

"This is Delta Flight, Beta Squadron, from the EGAS Dauntless, at your service ma'am!"

"What the hell took you guys so long?"

"Geeze, there's no hello, how ya doing, nothing? We had to wait for a new friend to accompany us here. It's such a long lonely trip."

Chapter 45

EGAS STARFURY

TAFT was preparing to fire the last of the missiles, and then ram the ship. He figured once he rammed and the ships were entangled he could then hit the Self Destruct. If he were lucky, he just might be able to find one of the Life Pods, and get off the ship before it blew. The Demon ships were just about close enough. He had his one hand poised over the pad that would drive the remaining engine to flank speed for the ram. The other hand was over the last button to fire all weapons.

Just before the last missile launch, he saw the enemy fighters quickly veer off to the port side. The D'mon ship tried a hard turn to his starboard. From behind him, flying incredibly fast appeared a Squadron of small sleek fighters. They dove in formation right in front of his view banked to the port and easily overtook the slower Demon fighters destroying them wholesale! Flying on his starboard side was a new ship he hadn't seen before. The ship was similar to the Starfury but larger! Along with the anti-air guns now on the Starfury, there are larger and longer turret guns. Taft realized it was one of the new Space Cruisers! *No wonder it took them so long to get here! They must have really rushed to get that big bad boy out of the shipyards.*

As he watched the ship's energy cannon fired huge pulses that collided with the fleeing ship. The pulses tore great gaps out of what had been Missile Launch Bays. As the ship continued to turn away from the salvo, the guns concentrated on the aft engine compartments starting an explosion that swept forward to engulf the entire ship!

Calmly replacing and locking the lid of the Self Destruct panel Taft read the name of the ship as it swept forward. It proclaimed the EGAS STALWART. The communication light on Taft's console was blinking. He pressed the receive button. The message came through with a lot of static probably due to the damage to his ship. "Starfury, this is Captain Zin of the EGAS Stalwart."

"Go ahead Captain Zin. This is Captain Taft of the Starfury."

"The enemy's space fighters within the system have been destroyed. The Dauntless will continue to fly Combat Air Patrols around the system. The one damaged ship that was in orbit around the planet, left in a hurry when we entered the system. The ship has enough of a start that I feel pursuit at this time not an option. The Stalwart will begin retrieval of Life Pods and rescue any other battle survivors. I shall be sending a shuttle over with a Damage Control Party to assist you in returning to orbit around the planet Romeo. Is there any other assistance we can provide?"

"No Captain Zin, thanks, and welcome to the Romeo system. I'm sure glad you made it in time!"

Taft sat back in his chair the tension beginning to melt from his shoulders. He looked around at all the damage to the Bridge and the empty crew stations. *I can't remember the exact words, but the ancient poem said something about taking brave ships into harm's way!*

Chapter 46

ROMEO

CAPTAIN Gin moved the Marines out slowly from the Center. They were on line, weapons ready, checking for survivors, wounded or prisoners. Pierce found Mills at the side of a blast crater not far from the destroyed automatic weapon. His armor and uniform torn and burned was still smoldering. The Corpsman gave him a shot of morphine but lowered his eyes to Pierce and shook his head. Pierce knelt next to Mills and he coughed and croaked through burned lips. "Can't a guy get a drink around here?"

With tears in her eyes, Yolanda lifted his head with her arm, pulled out her canteen and dribbled a little water in his mouth. Chuck swallowed painfully then coughed again harder leaving frothy blood in the corners of his mouth. Removing her arm gently Yolanda rolled up an empty sandbag cover and slid it under Chuck's head as a pillow. She then pulled a handkerchief out of a pocket and carefully wiped the blood from his mouth. Yolanda attempted to wipe the tears from her face with her sleeve as she spoke. "Now you hang in there Chuck. We're calling for a shuttle and you'll be up to the Dauntless soon. They have a whole hospital up there!" Mills coughed again and looked at her with pain-fogged eyes. "Did I get him Pierce? He was coming straight in at me. Did I get him?"

Pierce struggled as she gently clasped one of Mills' burnt hands, and then answered in a breaking voice. "You got him Chuck. He crashed right over there." As Pierce looked towards the fighter crash site, Chuck smiled once, and then his head rolled to the side in death. As the Corpsman closed Chuck's sightless eyes Yolanda choked back a sob and placed his hand across his chest. "You got him Chuck. You got him."

Phillips walked up as Pierce climbed out of the crater. With tears streaming down her cheeks she paused by John. "Chuck didn't make it." He put his good arm on her shoulder. "He was one hell of a Marine."

"Yeah he was one hell of a Marine. That's just what I'm going to write to his mother."

Wiping her face Pierce turned and glanced at Chuck's body one last time. She let John's hand fall from her shoulder. "I'm going to the Aid Station and check on Maryann. Can you finish the sweep with these guys?"

"Sure Pierce, go on ahead. I'll finish the sweep."

As Pierce left, Phillips walked up to the top of the outer perimeter. The Corpsman stepped up there with him curious as to where Phillips was looking. "Damn would you look at that?" From where they were standing, they could see a continuous line of Demon bodies. From where the man in gold hit the Demon line, clear out through the perimeter. The Sergeant Major climbed up on top of the sandbags with them. He gave a low whistle. "It sure looks like they got their ass kicked!"

To their left two Marines were tugging at the gold colored spear with the two Demon bodies impaled upon it. The spear had gone through the two Demons and pinned them to a large boulder. The Marines were trying to dislodge the spear so they could throw the Demon bodies into the common pit, dug by a small dozer. A shout came from Phillips' right. "LIEUTENANT, SERGEANT MAJOR, OVER HERE!"

Pulling his pistol from the holster, Phillips had a hard time keeping up with the Sergeant Major through the tangle of strewn bodies. A Sergeant and the Corpsman were standing between two bodies. One was a naked human male with a pair of identification tags around his neck. The other was a Demon that had one arm in a sling impaled to the sandbags by a bloody crystal sword. The Corpsman took a quick look at the two. "Lieutenant these two are still alive! The sword holding the Demon just went through muscle and skin. The other guy is breathing he just looks dehydrated and exhausted."

Phillips squatted in front of the two, and then turned to the Sergeant that called him over. "Sergeant, keep a weapon trained on that Demon as Doc pulls out the sword. Then shackle the Demon and take him to the Aid Station so the Surgeon can look at him. This guy looks like he was in charge of the attack. Captain Gin might be able to get some information out of him. Wrap this other guy up in a tarp and take him to the Aid Station too. He might be able to identify the golden guy."

It took four Marines to shackle the Demon and then not without lacerations from slashes of its claws. Finally, with a liberal use of duct tape around the hands and feet the danger from the claws ended. The Demon and the unknown man rode on stretchers. Three times on the way to the Aid Station at the Center, the Demon tried to break his bonds and rolled off the stretcher. After the third attempt, Phillips told the Corpsman to give him some sedation to quiet him down. The Corpsman pulled out a morphine cassette and as he injected the demon stated. "Basically Lieutenant this is an alien. You do realize this stuff could kill it."

"As far as I'm concerned it's a small loss. I'm not getting any more Marines injured moving this beast."

On the way back to the Center, John also pondered another puzzling occurrence. When the Corpsmen pulled the sword from the Demon's side the sword turned to dust the rusty color of the surrounding soil. A Corporal described the same result when the two Marines finally pulled out the spear that impaled the two Demons to the boulder. John wondered if it was a design built into the weapons or what. Perhaps it prevented an enemy from picking up the weapons and using them against the golden guy. The speculation ended at the arrival at the Center.

The Surgeon and the other Corpsmen were still busy caring for the minor wounded left at the Station. Several shuttles had come down from the Dauntless first thing this morning, transporting the most serious wounded up to the ship's Sick Bay. Finding Maryann with her knee splinted and bandaged John asked. "How are you doing Pug?"

"Doc said I'll be fine. There's no major damage. I'll just have to use the crutches to get around for a while. I'm sure I'll be running with the Platoon in no time." Then there was somewhat a sad and awkward moment when Both Hall and Phillips realized that with all the casualties, only about three out of every ten Marines from their Platoons had survived the battle. Certainly many of the wounded would now survive. However, a lot will go home without limbs or with the need of disfigurement repair. For many, to go from active Marine to Disabled Veteran was a terrible destiny. Even with the advances in biomechanical replacements and plastoskin. Maryann saw the figures on the stretchers and the Marines guarding them. "Who are these guys?"

John pulled back the blanket covering the first figure and the whole room became quiet as the Marines saw the Demon. Some grabbed for weapons that weren't there. Everyone slightly moved away from the thing. Maryann with her hand on the butt of the weapon in her holster asked. "Are you going to have the Doc try and fix it? Why didn't you shoot it?"

"Its sedated, besides it looks like the one that was directing the attack. Perhaps Captain Gin or the Intel guys from the ships can learn something from him. After all we really don't know squat about these things."

The Surgeon walked over and looked at the sedated figure. "Well, put it in that back room over there but make sure that it has plenty of guards. If that thing hurts just one of my guys I'll kill it myself!"

Phillips responded, "Sure Doc." Then he sent the stretcher-bearers with a four Marine guard into the far room. The Surgeon turned to the next stretcher that the bearers put up on the table before him. "And what do we have here?" The Doc murmured as he pulled back the blanket. The Surgeon looked over the young man that he estimated must be about twenty to twenty five years old. He has shaggy blondish brown hair and green grey eyes. His body is thoroughly muscled as though he has had vigorous physical training daily. During his examination, the Surgeon removed the only thing the man was wearing, a pair of identification tags. The Doc looked at them and commented. "I can't find any wounds on him. I don't think we have a Michael Stil with this Company. Who is this guy?"

Captain Gin entered the room and offered. "There was a Lieutenant Commander Stil assigned to the EGAS Inquisitive. When the Company searched for survivors and then remains, Commander Stil's tags were missing, though he was on the planet at the time of the attack. There were a few unidentified bodies in the Science Center. We thought they were civilians. It didn't help that the bodies were stripped clean and everything taken."

The Surgeon looked at the man and asked. "How old was Lieutenant Commander Stil?" Captain Gin thought about the question for a minute then answered. "I believe he would have been in his late thirties. I will have to check the EGAF records to be exact."

"Well, this man can't be a day over twenty if that. Perhaps DNA testing will be helpful."

"Very well Doc, help him if you can. Get him up and around perhaps he will tell us his name. Meanwhile I'll check with Fleet Command about Commander Stil." Captain Gin spotted Phillips returning from the room where he had just secured the prisoner. "Lieutenant, I've been told you've brought in a prisoner."

"Aye sir, he's in the next room bound and sedated. I have two Marines with him in the room and two more guarding the door. He has some wounds that Doc will have to take care of then perhaps we can get some information out of him."

"Good work Lieutenant. Let me know when he's ready for a little talk."

As Captain Gin left the room, the Surgeon directed the Corpsmen. "Get this guy on a heart monitor then put in two IVs. It appears he's acutely dehydrated." Turning to his Lead Corpsman, the Doc stated. "Come with me. We'll see what we can do for that thing in the next room."

A Corpsman fitted Maryann with a pair of crutches and she gingerly eased herself off the exam table. Since he had no other duties, John helped Maryann hobble over to what will be her new quarters in an abandoned temporary building. On the way there, they noticed the shuttles coming and going all around the compound. The shuttles brought fresh supplies and more Marines from the Dauntless and an EGA Supply Ship that had just arrived. The supply transport EGAS Harvest Moon had just arrived with the Space Destroyer EGAS Mars Revenge. As they looked at all the new activity, Maryann asked. How come none of the Alliance Ships have Giann names?"

"The Giann don't name their ships, they never have. The Giann consider that a quaint human affectation."

The Surgeon had just completed suturing the prisoner's wounds and resetting the shoulder when a Corpsman entered the room. "Doc I think you ought to come here and see this. We've got a little problem." The Surgeon removed his gloves and directed a Corpsman to finish bandaging the Demon. He then moved quickly to the next room and found a couple of perplexed Corpsmen. They were standing next to the unknown patient obviously puzzled. All of the remote electronic leads were in the correct position on the man's chest but the monitor displayed only interference. The Corpsman then said, "Doc that ain't all of it!" The guy turned and pointed to a pile of bent and dulled IV needles on the stand next to the patient.

Over an hour, later The Surgeon knocked on the door of Captain Gin's office in one of the other rooms left intact at the old Science Center. Captain Gin was standing behind some crates he was using for a desk speaking with female Officer. They were going over what looked like plans for the expansion of the compound and settlement. Captain Gin waved the Surgeon over to the temporary desk. Walking in coming to attention and saluting both Officers the Surgeon waited at attention. Captain Gin nodded and turned to the Doctor. "At ease Doctor, I'm glad you are here. I would like to introduce you to the new Commanding Officer. Colonel Kellogg is the new CO of Camp Mills. The name was selected to honor the Marine that died holding the line so the rest of us could fall back."

The Surgeon noted that the Colonel wore almost every decoration the Corps awarded. He came to attention and stated. "Lieutenant Farmin, I'm the Company Surgeon ma'am." The

Colonel with the gray streaked hair smiled easily and enquired. "Pleased to meet you Doc go ahead and stand easy, I'm not going to bite your head off. What can Captain Gin and I do for you?"

"Colonel, I don't know if Captain Gin has briefed you yet we've got this guy at the Aid Station."

"Would that be the prisoner or the man that wore Lieutenant Commander Stil's identification tags?"

"The man that was found wearing the tags ma'am."

Colonel Kellogg glanced at Captain Gin and then suggested. "Let's have a seat gentleman. They glanced around and each dragged up a crate to serve as a chair. "Well, what have you found Doc?"

"Nothing," Doctor Farmin stated with annoyance, "nothing!" The man appears acutely dehydrated but we can't get a needle to go through his skin to give him fluids. None of my monitors or sensor equipment can penetrate his skin. I tried X-rays and even the portable CT scanner and nothing can see inside of him!"

Chapter 47

THIRST

D EFENDER.
    He heard the voice but it sounded so far away.

Defender.

He was so very, very tired.

Defender.

His mind struggled sluggishly to become awake enough to respond.

Defender.

"Yes Teacher?" He croaked with a throat that felt covered with dust.

Defender, you must refresh yourself. Your Elemental level has depleted.

"I'm just so tired. I don't feel like I can get up."

Tell the Humans or the Giann; tell them you need water with the Element in suspension.

"Yes Teacher, I will tell them."

Colonel Kellogg with Captain Gin and Doctor Farmin trailing walked briskly into the room. One of the Marine guards stated. "Attention on deck!" Kellogg responded, "As you were Marines," and strode to the unknown man's bedside. A worried looking Corpsman attending the unknown man stated. "Doc, this guy's been mumbling to himself." Farmin took a light and examined the man's eyes. "Well that's a good sign considering we can't get any fluids into him."

He thought he could hear voices in the distance. Then a bright light seemed to be blinding him. He forced himself to open his eyes, and at first, he could only see dark figures above him. Slowly his eyesight improved and he could see men and one women standing around him. With a swollen tongue, he croaked, "Water."

Farmin nodded and directed a Corpsman to elevate the head of the man's bed. Then he picked up a water bottle and started to sprinkle small amounts of water into the man's mouth. The man closed his mouth and the water dribbled down his chin. The man slowly shook his head and tried to speak again. Farmin leaned in close to the man's mouth so he could hear what the man said, "Soil."

The Surgeon stood back and shook his head. "No that's clean water, it's ok to drink." The man's eyes closed then opened again slowly as he struggled to form a sentence. Finally, he whispered. "Put soil in the water." The Doctor looked up at the others and shrugged his shoulders. "He wants us to put soil in the water."

Captain Gin offered. "Do you think its delirium? On the other hand, perhaps he is not human. After all, you said his body make up is different. Will it hurt to do what he asks?" Farmin looked at the man and shrugged his shoulders. "No, I don't believe it will. Ask any of the Marines around here, they've eaten enough of the dirt around here to crap foxholes!" Farmin looked to the Corpsman across from him and nodded his head. "Go get a cup of fine soil and we'll stir some into his water."

Bottle by bottle, the man began to consume the suspension of soil and water. Eventually he had enough strength to hold the bottle himself and thirstily empty more. While the Corpsmen were busy mixing up suspension bottles for the man in bed. The Colonel, Captain Gin and Dr. Farmin paid a visit to the prisoner. Captain Gin explained the large bandages wrapped around the prisoner's hands. "Even sedated, the Demon tried to cut his bonds with his claws. I directed the Doctor to trim his claws so they are blunt.'

Colonel Kellogg noted that the large sharp teeth of the Demon looked quite formidable. The Demon struggled in its chains and snapped at anything that came too close. It growled and spat in its unknown language. Leaving the room the Colonel offered. "Well we sure can't understand it. Perhaps the intelligence guys on the ships can figure out what its saying."

"I can understand it."

Kellogg and Gin turned to the figure outside the doorway now sitting up still sipping muddy water. Kellogg looked at the man outfitted in green sweat pants and sweatshirt given to him by one of the Corpsmen. Kellogg and Gin once again returned to the man's bedside. "You can speak its language?"

"Yes."

"And who are you?"

"I am the Defender."

"The Defender, are you the only one?"

"Yes, at this time."

"Are you the one the Marines call the Golden Guy?"

"I don't know. Are the Marines your warriors?"

"Yes."

"I haven't heard your Marines call me anything."

"Was it you that fought and killed so many of the Demons?"

"If by the Demons, you are speaking of the Evil Ones called the D'mon. Then yes."

"Who are the Evil Ones that you say are called D'mon?"

"They are the warriors that you were fighting."

"Why did you help us fight the D'mon?"

"I am a Defender. The Defenders are designed to fight the D'mon."

"Are you human?"

"I was once human. Now I am bonded with the Element and I am a Defender."

Kellogg paused and just looked at the young man. He looked back and didn't appear to feel uncomfortable looking her right in the eyes. She knew that very little would intimidate this young man. *His eyes are big and bright green, happy and inquisitive. Almost as if, they were the eyes of a child looking forward to the future with confidence and trust. Naive and yet, not naïve, I can almost forget that this charming young man has killed hundreds of the most brutal creatures that the Corps has yet faced.* The Colonel considered what she had learned. "When you are stronger I would like to have you ask the Demon some questions."

"I can question the," the Defender paused then continued, "Demon for you."

Kellogg nodded with a smile then enquired. "Would you mind if one of my Officers asks you a few more questions? I would like to learn more about you Defender."

"I will answer when asked."

Kellogg raised an eyebrow at the response, and then smiled. "Good enough Defender. That's all I asked. I will see you again. If you need anything just ask. I will leave you in the very capable hands of our Surgeon." The Defender nodded in understanding and continued to sip on his cocktail. The Colonel with Captain Gin at her side left the Aid Station. Kellogg spoke with Gin on the way back to her temporary office. "Who do we have that we can spare to sit down and talk with this guy?"

"Lieutenant Hall is recovering from a leg wound and is currently on crutches."

"Perfect, have her record the conversations for EGAFMC Headquarters. We can hand a copy over to the intelligence guys on the Dauntless."

"Aye, ma'am I'll get right on it."

Chapter 48

FRIENDS

MARYANN received orders to report to Captain Gin at the new Company Headquarters building. The new HQ now located in a temporary prefabricated building is not far from the old Science Center currently under repair. Entering Gin's office and putting both crutches on one side of her body Hall came to attention and stated that she had reported as ordered. Captain Gin asked her to have a seat, and then explained what the Colonel desired. After the initial briefing Gin gave her a small recording device.

"I realize this man fought the Demons just as much if not more than we did. However, we still don't know a thing about him. We don't know if he is actually an ally or if he just had a grudge against the Demons. Until we find out his motivations it will be hard to trust him." Gin handed Maryann a sheet of paper with a list of questions printed upon it. "Here are a few questions the Colonel and I are wondering about. Get to know him over the next few cycles. Let him bunk with the Third Platoon and when you feel you finally know something about him turn in an after action report."

After assuring Captain Gin that she fully understood her assignment and that she had no further questions she left the HQ building. She tucked the list of questions and the recorder in her pockets and started hobbling over to the Aid Station. Maryann was in less than a stellar mood when she ran into Pierce on the way. "Hey Maryann, how are you doing? Do you feel better?"

"Well it sure would help if I could get off of these damn sticks. I have so much to do. My Platoon needs training and the new replacements need equipment. You know how it is, the same old BS. Then on top of that the Captain wants me to pal around with the guy found out by the perimeter and find out his life story!"

"Well I'm sure glad I didn't bump in to you on a bad day! Well just figure, whatever happens now you've seen worse. Aren't you curious about this guy?" Hall chewed her lip for a moment then admitted. "Yah, I guess so. I'm sorry about climbing all over you it's just a real pain doing everything at half speed. I'm used to being mobile, jogging everywhere and getting there quick. I guess it's the crutches that are really bothering me."

"Well, you won't be on them forever and you want your knee to heal correctly. I know it sucks but hang in there." Pierce glanced at her watch and added. "I have to get going. I have a whole bunch of replacements that are blinking their eyes at astonishment at the real world. I've got to straighten them out before my Platoon Gunny puts his boot up their ass."

"Yeah, well take it easy Pierce. It was nice running into you. Have fun, I have to go find my new best friend." Yolanda gave her a mock salute and spoke in her deepest voice gravely. "Well then. Good luck and good hunting!" Hall chuckled at the retreating form of Pierce. She was in a much better mood, as she hobbled up the stairs of the Aid Station.

Chapter 49

DEFENDER

M ARYANN entered the ward section of the Aid Station. Next door to the Science Center, the engineers were quickly assembling a large prefabricated building that would shortly be a Base Dispensary. It will have additional Doctors and staff with additional equipment arriving every day. She found the guy sitting in a chair by his bed reading a First Aid manual. Maryann approached and stopped across from his chair. As she watched, he would look at a page then turn immediately to the next. Maryann leaned her crutches against his bed and sat down on a corner. "Are you reading that or just scanning the pages?"

He stopped what he was doing and looked up at her with a puzzled expression. "I believe I am reading. I have been studying your written language for several days now. I have no scanner."

"It is possible to scan using only your eyes. Scanning usually only identifies certain words phrases or pictures."

"Why would you want to do that?"

"To save time and cover more text quickly."

"But wouldn't you lose some information?" Maryann nodded. "That's true, but that's the trade off."

"What is a trade off?"

Maryann thought about the question carefully then answered. "It's like in warfare when you give up stealth for speed." The man nodded and closed the book. "I understand."

Maryann rose from the bed placed the crutches under her arms then offered her hand. "Hi, I'm First Lieutenant, Maryann Hall." The man stood up, looked at the proffered hand and then at Maryann. She looked back at him and smiled. "Put out your hand like mine." As he repeated the gesture, Maryann grabbed his hand and pumped it up and down. "It's a hand shake. A gesture used for greeting and trust. Ages ago, when two warriors met peacefully they would shake each other's hand. The offering of the empty hand with no weapon demonstrates peaceful intent."

The man kept pumping her hand up and down so Maryann had to add, "You can stop now." He dropped his hand so she continued her explanation. "The hand shake is usually accompanied by a verbal introduction identifying your name." The man thought for a moment then asked. "Do all people have names?"

"Usually, do you have one?"

"I am the Defender." Maryann looked at the identification tags around his neck and asked. "What about the tags around your neck? May I see them?" He bent his head forward removed the chain with one hand and offered her the tags.

"These tags belonged to an Officer named Lieutenant Commander Michael Stil. He died on the first expedition to this planet. Did you know him?" The man shook his head. "No."

"Then how did you get the tags?"

"Teacher told me that the female that brought me to the dome put them around my neck."

"Who is Teacher?"

"He is the one that guided and trained me."

"Is he in the dome can I meet him?"

"No."

"Why?"

"He speaks to me in my mind." Maryann thought about that then asked. "Have you seen the Teacher?" He put the book he had in his other hand on a bedside table and answered. "No."

Maryann looked at the man with the greenish grey eyes and the brownish blond hair and thought about the file picture Captain Gin had shown her of Lieutenant Commander Stil. The resemblance was substantial. However, this man appeared to be about twenty solar cycles old. Stil's boy that was missing with his mother during the first Demon attack was about two or three at the time. She figured that would make the boy about five or six by now. The figures just didn't add up. Maryann even wondered about this, "Teacher." *Could he have developed the Defender to resemble Stil? After all, the Doc said the makeup of his body was certainly different from the humans.* Maryann gave a mental shrug and let those thoughts go. She handed the tags back. "Since you have no particular name, can I call you Michael?'

He nodded then offered Maryann his hand. She took the offered hand and shook. He gave her a huge smile and announced, "Hi, I'm Michael."

"Well Michael since the Doc is discharging you from here how about you bunk with Third Platoon? Do you have somewhere else you have to go back to?"

"No I have no other plans and I have no need to return to my place of training. My training is complete and I do have so much to learn about Humans and Giann. I would appreciate sharing your home." Maryann raised an eyebrow at that statement. "I don't know if I would call it home but your sure welcome to come. I do have one more question before we leave. I've wondered since we first found you. How come you can speak and understand our language?"

"I have access to every language the Old Ones recorded. Your language was recorded from the first group of humans that came to this planet."

"The Old Ones are they still here?"

"No the Old Ones are long gone. Teacher listened to the first visitors."

"I thought Teacher was in your mind?"

"Yes. He's in my mind, but also in the dome and in this planet built by the Old Ones."

Maryann nodded then once again mounted her crutches for the trip back to Third Platoon. Maryann noticed the eagerness, which Michael showed at the thought of coming along. *It's kind of like a kid looking forward to going to camp. Michael appears very intelligent even brilliant. However, in some ways it's almost as if he's slightly mentally retarded.* Once again Maryann shook her head and just headed for the door a very happy appearing Michael, tagging along behind.

On the way out, they passed the room where the wounded Demon is in chains. The two Marine guards came to attention as Maryann passed. Then Maryann heard the Demon howl and then make growling noises as Michael passed the door. Out of the corner of her eye, she saw Michael whirl around with a crystal knife in his hand. The guards taken by surprise quickly lowered their weapons preparing to fire. Maryann turned dropped her crutches put out her hands and yelled. "NO, STOP!"

For a moment, no one moved. Then slowly Michael returned the knife to the sheath on his arm and straightened up. The guards seeing him sheath his dagger slowly raised their weapons and clicked them to safe. The Demon growled again. To Maryann's surprise Michael growled right back spitting in the direction of the Demon. The Demon sat back in the corner put his head in his arms and whimpered. Michael turned to Maryann to apologize. "Sorry, we can go now. I won't hurt it." Maryann looked at Michael put out her hand and demanded. "Put out your arm. Where did you get the knife?"

Michael put both of his forearms forward. Maryann looked at his arms but the knife and sheath were gone! She looked confused for a moment then asked. "Where did it go? How did you do that?" Michael gave her a sad look then spoke as if he was talking to a small child. "I reflexively produce my weapons. If you like, I will show you."

"You're darn right you will. I'm sure you won't mind if we see if you're holding any other weapons at the moment." Michael stood still with his arms at his side passively. Maryann nodded to one of the Marines behind him and the Marine patted down his arms, legs, back and chest. The Marine even ran his fingers through Michaels shoulder length hair. Finished, the Marine shook his head to the negative and stepped back to his post.

Maryann stepped up to Michael leaned on her crutches and looked at his face closely. "I believe your ok for now but understand this; from now on while you are on this base you will not pull a weapon without my permission. Do you understand?" Michael lowered his eyes and his cheeks reddened. Maryann noticed he appeared to look confused and embarrassed. Michael quietly replied, "I understand Lieutenant Hall."

Maryann put two fingers under Michael's chin raising his head. "Then let's get going. Third Platoon is on the other side of the compound and I'm not real fast on these sticks." Michael's face brightened and he followed Maryann out the door to the compound. Outside they paused for a moment after Maryann came down the stairs on her crutches. Michael looked in fascination at all the activity.

On the plain where the Demon's had landed there was now a new large Plasticrete slab where shuttles were coming and going bringing even more supplies and troops. Everywhere there were prefabricated buildings going up. A new perimeter will extend for kilometers even enclosing the large shuttle landing area. Roads are graded and military vehicles of all types are coming and going. Maryann saw Michael's amazement and commented. "It's not exactly a small town any longer. Now remember we have to stay out of the way of the vehicles and dozers." As they started out across the compound, Michael walked right next to Maryann trying to look everywhere at once.

Being careful where she put the tips of her crutches Maryann continued with her questions. "Were you talking to that thing?" As they paused to let a loader go by Michael replied. "Do you mean the Evil One? Yes I can communicate with it." A large loader came rumbling along and Maryann and Michael paused to let it pass.

"What did it say?"

"It asked if I was the one that killed so many of his warriors."

"What did you say?"

"I said yes. I also said if the humans would let me, I would cut him up starting at his feet so he would die very slowly!" Maryann looked at Michael and noticed the cold seriousness of his face. "I believe you would Michael. Yes I believe you would." With the loader past, they slowly made their way to Third Platoon's quarters without further words. Maryann felt an involuntary shudder. *I believe this guy could be one dangerous Son of a Bitch.*

Chapter 50

HARRAK'S MOON

ANGELA didn't know how long she has been a captive. She had been on a ship kept in cells with the other women from the settlement. The cells were filthy and had only a hole in the floor for waste. Twice a day old D'mon women would bring a bowl of unknown contents for each woman. At first, no one would eat the foul smelling stuff. Those that would not eat were beaten. Even the old D'mon women were far stronger than the humans were. They are careful not to kill; they just beat the woman senseless. Eventually everyone learned to clean the bowl twice a day. Every morning one Old D'mon women would hose down the cells and the women the water going down the waste hole for recycle.

Angela knew she had been on the ship for quite some time perhaps as much as eighteen lunar cycles. She also knew there had been a battle because they could feel the concussions when the ship took damage and feel the outside weapons firing. Many times, she wondered who had won the battle and whom the D'mon had fought. Then time passed and the battle just became a dim memory.

Along with the other women, Angela had an examination by a D'mon she would call the "Doctor". The Doctor seemed angry when he found she no longer had reproductive organs. The old D'mon female, the Doctor's assistant, used an electronic translation device to tell Angela that female slaves are only valuable for their reproductive potential. Angela feared they would kill her. When they came for her the other women from the settlement cried and held on to her wailing until the Doctor let her stay.

Since then, the D'mon female gave Angela all the instructions for the other women using a translator device. One day when Angela told the D'mon female, she had some questions for the Doctor the old D'mon cuffed her across the mouth so hard she flew across the room. While Angela wiped the blood from her mouth, the D'mon female explained that for the Doctor talking to a female slave is, "beneath him." The old D'mon female dropping her head, also told her that she too was a slave. The Doctor kept her around to give the women slaves their instructions.

The old D'mon female confided in Angela one day. She told Angela that the Doctor was baffled as to why the human females were not conceiving. The D'mon use artificial insemination for which Angela was thankful. She learned that the D'mon warriors are so violent in their coupling that females from many species die. Since breed able female slaves are so valuable, the Doctor will not waste them coupling with the warriors.

Angela kept a secret very tightly. She knew why the women couldn't conceive and one by one warned all the women to keep silent. Since birthing a D'mon was so deadly and painful, it was an easy secret to keep. Most of the women with her were part of the Inquisitives crew. They had an injection of a very slow acting contraceptive before they left Earth. This was to prevent an untimely pregnancy while they were on the expedition. The science team members also chose the injection, all of them except for Angela.

Since the D'mon Doctor had no idea of the normal hormonal levels in the humans he had the female D'mon ask Angela how long was the average human procreative cycle. Angela lied and

said normally it was a few solar cycles but that it differed slightly
for each female. She also suggested to the D'mon that they
continue trying since someone was bound to conceive soon. She
told the lie since she knew if the Doctor considered the women
inconceivable, they would die.

Angela is now worried. Some time ago, the ship came into
orbit around an unknown moon. The women along with the
other cargo transferred down to a large stone and rock fortress
dug into a small round mesa on the moon. The D'mon female
told her this was the fiefdom of Harrak. On this moon, he hid
most of his spoils from the rest of the D'mon Fleet. The women
are in the slave holding cells in the lowest level of the fortress by
the kitchens. Keeping track with little scratch marks on a table
Angela figured they have been in the fortress for six to eight lunar
cycles. Angela calculated that along with the time aboard the
ship it must be about two solar cycles of captivity! She had no
idea how long the D'mon would accept the lie. Angela had heard
of the "Claw Kill," and now every day she wondered if the time
would run out for them.

Chapter 51

CAMP MILLS

MARYANN gave Michael a tour of the Platoon's new barracks and showed him where he could sleep. Maryann also introduced Michael to Sergeant Hill. Hill is the largest Marine in the platoon. Although he is a new replacement to the Platoon, Sergeant Hill has spent nine years with the Corps. Colonel Kellogg had suggested to Maryann that Hill could help keep an eye on the Defender when Maryann was not available. Michael's rack was in the back corner of the barracks and Hill's was right next to him. Hill admitted to Maryann that he was not pleased to have to baby sit the guy. However, when he found out the idea was Kellogg's there was no more argument.

The exposition of Michael's abilities began by him changing clothes. Michael asked if he could dress the same way as the Marines. Maryann had already thought about clothes. She was prepared to send Michael with Sergeant Hill to the uniform supply to put Michael in uniform. She was surprised however when as soon as Michael removed the borrowed sweat suit he appeared to be wearing the exact same uniform as Sergeant Hill. Maryann was concerned though when she noticed the uniform was exact right down to the sergeant's stripes and Corps Emblem. Maryann explained he could wear the tunic, pants, boots and hat but he could not wear the Corps Emblem or a designation of rank. Michael looked disappointed but Maryann patiently explained that the Corps gives those items to the Marines at special ceremonies once the Marines earned them.

Maryann then asked Michael to explain how his uniform appeared. Michael explained to Maryann and Hill that with the Element in his skin he could produce or duplicate any type of clothing that he had seen. He changed his uniform slowly so Maryann could see the Sergeant stripes slowly seem to dissolve away, the same with the Corps emblem. Michael was now standing there in a plain Marine tunic and pants with no markings, hat and boots. Maryann found it interesting that although Michael could wear any type of clothing, he preferred to dress like the Marines.

For further demonstrations, they moved outside behind the barracks. Michael then demonstrated his body armor. Maryann started filming with a portable hologram recorder. As she held the recorder in her hand, she asked what kind of punishment the armor could withstand. Michael seemed to be quite excited to explain. "Initially with adequate Element refreshment it can withstand all types of hand weapons right up to energy cannon fire. However, the larger the weapon blast the faster the armor uses up the Element. I extend the use of the armor and conserve the Element by using my speed to avoid weapon strikes."

Maryann had Michael demonstrate his speed by having Sergeant Hill pace out a hundred meter course across the compound. When Hill reached a hundred meters, he turned and waved. Maryann set her watch to timer then told Michael that when she said, "Go", he should run to the end of the course as fast as he could. Maryann put her thumb on the timer button and said, "Go!" Michael was a blur as he ran around Sergeant Hill and back to Maryann! Maryann taken by surprise pressed the button when he was once again standing next to her. Maryann looked at the watch and noted the time three point six seconds!

She looked at Michael standing there relaxed not even breathing hard. "Three point six seconds. I had expected you to only run to the far end."

Michael chewed on his lip and gravely answered. "Sorry, I misunderstood." Maryann shook her head and muttered, "Whew, that's ok, believe me." Maryann noticed that quite a few Marines around the compound had stopped what they were doing and were watching the three of them. They quickly noticed Maryann's hard look and went back to their duties. So that they wouldn't cause any further distractions, Maryann moved the three for them to an open area behind the Headquarters building. Once there, she turned to Michael. "Now, if you would please demonstrate how your weapons work."

Michael explained that his thoughts produced his weapons derived from the Element combined with his bone material. He showed how his saber appeared, then the spear and the dagger. Maryann had Sergeant Hill bring many different materials and Michael demonstrated how the crystal blades cut through them. The last demonstration was how Michael could heat his blade to cut through armor steel. Maryann noticed throughout the demonstration that Michael would pause to refresh with a water bottle filled with an Elemental suspension. She asked, "Does creating your weapons dehydrate you?"

"No, it uses up a lot of the Element stored in my body. The fluids I drink are a suspension of the Element. By continually refreshing myself, I can have an optimal amount of Element available for weapons or armor. A small amount of the Element is also required for my body's regular metabolism."

As the time passed Maryann's knee healed and grew stronger. Though she still required a slight brace with a bandage, she was able to return the crutches to the dispensary. Every morning Michael went through a training routine behind the

Headquarters building. Since Maryann also needed to exercise to build the strength in her knee, she would join him. As Maryann spent more time with Michael, Sergeant Hill spent more time with his Squad appearing only when Maryann was unavailable. Michael was never by himself, but he didn't object or seem to notice. Little by little, Maryann's knee grew stronger and the discomfort disappeared. Finally, she no longer needed the knee brace or bandage at all.

One morning after a sweaty and fatiguing workout, they both headed to the shower area at the same time. Maryann was long used to the Marine communal facilities. She was used to dressing and undressing with men or women present. After all, in the cramped ships in space, there was no privacy and everyone was used to politely minding their own business. It was now part of the culture since few starships had more than one shower room. What Maryann hadn't noticed was that Michael usually showered in the middle of the day alone. At that time of day, there usually wasn't anyone else present.

Michael had just mentally removed his clothes. He grabbed a clean towel to hang on one of the hooks by the shower entrance. He happened to glance over towards Maryann and stopped. Maryann had removed her workout clothes and had one leg up on the locker room bench. Her back was to Michael and she was bending over massaging her knee. It still got a little sore after a real demanding workout. Michael stood there frozen as he noticed the nice curve of her buttocks. His eyes ran up the curve of her flat stomach to the generous breasts, which hung down and gently swayed side to side with the rhythm of her massage. Michael noticed he began to breathe faster and he felt his body tingling. Michael looked down and found part of his body was swelling! Maryann hearing a gasp behind her stopped her massage picked up a towel and turned. "SHIT!"

Maryann hadn't even realized she had yelled. At the sound of the yell, Michael changed instantly to full body armor. His saber jumped into his hand looking for a threat. As Michael was scanning back and forth, trying to understand where the threat was coming from, Maryann began to smile and then ended up laughing. Wrapping herself in the towel, she explained. "It's ok; I didn't mean to startle you. But when I turned around and saw you standing there with an erection it took me by surprise." Recognizing there was no threat Michael sheathed his saber and was once again wearing his Marine sweat suit. He said hesitantly, "An erection?"

Maryann gave a sigh, and said. "You shower up and then wait outside. When I'm finished we're going to take a walk to the Dispensary to see the Doc."

"Why?"

"You'll see."

On the way to the Dispensary Maryann asked. "Why do you hate the Demons?" Michael looked at her with a puzzled expression. "I don't hate them."

"Perhaps I shouldn't have said hate. Why do you fight the Demons?"

"I am a Defender. The Evil Ones are the enemies of the Old Ones. As a Defender I am trained to fight the Evil Ones."

Maryann stopped walking and looked up at his face. "It's as easy as that?" Michael gave a shrug of his shoulders. "It's not always as easy but that's why I'm here.

"You spoke about the Old Ones. Did they make the domes?" Michael nodded and they resumed their walk. "Yes, the Old Ones made the domes."

"What are the domes for?"

"The domes are for producing Defenders."

"How are they used?"

"A child is placed in the dome. The Element bonds with the growing body. Once the child is full grown they are trained as a Defender." Maryann stopped short again and sputtered. "Why that's barbaric!" Michael looked down at her face in alarm. "What do you mean? Your Marines are they not trained as warriors?"

"Yes they are. However, we train them after they are adults. They make the choice whether or not to become a Marine!"

Maryann looked around as if she had just noticed they were standing still. Michael appeared a little confused as to why she was upset. Maryann just pointed with a nod of her head. "Come on let's go. It's not your fault what people did on this planet thousands of solar cycles ago." As they continued the walk, Maryann had another train of thought. "What about the Element?" Maryann also noticed that Michael had unconsciously walked with his hands clasped behind his back just like her. Her first thought was, *is he mimicking me?* Maryann let her arms drop to her sides and in a few moments, she noticed Michael did the same. *It's almost as if he's trying to fit in by doing whatever I do.*

Finally, she stopped again. "Michael why do you have to make every move I do?" He thought for a moment then replied. "Don't friends do everything together?" Maryann put her hands to her mouth to keep from laughing aloud. "Michael, doing everything together is a general term. It doesn't mean doing everything the same with the same movements. It means interacting together and with the surrounding area as two people that are friends. Do you understand?" Michael nodded a "yes", and they continued walking. Once again, Maryann went back to her train of questioning. "Again, tell me about the Element."

"What would you like to know?"

"Where's it from?"

Michael gestured with his hands as he walked. "It's all around us." Maryann stopped again and kneeled on one knee.

She picked up a little of the reddish brown dust and let it slip through her fingers. "Can it be found anywhere else? On any other planets or places"

"Not as far as the Old One's records show." Standing and brushing the dust from her hands Maryann looked into the distance at the surrounding mountains with the slightly different colored vegetation and thought how much Romeo reminded her of Earth's American Southwest. "Did the Old Ones make the Element?" Michael shook his head. "It's more like the Old Ones developed here because the Element is here."

About ten meters from the Dispensary Maryann suddenly stopped again. Michael took two more steps then turned around and waited patiently. Maryann stood there looking at Michael with a speculative expression. After a few moments, Maryann had seemed to reach a conclusion. "Michael, along with the women that are missing from the Inquisitive expedition, Michael and Angela Stil had a little boy who is missing too. The boy would be about four or five Solar cycles old. Although you appear to be about twenty to twenty five, I believe you could be Michael Stil Junior. Do you know how long you were in the dome?" Michael thought about the question then offered. "I'm not sure. My first memory is waking up just as I am. "Maryann thought about that as she continued up the steps of the Dispensary. Once inside Maryann stated. "We've got to find the missing women, they're the key!"

Dr. Farmin was in his office completing paperwork when they knocked. He said, "Enter," and put his pen aside. Once Michael and Maryann had entered the room he asked. "Well Lieutenant what can I do for you?"

"Well Doc, it's actually for Michael here."

He looked back and forth between them and asked, "Michael?" Maryann sat down in the one chair Farmin had across from his desk and explained. "Yeah Doc, I needed to call him something besides Defender and I figured since the ID tags said Michael, it would be as good a name as any." Farmin looked at the tall young man and asked. "Well what can I do for Michael?" Michael didn't answer he just looked toward Maryann. She quickly piped in. "Well Doc, Michael appears to be full grown and he has a whole lot of knowledge but not a lot of human knowledge."

"What do you mean human knowledge?"

"Yeah, how would I put it? Like human sociological relationships and such. Ah, like relationships between men and women." Maryann quickly recapped what had happened in the changing room. The Doctor sat back in his chair and smiled. "Oh, you mean like sex?" Maryann looked a little embarrassed and nodded. "Yeah I guess so."

Farmin pushed back his chair and looked through the disk library in the small cabinet next to his desk. He pulled out a disk and handed it over to Maryann. "This will get him started but it's only anatomy and physiology. I'll have to down load some texts from the Dauntless' library about human sociology and sexuality. The EGA Navy and Marine Officer's Manual will also help him to understand the rules and regulations that guide military personnel. Michael can pick them up in a cycle or so." Maryann handed the disk to Michael and thanked the Surgeon. She also promised to return with Michael to pick up the other disks so Michael could round out his education.

Chapter 52

PRISONER

EARLY the next morning Maryann responded to the request to report to the Commanding Officer at Headquarters. She brought Michael as well as her report, the disks of Michael's abilities, his armor, weapons and the ever stoic Sergeant Hill. Maryann asked Michael to wait for her outside the office and he patiently took a seat on a bench next to Sergeant Hill. Maryann knocked on the door and listened for the crisp, "Enter."

Maryann found Captain Gin along with the Surgeon, Dr. Farmin already in the office. Colonel Kellogg was leaning against one corner of her desk and she informally directed Maryann to a seat next to Captain Gin. Colonel Kellogg asked Maryann how her leg was mending and with the Surgeon nodding in agreement, Maryann explained that with a little more physical therapy she would soon be back to full duty. Colonel Kellogg then asked for her assessment on the Defender. Maryann gave a short verbal brief and turned over all disks and recordings to Captain Gin. At the completion of her report, she spoke about giving the Defender the name Michael. The Colonel sat quietly then asked if the Defender had agreed to the name. Kellogg then mentioned that the first name Michael is acceptable but that at this time the Defender's last name will be open pending definitive proof of his lineage.

The Surgeon gave a short report on his assessment of Michael's physical nature and explained the Defender's need for further education. In his explanation, Maryann noted that Dr. Farmin mercifully omitted the locker room story. With both reports concluded, the Colonel then asked the Defender to join them. Kellogg started with a direct question for him. "Defender, Lieutenant Hall is referring to you today as Michael. Do you find this acceptable?"

"Yes, that is the name on my identification disks."

"Very well, Michael it is. Michael I've been told you have a good working knowledge of the Demon's language."

"Yes sir, that is correct."

"We have some questions for the captured D'mon. Would you have the time to come with us and translate?" Michael smiled and answered, "But of course sir!" Kellogg looked at Michael for moment and then added. "By the way Michael, being that I am a female Officer I'm referred to as ma'am, not sir." Michael blinked once as if storing information to memory and apologized. "Yes ma'am, I'm sorry." Colonel Kellogg glanced at the other officers then stated. "Well folks shall we go have a conservation with a Demon?" The group left for the room that holds the captive, with the large Sergeant Hill silently falling in behind.

Besides the chains that the Demon wore the last time, Michael saw he now also had a metal crossbar added to the manacles. Captain Gin explained to the Colonel how the Demon even with trimmed claws kept slashing at anyone that came within reach. The crossbar made sudden movement clumsy at best. There had been no new injuries since the bars addition to the chains.

When the Colonel, Captain Gin and Maryann entered the cell, the creature snarled and rose to its feet defiantly. Then Michael entered the room. The demon's eyes went wide with fright upon seeing Michael. It backed into a corner and sat as though terrified. Michael walked right up to the Demon and squatted in front of the creature his face a neutral mask. Maryann stood diagonally across from the Demon in the other corner. One hand casually rested on the butt of her side arm. Sergeant Hill brought in chairs for Colonel Kellogg and Captain Gin then stepped to the far side of the cell. Hill's right hand also hovered close to the weapon in his holster.

The first questions the Colonel wanted answered was who they were and why they attacked the Inquisitive and the settlement. To Maryann the exchange between Michael and the Demon sounded like a series of grunts, growls and howls. This went on for some time before Michael gave them an answer. "They call themselves the D'mon. They had an ancient sensor left orbiting this planet, which let them know of the arrival of a breed able species. The D'mon Fleet needs the technology, materials and females of conquered species. Their Fleet travels from system to system conquering as they go."

Colonel Kellogg listened patiently to the translation then stated. "So basically these creatures are nomadic parasites. They produce nothing they just destroy and take the spoils from other species." Michael nodded in agreement. Kellogg with a disgusted look at the Demon added. "Then I personally, won't have a lot of heartache over killing them."

"Now," continued Kellogg. "Ask him why they only took the human females and what did they do with them." Michael continued the macabre conversation with the Demon then translated. "The human females were taken because the DNA is compatible for breeding. The Giann DNA was not. They are prisoners on Harrak's ship, the one that got away."

"Does he know where this Harrak would take them?"

After another quick translation, Michael replied. "He says most likely to Harrak's moon. Harrak has a fortress there and after the defeat here, Harrak wouldn't return to the D'mon Fleet."

Colonel Kellogg rose from her chair and stated. "I have enough for now to send a preliminary report to EGAF Command. Captain Gin, please continue the questioning with the Defender. Find out all that you can about this fortress and the D'mon Fleet. I shall hold Officer's Call tomorrow morning in the HQ conference room. By then I should have some direction about how we should proceed."

After Colonel Kellogg had left, Michael, Gin and Hall continued the questioning making a rough but detailed map of Harrak's moon and the fortress. By the end of the day, they felt they also had all of the information they could glean from the prisoner about the moon and the D'mon Fleet.

Chapter 53

HEADQUARTERS

(EGAFMC, Camp Mills)

MARYANN with Michael in tow wasn't very surprised to find the conference room in Headquarters full. Along with the Marine Officers in the room were the Commanding Officers and the Executive Officers of the EGAS Stalwart and the Dauntless. Counting the Sergeant Major and Dr. Farmin, they found standing room only. Maryann and Michael stood quietly in the back with the other Junior Officers. Everyone seated came to their feet when Colonel Kellogg entered after which the Colonel exclaimed, "As you where." The Colonel started the meeting by asking Captain Gin and Maryann to bring everyone in the room up to date on the information learned about the D'mon including what they learned about Harrak's moon. Once the briefing was completed, Colonel Kellogg explained the direction she had received from Headquarters.

"Ladies and Gentlemen, I have been in constant communication with both EGA Fleet and EGA Fleet Marine Corps Headquarters. My orders are simple. I am to mount a rescue mission to the place called Harrak's Moon. There recover the female Civilian and Fleet personnel that have been abducted by the D'mon. The destruction of the fortress, ships and or

D'mon personnel is secondary to the rescue of our personnel. I have authorization to bring along one non-military being, the D'mon called Parek. He is now a prisoner at Camp Mills."

Maryann immediately put up her hand. Kellogg looking displeased at the interruption asked. "Do you have a question already Lieutenant Hall?"

"Yes ma'am. If we take along the Demon, we will have to take along the Defender to translate for us. I also feel the Defender would be invaluable as I am assuming you are planning a Marine assault on the fortress."

With a suffering look, Kellogg replied. "Lieutenant you're getting a little ahead of me. Indeed, I had said I have authorization to take one non-military person on the mission. However, if I had time to explain I would also have stated that I have authorization to offer the Defender now known as Michael a commission as a Second Lieutenant in the EGA Fleet Marine Corps." The Colonel turned to Michael, "Defender?"

Michael slowly came towards the front of the room considering his answer. Reaching a spot a step away from the Colonel, Michael stopped. He looked from the Colonel back to where Maryann waited a big smile on her face. Then he began to speak forming his answer. "Colonel Kellogg, I would like to thank the EGA Fleet and the EGA Fleet Marine Corps for their offer. Unfortunately, I must decline a direct commission into the EGA military forces."

The room was extremely quiet as Michael continued. "Indeed, although I am part human. Part of me also belongs to this planet you call Romeo. My engineering and training designed me to be a Defender of this planet. Even though I am the last Defender, I am never less the sum total of the defense forces of this planet. My obligation as a Defender thus supersedes any off world commission which I may be offered."

Michael noticed some of the sour looks he was receiving from some of the Officers present. He also saw a look of disappointment from Maryann. However, he continued. "Dr. Farmin was kind enough to offer me some disks to further my education. Two of these were the EGA Fleet Manual and the EGA Fleet Marine Corps Manual. In both of these manuals, there are passages that describe a 'Honorary' commission for Foreign Officers of allied planets. Since I am the last Defender of the planet Romeo, I can state that the planet Romeo is now an ally with the EGA in the war against the D'mon. In this capacity I would be proud to accept an Honorary Commission in the EGA Fleet Marine Corps!"

The room was deadly quiet, and then Colonel Kellogg broke out in laughter! Shaking her head the Colonel declared. "I was told how intelligent you are son, and such a quick study! I will offer you an Honorary Commission in the EGA Fleet Marine Corps as a Defender, Second Lieutenant Grade. I hope you realize this makes a historical change in both the Fleet and Marine manuals under designation of rank structure. I shall notify Command of the changes and from now on, Defender will be a proper title in the EGAFMC. You will wear the uniform of a Marine Officer which has the two gold bars of a Second Lieutenant."

To everyone's surprise in a blur Michael changed his clothing to match the Marine Officers uniform complete with two gold bars. Kellogg turned to Captain Gin once again shaking her head. "Even though I know how he does that, it's still an amazing thing to see."

Chapter 54

EGA GRAND COUNCIL CHAMBER

(Earth)

WINGATE Toath seethed with anger and it took a great amount of self-control to appear calm and disinterested in the proceedings. The Council briefing concerning the battle in the Romeo system and the declaration of war with the D'mon had taken all morning! When presented with the evidence of the ferocity and aggressiveness of the D'mon warriors Toath made a recommendation to the Council. After viewing the disks of the capability of this Defender, Toath had just suggested that the Fleet could use more of them.

Of course, this issue brought out a whole host of moral and ethical arguments. The first important issue is the fact that the domes only respond to the placement of human children. One of the Giann council members is currently presenting the argument that the current Earth laws since the twenty-first and twenty-second earth centuries have outlawed the use of human ovum for cloning purposes. His argument is the bonding with the Element changes the physical being thus altering the species. This would put the use of human infants to develop Defenders under the same category as cloning the ovum. What is worse, he pointed out that the cloning procedure at least does not alter the initial subject.

Toath sat and fumed. As he sat and watched more and more Council Members nodding their heads in agreement, Toath thought. *Why is the damn Baldy so concerned with human infants? The Baldys always have to make sure they have control of the moral high ground. Since they were a few years ahead of us in space travel, they feel free to treat humans like ignorant savages. Doesn't the fool know there are places on earth where mothers give up their infants free? I'm sick of the way the damn Baldys run roughshod over the Council!*

Chapter 55

CAMP MILLS

(Operational Planning)

For fifteen planetary cycles, the planning and preparation went on for the raid on Harrak's moon. On the morning of the sixteenth, they attended the follow up brief at the Camp Mills Headquarters. The Military planners directed that Hall's, Phillips' and Peirce's Platoons would augment one Platoon of Marines from the Dauntless to make a Company sized raid. Captain Gin would lead the attacking Company. Due to space constraints on the ships involved, Hall's Third Platoon and Phillips' First Platoon would travel on the Space Cruiser EGAS Stalwart along with the Defender and the prisoner Parek.

Since the rescue of the women was paramount, the Dauntless and the Stalwart would wait outside the system where Harrak's moon was located. The Marines would fast drop to the moon in combat shuttles escorted by Banshees. This drop would come in on the side of the moon away from where Harrak's ship the Conqueror and the fortress are located. Long-range Banshee patrols from the Dauntless have reported that there are no Demon fighters flying patrols around the moon or system. The planners surmised that since Harrak was feeling safe on his home turf he was relying on sensors to warn him of possible threats. The Banshees would take advantage of that by jamming the sensors on the way in.

Parek's information said there are four entrances. These are located at the base of a small flat-topped mesa that contains the fortress. The only rear entrance is closest to the kitchens the slave cells and birthing rooms. He also said this entrance is hard to find since the Demons dump their trash directly out of this hatch on to the moon's surface. Third Platoon, with Hall the Defender and the prisoner Parek will as quietly as possible breach the rear hatch. Parek will show them the way to the cells that contain the women. One Squad of Third Platoon will carry extra pressure suits. Those Marines will all be Giann for the ease of carrying the extra weight. Each Marine will help a woman to suit up and assist her with the trip back out to the shuttle.

The Demon Parek will be the responsibility of the Defender at all times. The Demon had promised his cooperation but many of the Officers were skeptical of his motivations. The Defender explained. "Since his claws are cut short he will be immediately killed by any of his own. In addition, if he doesn't help us, I will kill him. I have promised him that the death will be very painful."

Once the Third Platoon has made contact with the captives, the three other Platoons will stage frontal assaults on the other three entrances. The Stalwart will engage the D'mon warship and the Banshees from the Dauntless will take out any anti-air batteries located on the outside of the Fortress. A reserve Combat Air Patrol of Banshees will engage any enemy space fighters that make an appearance. The CAP will also provide security for the returning shuttles.

Once the Third Platoon has withdrawn from the fortress with the captives, the other three Platoons will disengage and retreat to their shuttles. The planners stress that the rescue of the captives is the primary mission. A prolonged battle with the fortress defenders may give time for the D'mon Fleet to intervene. The planners described the Operation as a pure snatch and fly.

Chapter 56

OLD SINGAPORE, STATE OF EAST ASIA

(Earth)

THE flying limousine landed atop the tallest building in Old Singapore. The massive black and silver structure is the headquarters of the PTS Corporation. Standing in the shade of a silver awning is Justin Marrt the Chief Executive Officer of the PTS Corp. He stands stiffly in the Singapore heat the sweat traveling down his neck into the collar of his five-thousand, credit pale red suit. His black hair and thin pencil mustache make him look decades younger than he really is. The slight olive shape of his eyes is the only clue of his mother's Asian heritage. His father a European space freighter Captain had disappeared in space long ago. Marrt may have been just another Singapore salary man if he hadn't bloomed under the wing of a very powerful mentor.

Only one thing would bring him out of his luxury office suite on a hot humid day such as this. The long black limo flyer landed with the back passenger door exactly at the end of the red carpet that leads out from the shaded lift awning. Standing slightly behind Marrt and to his right is the man with no name. Very few employees of PTS Corp. have ever seen the man let alone know his name. He is the head of PTS security and the men that work for him just know him by his title "Alpha". Alpha also controls all of the PTS "Black", projects and is only answerable to Justin Marrt. The tall thin man in an impeccable black suit stands calmly behind Marrt seemly impervious to the heat and humidity.

Marrt and his Security Chief walk briskly to the end of the carpet as the limo's hatch swings open. Both Marrt and the man known as "Alpha", bow as Marrt's mentor steps down from the Limo. Rising Marrt implores, "Welcome to Singapore and PTS, Councilman Toath. I hope your journey was tolerable." Toath dressed in a single-breasted light linen suit grunted, "Barely."

Marrt led Toath to the private lift, which will carry them down to his office suite. Holding the door to the lift open are two PTS security personnel in black uniforms and the PTS logo on the left breast of their black body armor. Energy rifles hang barrel down across their backs, pistols in holsters at their hips. Once Marrt and his guest have entered the lift the guards will once again stand with back to the lift with rifles at port arms. The man called "Alpha" prefers actual physical security at all entrances and exits to the building. He feels counting on electronic security is foolish. The three of them entered the lift and seconds after the doors closed arrive at the lower office suite.

The office suite appears to be the top floor of the massive building, but it actually is several floors down. Above the suite is a large hanger for Marrt's private limo flyer and security and communications rooms filled with security personnel that monitor the equipment around the clock. PTS security personnel likewise staff the floor below the office suite. The whole floor has a modulating current flowing around it, which protects it from unwanted surveillance. The suite has a private elevator, which descends to a security room on the building's lobby level for quiet egress. There is also another elevator, which descends below to a public office. This office contains a secretary that greets Marrt's business clients. The ornate office with gilded chandeliers and leather furniture is the place most of his clients believe is his office. Only a very few trusted people know of Marrt's upper luxury suite.

Marrt walked out of the elevator straight across the plush carpet floor to a mahogany bar on the far side of the suite. The bar contains every major brand of top shelf liquor found on Earth. Toath walked over and settled into one of the large leather divans in front of the expansive panel of windows that overlook the Old Port of Singapore. Marrt has his suite filled with priceless paintings statues and artifacts but Toath always prefers the view of the port. Marrt picks up a crystal carafe and pours two tumblers half full with an exquisitely aged single malt scotch. The Security Chief known as Alpha, glided silently across the floor and calmly stood with his back to a wall where he could see both the two men and the elevators. Marrt brought the two glasses of scotch from the bar and handed one to Toath. He then sat in a matching chair to Toath's left.

For a short while, both men just sip their scotch and look out over the old port. Now that Earth's States use, null-gravity transports to move cargo between the continents the old sea going ships are long gone. The only boats actually in the water these days are pleasure craft most of them are of the sail variety. The boats with their colorful sails made a sharp contrast to the slums built around the old port. Marrt knew whatever had brought Toath all the way to Singapore to see him personally must be extremely important, since most of their general business takes place by hologram conference. He has been intensely curious since hearing of Toath's visit, but he knows better than to ask.

Without a word, Toath reaches into his jacket and removes two items. The first is a leather cigar holder. He opens the holder and offers a cigar to Marrt. Marrt accepts one of the Ashton

Maximus double coronas and raises an eyebrow at the other item in Toath's hand. Toath takes one of the cigars for himself and makes a come here gesture with his other hand. Alpha leaves his place by the wall and glides over to Toath. Toath gives Alpha an information disk labeled, "EGA Council property, Top Secret".

While Marrt and Toath are cutting their cigars, Alpha takes the disk and inserts it into one of the terminal slots in Marrt's private desk. Marrt presses a button on the side of his chair and the windows they are looking out gloss over and become a huge monitor screen. Toath and Marrt puff on their cigars as they watch all the Council briefing information about the Defender named Michael.

Chapter 57

EGAS STALWART

I n the Stalwart's Landing Bay, John and Maryann were going through the last equipment and weapon checks with their Platoons. It had taken the ships almost a lunar cycle to reach their position just outside the system where Harrak's moon is located. John noticed that Maryann in addition to her normal combat gear carried a two-liter pressure sealed soft-sided water bag. Phillips picked up the bag, "What's with the extra bag Pug? Going to the beach?" Maryann smiled as she retrieved the bag from Phillips and placed it back with her gear. All she said in reply was, "Just in case."

Combat in armored pressure suits is cumbersome and difficult at best. The Marines train to fight in the suits giving them an all environment capability. To do this the Marines spend long hours training on the surface of Europa until combat in the suits becomes second nature. In contrast, Michael stood quietly to one side watching John and Maryann with a relaxed expression. His Elemental battle armor appears just a little thicker than his uniform. His armor was still gold in color but it had two new green patches on his shoulders each with a single gold bar. On his collar like the Giann Marines, there is the globe anchor eagle and stars insignia of the EGAFMC.

Maryann finished with the last minute checks, strode over to Michael. "Are you sure you don't want to take an energy weapon with you? It may come in handy if you want to reach out and touch someone at a distance."

"No thank you, my weapons are adequate. I do believe that inside a structure most warfare is at less than ten meters." Maryann nodded but added. "I'm hoping that we don't get into a major battle inside the place. I'd like quiet in and quiet out."

"That would be the easiest," agreed Michael. Then Michael asked something that surprised Maryann. "Do you like Lieutenant Phillips?" Maryann looked closely at Michael then answered. "John Phillips is a good friend of mine. I like him a lot. Are you asking if we are romantically involved?"

"Well kind of, you're always talking and smiling at him. Is he your boy friend?"

Maryann rolled her eyes and stated. "Look Michael, we're just friends and it really isn't any of your business. Certainly now isn't the time or place to be discussing this." Maryann saw the sad look in Michael's eyes as he looked down to avoid looking at her. She quickly changed the subject. "When your Elemental helmet field is in place will it interfere with your communication ear piece?"

Michael now has an earpiece with a tiny microphone just like the other Marines. The ear communication receiver/transmitter would allow him to communicate on both individual and ships communication bands. Michael activated his Elemental helmet and asked Maryann over the comm. line. "Well what do you think?" Maryann smiled and replied. "Traditionally in the Corps, we say radio check over." Michael looked at her and questioned. "What's a radio? And why would I check it?" Maryann looked up at the ceiling of the hanger deck as if looking for guidance. "A radio is an ancient communication device. When you check it you're asking if it works correctly." Michael inquired again. "Is my radio checked?" Maryann noticed the Platoons were boarding the shuttles so she just shook her head and picked up the last of her gear. "Yeah it's checked, let's go pilgrim." Walking behind her up the shuttles extended loading ramp Michael asked. "What's a pilgrim?" Maryann didn't answer she just kept on walking. Finding her seat, she strapped the water bag to the bulkhead behind her.

Michael strapped in next to Maryann so he was facing Parek. Sergeant Hill next to Parek, had strapped Parek to the seat earlier. Michael and Parek sit in the last two seats next to the loading ramp, which had just closed with a hiss. Michael eagerly looked around for this is his first ride in an EGAF combat shuttle. The back compartment of the shuttle has two long rows of seats facing each other. These are along the walls starting at the bulkhead that separates the pilot's cockpit from the back troop-carrying compartment. There is ample room for a full Marine Platoon even in pressure suits. In the center of the aft compartment, a ladder leads up to a copula where a crewman operates a double forty-millimeter energy cannon. There are two more energy cannon in the nose of the craft along with pilot controlled missile launchers.

Michael looked at the D'mon sitting in his ill-fitting pressure suit. With the horn cut off the top of his head and his claws trimmed, he looks a little smaller inside the pressure suit. Michael noticed Parek's nervousness. The way his lips pulled back from his uneven teeth and his cold eyes constantly glanced at the armed Marines in the shuttle. Michael couldn't help but notice that except for Hill, the other Marines kept as much distance as possible between themselves and the Demon. The iron look of their faces with the weapons held tightly across their chests gave Michael no doubt, if Parek made a wrong move it would be his last.

Michael felt a bump then the weightless pull on his straps as the shuttle left the Stalwart. Pulling into formation with the shuttles from the Dauntless, they would fly into the system fast keeping the bulk of the moon between them and the fortress. During the short fast trip, the accompanying Banshees will jam any sensors until they reach the surface of the moon. As soon as the shuttles reached the moon's surface, the jamming will stop. The planners hoped the short time the sensors were jammed would mimic a malfunction. Parek told Michael the equipment in the fortress is old and not well kept. He stated Harrak's sensor arrays malfunctioned all the time. The Marines were betting their lives on this information. Michael believed Parek only because Parek knew he would be on the shuttle with them.

Reaching the moon's surface the ships began flying towards their target just meters above the surface matching the Moon's contours and staying below sensor range. Upon reaching the moon, Maryann ordered the Marines to close helmets and pressurize suits in case of accident or enemy fire. Michael was thankful Sergeant Hill had already put on Parek's helmet. Releasing his straps and trying to help him with the shuttle bouncing up and down in the erratic flight would have been difficult.

Chapter 58

PTS CORP.

MARRT didn't bother to ask how Toath got the classified disk. When it was over Marrt rose and refilled their glasses at the bar. The significant aspects of what he had just seen were not lost on the CEO of PTS Corp. Handing his glass back to Toath, Marrt sat back down and waited for Toath to speak. Toath sipped his scotch and looked at Marrt with a slim smile. Eventually Toath stated, "I want a Defender." Marrt without surprise asked, "How?"

"There are additional resources being sent to Romeo. Ships, troops, and a lot of additional equipment to build a ship repair Facility, in orbit around Romeo. I own an agricultural subsidiary called Greenleaf Global. A team from Global will be shipping out on a supply ship called EGAS Harvest Moon to set up a agricultural research station on Romeo. This station will just happen to set up near one of the other domes on Romeo. I have gotten the Councils permission since the hostilities with the D'mon to send armed private security for the Greenleaf Global station. That security will come from PTS Corp., with your permission of course."

Marrt gave a smile, a nod and added, "of course, it's a privilege."

"Good, now PTS will have two missions on Romeo. First, you will of course ensure the Greenleaf station is secure and that your security perimeter happens to include a dome. Second, the security group will accompany a pregnant woman to Romeo. No one is to see or talk to this woman. I have spent many credits bribing the Captain of the Harvest Moon to get the woman to Romeo. She will not be on the ship's manifest of passengers." Toath pointed out of the windows that had reverted to plain glass after the disk had finished towards the slums around the harbor. "The woman, I hope, can be found locally."

With another smile, Marrt responded, "of course."

"A Physician and a Nurse from PTS will accompany the woman and deliver the child on Romeo. They also will be off the manifest. After the delivery the child will be placed in the dome."

"And the child's mother?"

Toath sadly shook his head, "there are a lot of complications associated with childbirth." Marrt nodded, "I understand."

Toath finished his drink and placed the empty glass on a table next to the chair. "The security team will monitor the dome and when the Defender exits, we bring him here. I shall arrange to fly to Romeo in my own ship and pick you and the Defender up personally. I can always call it a fact-finding tour. I'm sure the Council will authorize the tour."

"I see at least three loose ends, the Doctor, the Nurse and the Captain of the Harvest Moon."

Toath rose from his chair and stretched. "The Doctor and the Nurse need not leave Romeo and the Captain of the Harvest Moon can have an accident, space flight is quite hazardous." Marrt nodded his agreement and left his chair putting his empty glass on the bar. Toath walked over to Marrt and offered his hand. "Then we have an understanding?" Marrt took the hand and shook, "of course!" Toath moved over to where the Security Chief had entered the disk and pressed the disk release button. He put the ejected disk back in his pocket and walked back to the elevator. Turning he stated, "Then I shall see you once you have the Defender." Both

Marrt and his Security Chief nodded and Toath turned once again and entered the lift heading back up to the flying limo.

After the doors closed, Marrt turned to his Security Chief. "I want you to handle this personally." Alpha stood in the middle of the suite with his hands clasped behind his back. "If that is what you wish."

"Use your connections with the Singapore underground to find a suitable woman that won't be missed. Take Doctor Dau with you; make sure that the woman is pregnant with a male child." Alpha made a small cough and covered his mouth with his fist. "What if Dau has the opium sickness?" Marrt walked over to a large painting between the bar and the lift doors. He pulled the painting, which hung on hinges like a door. Once the painting swung open, Marrt put his hand on a glass plate in the middle of a safe door hidden behind the painting. The door to the safe opened at his touch. Inside the safe are stacks of credits a hand weapon and several clear bags full of white powder.

Marrt picked up one of the bags closed the door to the safe and returned the painting to its original position. Turning to face Alpha, he tossed the bag to him in an underhanded throw. With the speed of a striking cobra Alpha snatched the bag from the air and placed it into an inside jacket pocket. Marrt followed with, "Everyone knows about Dau's nasty habit. Let him have a taste to keep him quiet. Then after the child's delivery, perhaps Dau and his Nurse could over indulge a bit." Alpha smiled and stated, "If this is what you wish."

With his orders complete, Alpha bowed slightly to Marrt, turned and seemed to glide to the other set of lift doors, which will carry him down to the bottom lobby of the huge building. Just before the doors opened, Marrt said one more thing. "Oh yes, this will be called Operation Gabriel." Without turning, Alpha nodded and entered the lift.

Chapter 59

THE DOCKS

Old Singapore

WIN Ling is twenty-two solar cycles old. She has been working as a house cleaner for the Fat Merchant since her husband went away to work as a mine laborer on Europa. The Fat Merchant's wife seems to beat her for the smallest issues, which seem to pop up more and more often. Win Ling is not happy and hates the job and the abuse, but jobs are hard to find and she has a room and meals that are included with the job. Until her husband returns with the money he is saving on Europa, Win must do her best to take care of herself and the little one she knows she is carrying. She has had the morning sickness for almost a lunar cycle now and the old woman that cooks told her she is carrying a little bundle of joy.

Win sits in the kitchen of the large house after a long day of work. She listens to the old cook talk extensively about the old days and the many husbands she has out lived. Win tries to be polite but her eyes are drooping with fatigue after her small meal and the long day of work. They hear the Fat Merchant curse as someone rings the visitor bell. "Damn, what can this be at this time of the night?" The old cook peaks out of the kitchen door as the Fat Merchant opens up to let the three people in the house.

Ton Do, known as the Fat Merchant due to his enormous girth opens his front door ready to show his wrath to the unwelcome visitors. Opening the door his eyes grow large with fright as he recognizes the thin man in the black cloak that many call the "Bringer of Doom." The Fat Merchant stumbles backwards into his living room to let the visitors enter. He sputters, "Mr. Alpha good evening, it's so nice to see you again. Please come in to my poor house. What pray tell can I do for you?"

Alpha glided through the door looking around the gaudily decorated room with distaste. The Doctor and his Nurse followed close behind. Alpha stopped in the middle of the room and quickly came to the point. "I understand you have a house keeper here that is married to a mine laborer on Europa." The Fat Merchant stuttered again sweating profusely. "Of course, of course her name is Win Ling. But she is a poor house cleaner at best; she can be of no significance to you!" With a scowl, Alpha replied. "You don't tell me fat man what is significant to me!"

"But, I only meant . . ."

"Silence, I come here with a very lucrative business proposal for you. The woman Win Ling will board a space freighter where she will go to her husband on Europa." Seeing his lie accepted in the face of the Fat Merchant, Alpha continued. "I will pay you twenty-five thousand credits for your inconvenience and your silence about this transaction." Alpha could almost see the shrewd bargaining thoughts flying through the fat man's brain. "Oh, I don't know Mr. Alpha she is such a valuable . . ."

"Enough, I will give you fifty-thousand credits, but we must complete a little blood test on her before she can go."

"A blood test . . . ?"

"Fifty-thousand credits final offer and the blood test must be successful before payment."

"I don't know why you would need to test her." Alpha pulled a large bag from under the black cloak he is wearing. He throws the bag on the floor in front of the fat man and the bag spills gold credits all over the floor at the man's feet. The Merchant's wife that is peeking down the hallway at all of the commotion runs into the room falling on her knees quickly picking up the spilled credits. "Ton Do, you foolish fat man don't be impolite to Mr. Alpha. You know that skinny cleaning girl can't do good work. I think it's a good idea that Mr. Alpha wants to take her to her husband. Go get the girl and we'll see if she can pass Mr. Alpha's blood test." The Fat Merchant seeing his wife scrambling for the credits just replied, "Yes dearest." He moved quickly for a man his bulk through the kitchen doors to fetch the housekeeper.

The Fat Merchant barreled through the doors knocking down the cook that had been trying to listen to the exchange. He ran over to Win Ling and grabbed one arm to pull her with him into the living room. She tried to struggle but the man has too much strength for her she tries to protest. "Mr. Ton Do please, where are you taking me?"

"Come with me to the living room! A man is going to take you to join your husband on Europa but he has to test your blood first!" She looked at him in fear. "Test my blood, but why?"

"Don't ask questions it's for your own good now come on!"

The fat man pulled her into the living room and plopped her down on an ornate oriental couch. He dropped her hand and backed away watching the Doctor and the Nurse come forward with some tubes to take some blood. Alpha stepped back by the door as they drew some blood out of her arm while Win Ling sat passively appearing confused and overwhelmed at the same time.

The Nurse pulled a small machine from the bag she carried on her shoulder and the Doctor handed her a tube of blood that she placed in the machine. The Doctor watched the view screen of the machine and after a few moments looked up at Alpha. "It is a male child." Alpha made a let's go motion with his head and the three of them with Win Ling in tow left the Fat Merchant and his wife crawling on the floor picking up the dropped credits.

Chapter 60

THE FORTRESS

"Iт's not my fault!" Whined the D'mon Doctor as he avoided the Prime's glare. Harrak spat as he paced the rough rock floor. "I don't care whose fault it is you miserable piece of dung. If you can't get one of them to conceive within three sleep periods, I will give them to my warriors. The warriors are getting restless sitting here waiting for the ship repairs to be completed."

Harrak looked at the elder warriors sitting at a long table feasting on bloody meat. With each passing growth cycle, he heard more and more grumbling. He knew it wouldn't be long before one of them challenged him. He felt confident he could kill any of them but to waste good warriors with infighting was frustrating and not that rewarding. Harrak suddenly turned from his thoughts back to the quivering scientist. "Go back to your labs and do something useful. If I don't see any results by the end of the three periods your usefulness to me will have ended!"

Harrak sent him on his way with a kick that launched the smaller D'mon half way towards the door. The Doctor hit the floor rolled once and scrambled to his feet quickly making his exit. One of the young warriors ran into the room and quickly saluted the Prime dropping to one knee. The warrior spoke loudly with the importance of one that had vital information. "Prime, the sensors went off line again!" Harrak grabbed a half raw birds leg off the large tray on the table. He tore off a large portion of the meat bones and all with his sharp teeth, "And?" He spit out between mouthfuls.

"They were off for a short period then came back on all by themselves!" Harrak almost choked on the meat as he laughed. "And what now, oh great warrior should I do?" Harrak asked sarcastically. The young warrior suddenly not as confident as before stammered. "But I was told by the Sub Prime to make sure you were aware of the problem." Harrak pleased at the discomfort of the previously self-important messenger played to the audience of the elder warriors at the table. "So they came back on all by themselves! So you didn't even have to use any of your renowned technical skills to fix them?" The old warriors howled and hooted in laughter! The young warrior paled and squeaked out a reply, "N . . . no Prime."

"THEN QUIT BOTHERING ME WITH THESE STUPID INCIDENTALS," Roared Harrak! The young warrior backed up three steps before turning around and running for his life out of the room. This brought about another round of laughter from the table. Harrak sat down in his seat at the head of the table shaking his head.

Chapter 61

HARVEST MOON

Dr. Dau sat in the small desk chair in his cabin on the Harvest Moon. The small cabin has two small bunks that fold down from the metal bulkhead a small desk attached to the opposite bulkhead and a door that leads to the tiny private bathroom with sink and sonic shower. Above the desk are storage cabinets where Dau put his luggage. Dau would fold down the bottom bunk only when going to sleep. The cabin is so small that the bunk would barely leave room to pull out the desk chair if he kept it down while he is awake. The walls, painted a pale green color are like the rest of the ships interior. Dau remembered reading somewhere that the color is supposed to be soothing to the eye.

Dau opened the top desk drawer and pulled out a small black bag. The bag contains an auto injector and a small heating unit that liquefies the small amount of opiate that he puts into the auto injector. His day has gone well. After breakfast in his cabin, his routine is to go to the larger cabin where the pregnant woman and the Nurse stay. The PTS guard silently unlocks the door and allows him to enter. It has been six lunar cycles since the Harvest Moon left the Earth system traveling in a convoy with other EGA military ships to Romeo. The woman's pregnancy is progressing well. The woman is depressed but passive since she realized the ship wasn't traveling to Europa. The day she found out through a slip of the tongue by the Nurse, she was angry and combative, but after a few cycles tied down to her bunk, she acquiesced.

Dau hummed an old Asian tune as he prepared what he thought of as his little tension reliever. When he was younger, Dau was a talented physician. He had everything he wanted a beautiful wife two children and an exciting job on an epidemiology team that traveled to rural areas of the State of East Asia to identify and treat new diseases. Then that fateful call about a small village near a remote military base that had people dying within a cycle or two. For some reason his wife was very anxious about this assignment and pleaded with him to use some of the many vacation days he has on the books. She said let someone else go. Then asked why he was the one that had to go. He told her not to worry he would be back in just a few cycles.

That was the last time Dau saw his wife and children. Before containment was completed a few of the frightened villagers escaped to the city trying to leave the province. The epidemic spread quickly and before Dau could return his wife and children died. Dau was even more disheartened when he found out the virulent organism came from a biological warfare unit of the old Asian military. To drown his sorrows Dau first used alcohol but then he found opiates were the only substance that would help the pain go away.

Dau finished making his own personal cocktail for injection, he thought. *I wonder why Alpha hired me just to come all this way and deliver a baby. If there are military on Romeo then there are Doctors. There is even a Ship's Doctor on the Harvest Moon. Why all the secrecy and if this is all so secret what happens to me my nurse and the pregnant woman after the child is delivered. I was so happy to receive all that money and the half-kilo of opiate I didn't even ask about a return trip back to earth. I just assumed it would be a round trip. When I've asked, the response has been, Shut up, do your job. When I get to Romeo, I have to keep my wits about me,* Dau thought, just before he placed the auto injector to his neck and had no further worries for the day.

Chapter 62

PRAYERS

Angela was ladling food into rough wooden bowls when the Doctor came stomping into the room. Seeing his mood, Angela quickly filled a tray with the bowls and tiptoed down the small passageway containing the women's cells. She could hear him snarling and growling to the old female D'mon and knew that with his temper it was a good time to be out of the room.

"What does he expect of me?" The Doctor hissed. "I am a specialist. I have studied hundreds of species! Can I help it if when that moron's idiot warriors took the technology off that planet they destroyed all of the knowledge disks?" They thought they were worthless! Those warriors are dumber than animal dung! How am I to know when these females will conceive? How can I make sure one conceives in the next three sleep cycles?"

The female D'mon to who at that point had said nothing asked. "Why do you have to make sure one conceives within three sleep cycles?" The Scientist kicked a chair against the wall. "It's because that mindless rabid beast Harrak has finally lost his patience. He said if one of them doesn't conceive within three sleep cycles he's going to give them to his warriors!" He turned to his lab and kicked the chair again on the way out. This time the chair splintered and broke.

After distributing the food, Angela returned to the kitchen area. She found the old female D'mon picking up the pieces of the chair. "What was that all about?" The old D'mon put the pieces of chair in the trash and replied. "I'm afraid that Harrak's patience has run out. He told the Doctor that if one of the human females doesn't conceive within the next three sleep cycles he will give them to his warriors." Angela paled at the news. She knew none of the women would conceive. She knew the women would die. She sat at the dirty table and put her head in her hands. *What could she do?* For the first time since becoming captive, she felt overwhelming hopelessness. For the first time since her capture, Angela clasped her hands together and prayed. *"Please Lord Creator, only you can help us now!"*

Chapter 63

FEAR AND COURAGE

As Third Platoon advanced slowly through the trash outside the rear hatch of the fortress, strict communication silence was enforced. The moon's surface littered with broken equipment, old crates and boxes the remnants of stolen technology used and discarded. The piles of trash are everywhere. The Platoon moved from cover to cover slowly so they wouldn't kick up dust in the low gravity of the Moon. About one hundred meters away from the hatch, the Platoon stopped. Fourth Squad slowly crept forward to the hatch and went about their assignment of disabling sensors and cameras covering the hatch. It only took a few minutes before Fourth Squad took up defensive positions around the hatch and signaled with hand signals the job is complete, hatch secure. Maryann led the rest of the Platoon to the hatch. Maryann stood by as Sergeant Hill and First Squad prepared to enter the hatch. Maryann looked over to a Marine with Fourth Squad that was holding an electronic scrambler override. He placed it next to the electronic security box that controlled the hatch from the outside. Once Maryann was sure Hill and his Squad was ready, she nodded at the Marine and he pressed a button on the override.

The outlined plan was for Maryann the Defender, Parek and three Squads, to enter the fortress. Once through the hatch one Squad would deploy and defend the hatch until the others returned. Parek and the Defender would lead the Marines to the detention area. One Squad will secure the detention area while Maryann and one squad of all Giann Marines freed the women and got them into pressure suits. On the way out Maryann would help the Squad with the women while the Defender and his Squad covered the retreat to the hatch.

Even the best made plans begin to change quickly. After the hatch cycled and opened they found the inside portion of the hatch was too small for more than one Squad at a time. Sergeant Hill squeezed into the double-sided hatch with his Squad and the Defender. Maryann tapped her foot with impatience, as she had to wait for the hatch to cycle for the next Squad. On the inside, there was another surprise. From the drawing Parek had made they expected two passageways running away from the hatch. The room filled with rank smelling D'mon pressure suits had three entrances! When Maryann arrived with the Second Squad, she talked over the change with Michael and Sergeant Hill as they waited for the last Squad to enter.

She whispered that perhaps she should split one squad and leave more Marines here. Michael pointed out that with the Giann Squad burdened on the way in with extra suits and on the way out with the women that a full Squad is required for security. Hill nodded in agreement with the Defender. Maryann instructed the Sergeant in Third Squad to break down the Squad into three Fire Teams one for each passageway. Everyone was then surprised when Michael quickly without warning grabbed Parek threw him to the ground and held his dagger to the Demon's throat. "Are there any more surprises we don't know about?"

Through his opened helmet visor, Parek cowered and whined. "I've only been in this area once and that was a longtime ago. This is the slave area, you're lucky I was here at all!" Michael put his face very close to Parek's open helmet and whispered. "If there is any type of trap up ahead you will die first!" Parek paled, the sweat dripping from his face down his neck.

"There are no traps Defender. You can trust me!" Michael rose and pulled Parek erect with him. He asked Parek, "Which way?" The D'mon pointed to the passageway on the right. Michael grabbed the back of Parek's suit and pushed him ahead stating, "Let's go."

Maryann and the two remaining Squads followed Michael and Parek down the passageway. They moved from section to section using the large steel support beams where the sections come together as cover. Half of them on one side of the passageway half on the other. As Michael approached a four-way intersection, a warrior walked around the corner right in front of him. Michael's spear was instantly in his hand. As the spear extended it went through the warrior's throat. The D'mon died with a quiet gurgle. Retracting his spear Michael grabbed the falling warrior and passed him back to the other Marines. Replacing his spear in its holder Michael hissed at Parek, "How far?" Parek stammered back, "Not far, the passage to the right."

Maryann broke down her security Squad into three Fire Teams. She left two Fire Teams with Sergeant Hill at the intersection and took one with her. As the group left, following the Defender and Parek, Hill spread his Marines out covering the two passageways considered hostile. He took one Fire Team his Corporal the other. They laid down taking cover behind the support beams and started to wait. Michael led the remaining group down the passageway to the kitchens and the lab.

Chapter 64

GREENLEAF GLOBAL STATION

(Romeo)

ALPHA with two guards accompanied the woman, the Doctor and the Nurse into the covered rover, which will carry them from the shuttle landing-pad to the small dispensary on the agricultural compound. The half-kilometer ride to the gate of the compound on the dusty road took just minutes. The rover stopped at a guardhouse just outside of the main gate to the compound. The guards wearing black combat armor with the small silver shield emblem emblazoned with the initials PTS came to attention when they recognized Alpha. The rover continues through and Dr. Dau looked out a small tinted window where he sits in the back seat next to the pregnant woman.

As the rover passes through the gate, Dau looks at the four-meter high titanium fence that seems to go on for kilometers. He can see that there are guard towers at intervals along the fence. Parked inside the gate on either side of the road are two matching black Armored Personnel Carriers. The APC's each have dual forty-millimeter energy cannon in turrets crewed by more guards in the black combat armor. As the rover continued up the road to the dispensary Dau took one more glance out the back of the rover as the large metal gates swung shut.

There are many buildings scattered around the compound along with tractors, warehouses and different types of rovers. Set a little to the side away from the other buildings is the dispensary. The dispensary is the shape of an H with two wings connected by a central enclosed hallway. The rover drove around to the back entrance and stopped by the door in a cloud of rust colored dust.

Alpha and the driver got out of the rover first then the two guards opened the side doors next to their seats and stepped out. They folded the middle seats down so the three in the back could exit. While the guards assisted the women out on the dispensary side of the rover, Dr. Dau stepped out on the other side. As Dau stretched upon exiting the rover, he noticed a gold-brown dome about one-hundred meters behind the dispensary. He had only a moment to wonder what the dome was before he heard Alpha state. "Right this way Doctor, there's no time for sight-seeing."

Chapter 65

EXPOSED

ANGELA sat morosely at the table while the old D'mon female paced back and forth wringing her hands. "IT WAS YOU," shouted the Doctor! He strode into the room from his labs with his claws extended. "It was you! You lied to me!" Angela just sat there in shock, tears running down her face.

"I rechecked the hormonal levels of the females and they haven't changed! You lied to me!" It seemed to Angela that the Doctor was moving in slow motion as he strode towards her with claws extended. The female D'mon ran forward and yelled. "No!" The female moved between the Doctor and Angela. Without breaking stride, the Doctor backhanded the female so hard she flew across the room hit the wall and crumpled in an unmoving heap. Angela cried out in terror as she saw his clawed arm descending! Then everything stopped!

The descending arm flew harmlessly past her spewing blood across the table. The D'mon Scientist looked in astonishment at the bloody stump of his arm just as the crystal blade severed his head. The D'mon's body paused for a moment before collapsing back upon itself. Angela looked up in shock and saw a man that resembled her husband standing before her in golden armor. The air around his head had a golden shimmer and he was holding a bloody crystal sword. Angela whispered, "An Angel!" She then promptly passed out, her head making a thud as it hit the table.

Maryann ran quietly across the room and looked quickly around the corner towards the slave cells. She turned quickly and waved the security Fire Team to the other passageway leading to the labs. The three Marines quietly entered the passageway to clear it of any enemies.

The squad of Giann Marines entered the kitchen and followed Maryann's lead down the passageway to the cells. Michael felt the pulse of the women at the table to ensure she was alive. He then gently picked her up and placed her on the floor. Michael heard a noise to his left and quickly turned with his dagger in hand. He saw the old D'mon female sit up shaking her head. As he started to rise, he felt a hand on the arm that held the dagger. He looked down and saw the women he had placed on the floor holding his arm.

Angela looked up at him and croaked, "No please, she helped me!" Michael looked down at her for a moment then the knife disappeared. Angela noticed that the man's head no longer shimmered. She looked at his face and asked, "Who are you?" Michael looked back at her, his eyes gentled and he said, "I am Michael. I am a Defender and also a Marine." Angela looked confused for a moment and then asked, "Michael?" Before he could reply, Maryann came back in the room. She saw that the woman on the floor wasn't injured and turned to the female D'mon. Angela pulled on Michael's arm and he helped her sit up. Once again, Angela pleaded, "Don't hurt her. She's been helping me and the others to stay alive."

Maryann pulled her faceplate up into her helmet and noticed that the energy rifle that hung on a sling at her side was pointing at the D'mon. She lowered the weapon and spoke to Michael. "Defender we need to get this woman into a suit fast. I don't know how much longer our luck is going to last."

Parek had removed his helmet and placed it on a counter seemingly to scratch his head. Behind the helmet was now hidden a communications control station. While no one was watching, he took one hand and opened a small door in the console. Just as he pressed the button, a Marine from the Fire Team that searched the labs stepped in saw him and shot him through the head. The Emergency Claxon sounded all through the fortress. Maryann just had enough time to say, "Well it looks like we're in the shit now!" Before breaking communications silence keying her helmet mike to inter ship communications and yelling, "DAUNTLESS, STALWART, THIS IS HALL. WE'RE IN! GO! GO! GO!"

Maryann then switched her communications band to her platoon. "Ok folks, you know their coming. I need you to hold your positions until we can get these people out of here! Good luck and good hunting, Hall out." Along with small arms fire, Maryann could hear explosions in the distance. That would be the other three Platoons assaulting their assigned targets.

Chapter 66

HARRAK

JUMPING to his feet knocking over the bitter ale he was drinking, Harrak raced for the Control Center in the next room. Glancing at the monitors, he roared, "WHERE DID THESE BEINGS COME FROM?" The Sub Prime on duty in the control room answered in a quaking voice, "There are two ships coming in fast. One looks like it carries fighters! There are four shuttles on the moon outside the fortress with warriors attacking three of our entrance hatches. It seems the automated defenses are keeping them at bay."

"And what are these?" Harrak pointed at four monitors that displayed nothing but static.

"Those are the monitors from the rear garbage hatch."

"FOOL," Harrak screamed! He backhanded the Sub Prime across the face knocking him over a chair. Harrak picked up the communications microphone and directed. "Four Claws of warriors proceed to each hatch destroy these attackers!" He then pressed another screen and was immediately looking at the frightened face of a young Sub Prime on the bridge of his ship the Conqueror. The Sub Prime stammered, "P-Prime we're under attack! The repairs aren't yet completed and a large war ship is attacking us!" Harrak saw a large explosion blow the Sub Prime back from the screen then the screen went blank. He switched to another monitor that displayed the ship from the outside. Harrak watched in frustration as the EGA Cruiser flew by pounding the ship with missiles. Explosions started in the bow and continued all along the ship until reaching the engines. The ship exploded with a massive concussion destroying all the supply and refit buildings in the area.

Harrak enraged, moved to another monitor, which was the fortress's docking bay. He could see warriors running back and forth with hoses fighting fires and moving debris. One of the warriors stopped in front of the communications console and Harrak yelled, "REPORT!"

The cut bleeding and blackened warrior shouted above the din. "Prime with the first alarm we tried to launch all of our remaining fighters! The fighters that made it out were destroyed by the little needle ships. Then a large vessel launched a missile into the entrance of the Launch Bay. The missile destroyed the entrance and we're trying to contain fires and plug holes so we don't lose any more of our atmosphere!" Grimly Harrak inquired, "What about my personal fighter?"

"Prime your personal fighter is still on the individual launcher at the back of the Bay. The small armored launch doors haven't been touched."

"Good make sure it's fueled and armed I may have to lea—," Harrak corrected himself. "I may have to go out there and fight these cowards myself!" The warrior bowed and replied, "As you wish, Prime."

Harrak turned off the monitor and began to pace the control room. On the monitors, Harrak could see the warriors boiling out of three entrances fighting with the attackers. However, as he paced he wondered about the back hatch. *What's happening back there?* With fear and anxiety, growing Harrak turned to the Sub Prime in charge of communications. The Sub Prime with a large bruise where he was last hit looked at Harrak suspiciously.

Harrak ordered, "Contact the Elevated Prime. Tell him we are under attack by an unknown belligerent species. Tell him there are only two ships but they are carrying fast new fighters that would be well worth capturing." Harrak thought. *That will bring them running to my aid!*

Chapter 67

EGAMC HEADQUARTERS

Camp Mills

Lieutenant Colonel Maxwell Silverton sits behind a mound of reports. He is diligent in his duties and though he would rather be anywhere else in the universe, he will have the reports completed and signed by the end of this cycle. Silverton has short grey balding hair and this is his thirtieth solar cycle with Marines. Silverton has never been in combat. That is not by his choice it's just that when anything happens in the Marines he happens to be administrating somewhere else. He is a by the book man that many have said privately is too old to be just a Lieutenant Colonel.

Silverton does have an invaluable talent. He is a very good administrator. If you want every, I dotted and every T crossed, he's the man. That's why Kellogg brought him with her as her Executive Officer to the Romeo system. Since Colonel Kellogg is with the Harrak's Moon Operation, Silverton is now in charge of the rapidly growing Camp Mills. Most of the paperwork comes from the fact that Camp Mills must expand to house a full Marine Division by the end of next solar cycle. The supplies and Marines flow into Camp Mills daily. Silverton sadly reflects that nothing in the military is without paperwork.

The knock on his door is a glad interruption and he cheerfully calls, "Enter." Lieutenant Hernandez his adjutant briskly enters the office with photos in his hands. "I have the photos from the Banshee high fly over sir." Hernandez handed the photos to Silverton and added. "It does look a little strange for an agricultural station." Silverton looked carefully at the photos one by one. No one was particularly happy when the news came down the chain of command that a civilian company called Greenleaf Global has authorization to set up an experimental research station on Romeo. Colonel Kellogg thought it was a little unusual when they put the station a thousand clicks away from Camp Mills coincidentally near another dome.

Then of course, there has been no contact from the station. Usually if a civilian contractor sets up shop in a war zone, the contractors most always send a liaison to the nearest military commander to keep the lines of communication open. There hasn't been a single peep out of Greenleaf Global since they landed. That peaked Colonel Kellogg's interest in Greenleaf Global. Before she left on the operation, Kellogg asked Silverton to keep an eye on Greenleaf Global for as she put it, "Something just doesn't smell right here." Silverton pushed some of the data disk reports to the edge of his desk so he could spread out the pictures and look closer.

He looked at the very large fenced perimeter with the guard towers and noticed some parked APCs. He did note the large flat plowed areas that appeared to be agricultural fields of some type. Parked around some of the prefabricated buildings are rovers and farming equipment. Silverton thought the large H shaped building not far from the dome is unusual. The dome at Camp Mills has a two hundred meter perimeter fence around it as per orders from the EGA Council itself. The Council placed a moratorium on any scientific or other investigation of the Romeo domes. All personnel, whether they be military or civilian must keep at least two hundred meters away from the dome.

Silverton placed the picture in a scanner so he could better gage the distance with computer enhancement. Sure enough, the dome turned out to be ninety-seven meters from the building with no protective fence around the dome. Silverton a man to follow the letter of regulations turned to Hernandez. "Lieutenant, I would like to have a combat shuttle available for a flight to the agricultural station. I will take a flight out there personally in a few cycles. By then, the lunar cycle's reports are finished and I will have a free cycle to speak with the Greenleaf Global people." Hernandez responded with, "Aye, sir", and then asked. "Do you anticipate any problems with their security people?"

"No I don't, but I'll take a Squad of Marines with me and I always have comm. with the Banshee Combat Air Patrols. Inform Sergeant Major Min to clear time from his schedule so he can accompany me."

Hernandez nodded acknowledgement turned and left the office. Silverton smiled and stacked the pictures together. He thought. *The little jaunt up there to clear up this little misunderstanding with the civilians is just what I need to get out in the fresh air for awhile.*

Chapter 68

HOLDING THE LINE

A SHORT time after the alarm in the fortress started the Marines at the intersection of the passageways could hear what sounded like growling and snarling coming out of speakers in the walls. Sergeant Hill left with the Fire Teams at the intersection had four Marines covering one corridor while he and the other three Marines covered the second. The passageway behind them led back to the Squad holding the hatch and the passageway to the right was where the rescue party went. After the noise on the speakers stopped, Hill could hear what sounded like hundreds of feet running towards them down the two passageways. Sergeant Hill clicked the safety on his weapon to off and stated. "Ok folks here they come. Aim low and remember short controlled bursts. We have the advantage they don't know we're here." The Corporal watching the other passage way added, "Yet!"

Hill estimated that the length of the passageways were about fifty to seventy-five meters before they made a turn. That isn't a very long distance especially how fast the Demons ran when they fought on Romeo. He wondered about shooting out the lights around the intersection but the light strips ran along the ceiling. If they shoot out the ones near the intersection, the light in the passageways in the rear would highlight them from behind. He also considered that the women traveling along this route wouldn't have the advantage of the night vision lenses the Marines have on their helmets. *Dragging women in pressure suits that also can't see where they are going would make it one big goat rope!*

The drumming feet became louder and then in a moment a mass of Demons came down both passageways. Sergeant Hill yelled, "FIRE!" The Marine's weapons leveled the first groups of Demons rounding the corner. They piled up as they dropped stopping the ones behind in confusion. The withering fire killed more of them before they were able to push the others behind them back up the passageways. "That was easy," cheered the Corporal! Putting a new magazine in his weapon Sergeant Hill grimly replied, "This time they'll come out shooting!"

Chapter 69

RESPONSIBILITIES

Maryann walked to the corridor leading to the holding cells. She saw the patient Giann Marines helping the exhausted women into their pressure suits. Maryann could see the confinement had taken its toll. Even the women that were crew on the Inquisitive were struggling. "This is taking too long," Maryann muttered to no one in particular.

Just then, she heard the sound of weapons fire coming from the passageway that led back to the hatch. She looked at Michael watching the passageway leading to the scientific labs and stated. "They're hitting the intersection!" She gave a hand signal to the fire team she brought along for extra security. "Quick they're going to need help!" The team exited the kitchen towards the intersection at a trot.

As Angela struggled into her suit the female D'mon, clasped her crude translator and rose from the floor. From where she stood, Maryann had her weapon trained on the D'mon. Angela put up a hand and spoke to Maryann, "it's ok, and she won't harm me." The D'mon helped Angela hold her suit up while she fastened all the fast seal closures. While holding the suit the D'mon spoke through her translator, "Please take me with you!" Angela stopped and looked at the pleading alien. "Please take me with you. I am not a warrior. I am a slave too! Harrak will kill me after you go!"

Angela saw the tears beginning in the large D'mon eyes and looked to Maryann. In a determined voice, Angela stated, "Lieutenant, we have to take her with us." The D'mon female spoke again. "If you can't take me then kill me! Harrak will see to it that I have a slow and painful death!" Maryann started to raise her weapon then stopped. Michael his saber in hand stepped away from the passageway to the labs and interjected, "She is one of the Evil Ones! You saw what happened when we trusted the last one!" Angela pleaded again, "She helped us. She doesn't deserve to die!"

Maryann began, "We don't even have a suit for her." The D'mon pointed at the body of Parek slumped in a pile by the wall. Angela looked at the body and then spoke quickly. "The D'mon that was with you was shot in the head. The suit is still intact!" Maryann listened as the battle at the intersection sounded to be increasing. Finally, she rolled her eyes and said, "Geeze what else?" She pointed at Parek's body with the barrel of her weapon, "Make it quick. We've got people dying out there!"

Angela grabbed the helmet for her suit and ran with the D'mon to Parek's body. Helping the D'mon to open the suit and remove the body Angela commented, "It's got blood all over it but the suit will work just fine. It's a good thing your horns are so small we don't have time to make adjustments!"

Chapter 70

THE BIRTH

"Push now Win Ling, push." After nine hours of labor, the moment had finally arrived! Win Ling grunted with pain and exhaustion. The sweat rolled down her face plastering her black hair against her temples. The Nurse dabbed at the sweat with a cool towel. "His head is almost out you must keep pushing Win Ling!" Dr. Dau sits on a small stool at the foot of the birthing chair covered in gown, mask and gloves only his eyes are exposed. "Breathe deeply and blow in short puffs as you push." In another great effort, Win Ling puffed and pushed.

"Here he comes! I have him, Nurse Chang quickly bring a towel and take the child! Good job Win Ling it's a healthy baby boy!"

Win Ling watched in relief as the Nurse wrapped the baby in a towel after Dr. Dau cut the umbilical cord. She didn't notice as one of the security men opened the roller valve on the small IV bag that is hanging piggy back to her IV. In her greatest moment of joy, the medication worked quickly and she didn't even feel the Doctor finish the delivery of the placenta. Her eyes closed and the sleep came quickly.

Alpha stands just inside the door of the room. After the Nurse cleans up the child and swaddles him in blankets he speaks. "Bring the child, follow me." The Nurse follows Alpha out the door of the delivery room towards the back of the dispensary. She is scared and surprised when Alpha continues out the back door of the dispensary and walks toward the dome. Reaching the dome Alpha instructs. "Touch the side of the dome. A door will open for you. Inside the dome, you will find a cradle. Place the baby in the cradle then come back outside. Do you understand?

The Nurse shaking with fright nods then slowly steps forward toward the dome. She tucks the child in the crook of one arm and slowly reaches out and touches the dome. A door opens and she steps back in fright. She looks back at Alpha and he nods, "Go on." She slowly steps into the dome and sees the cradle on a short pedestal in the middle of the dome. She stops and looks around the dome once. The yellow light inside the dome feels very calming the walls themselves seem to have a soft glow. The smooth walls of the dome are the same tan and rust color of the soil outside. She glances out of the open door behind her and sees Alpha making pantomime movement with his hands of placing the baby. She can hear him say, "Go."

The Nurse nods toward Alpha in understanding and turns once again to the task. She looks down at the baby boy sleeping in her arms and begins to cry. His eyes open and one of his tiny hands holds on to her thumb as she places the boy on the cradle. She gently loosens the tiny grip and tucks the baby's arm back in the swaddling blankets. Her tears make tiny pools as they fall into the ancient dust of the floor. The baby on the cradle pulls one of his little arms out of the blanket and puts his fingers in his mouth. Contentedly sucking on his fingers the now drowsy baby falls fast asleep. Standing up and wiping the tears from her face the Nurse turns and leaves the dome. The door closes behind her.

Chapter 71

THE INTERSECTION

THE Demons came out shooting! The Corporal died with a surprised look on his face as the warriors advanced behind a volley of fire. The other Marine at the same entrance started rolling grenades down the passageway as fast as she could. Just when she was going to run the other fire team arrived and shot over her laying down a withering fire. She yelled, "GET DOWN!"

The Marines hit the stone floor just as the grenades went off! The concussions from the explosions ran both ways through the passageway. A thick piece of the metal ceiling fell like a cleaver taking off a Marines arm at the elbow. He rolled back against the wall and grabbed the stump with his good hand while calmly noting his severed hand still grasped the handle of his weapon on the floor. Sergeant Hill pulled the Marine back around the corner. Unzipping the man's armored pressure suit he pulled out the Marines belt, and pulled it taunt around the wound above the amputation. The makeshift tourniquet stopped the bleeding so he opened an aid kit, put a dressing on the stump, and sealed the suit over the stump with plastiseal. He then gave the man a shot of pain reliever. The wounded Marine obviously in shock mumbled. "I only came here to give you a hand."

Sergeant Hill zipped the man's suit closed again and looked at his pale face. "Hang in there son. The Lieutenant will be back with the captives soon and we'll get you out of here." The

Marine with his eyes getting heavy just said, "Sure Sarge." Then he quietly passed out. Hill with his back against the wall rolled and peaked back around the corner. All he could see was smoke debris and bodies. He reached into the passageway and grabbed the Marine's weapon and the severed arm. He put the arm in a plastic self-seal bag from his pack. Hill then strapped the arm to the front of the Marine's suit with plastic zip ties. A Marine watching from across the corridor asked, "What ya doing Sarge?"

"I don't know if the Medics can do anything with it but I'll be damned if I'm going to leave it for the Demons!"

Hill heard weapons fire coming from the other passageway. He rolled across the intersection and looked. The Marines weren't firing. The Demons at the other end were systematically putting out the lights in the passageway. Watching the lights go out one by one, Hill commented, "I had a feeling they would figure that one out eventually."

Thinking for a moment Hill came to a decision then explained his plan. "Let's give them a hand getting the lights out." Pointing to the female Marine, he continued, "MacDougal you go back down the passageways knocking out the lights. When the lights go out, everybody go to infrared visors. Let's see how well the beasties do in the dark!" He grabbed the female Marine by the elbow, "Mac, when you reach the Lieutenant. Advise her we're on infrared." She nodded, slid back from her position and started down the passageway towards the kitchen and labs taking out the lights as she went. Grabbing his sidearm Hill rolled back to the other passageway, "Ok guys; let's take out the lights around us!"

Chapter 72

MAIN GATE

(Greenleaf Global Station)

Lieutenant Colonel Silverton stands in the hot sun and feels his anger rising. He asked the pilot of the combat shuttle to land fifty meters from the main gate of the station instead of at the Greenleaf Global shuttle pad. Although the landing had blown up a lot of dust, Silverton wanted to make two points. The first point being the acting CO of Camp Mills was not going to walk a half of a click to speak to some civilian contractor that should have given him a courtesy call in the first place. The second point being as acting CO of Camp Mills, he can land his shuttle any damn place on the planet he wanted.

The two PTS guards in combat armor stand at port arms with their weapons behind the pulled down metal pole that blocks the way to the main gate. "I'm sorry sir; did you communicate with our administration personnel your request to visit the station?" Silverton took a deep breath and glanced at Sergeant Major Min that stands to his right. The tall Giann stands impassively giving no clue to his thoughts. The Marine Squad behind the Sergeant Major half of them human and the others Giann watched with nervous interest. The Squad armed with holstered hand weapons only couldn't fail to notice all of the firepower carried by the PTS guards backed up by the guard towers and parked APCs.

Fighting his anger Silverton stated. "Let me speak with the person in charge of this station, NOW!" The guard spoke softly in his helmet comm. and after a few moments stated, "Our Commander will be with you shortly." Placing his hands on his hips Silverton waited impatiently as the large gates to the station slowly swing open. He sees a tall thin man wearing a long black coat seem to float as he walks from the gate to stand between the two guards.

Having heard the shuttle land outside the gate Nurse Chang looked apprehensively out of one of the front windows of the dispensary. She sees Mr. Alpha go down to the gate then the gate opens and he walks outside. Before she could see any more, a guard from the front door walks over and stands outside the window. He taps on the glass with his weapon and warns, "Away from the window."

The Nurse jumps back from the window and hurries down the hall to Dr. Dau's room. Forgetting to knock Nurse Chang quickly opens the door. "Doctor Dau I'm so sorry for the interruption . . ." She puts her hand to her mouth so she won't scream. Dr. Dau is sitting in a white plastic chair on the table next to him is his small black case that carries his auto-injector and a half empty plastic bag with white powder. The little heating stove for melting the opiate still has a blue flame running on the table next to him. Dr. Dau's head is back and his open eyes stare blankly at the ceiling his mouth open. At a glance, Nurse Chang knew he is dead.

Closing the door the Nurse runs down the hallway to the room where they keep Win Ling. She opens the door and is happy to find Win Ling looking at her with sleepy eyes. Nurse Chang runs to the side of her bed and starts removing the tape from her IV site. Alpha wanted her sedated since the delivery three planetary cycles ago. Pulling out the catheter from her arm Nurse Chang instructed. "Win Ling we have to get out of here! Dr. Dau is dead and I think Mr. Alpha will kill us too! Parked at the back of the dispensary is a large rover. The workers here have been putting stems of local plants in transport cases to go by shuttle to a space freighter. We must hide in the cases and get to the freighter it's our only chance."

Nurse Chang sat Win Ling up in the bed and tried to get shoes on her feet. Still medicated Win Ling lay back on her side. "I'm so tired. Where is my baby? I want my baby. I can't leave without my baby." Nurse Chang put the shoes on her feet then put her legs in scrub pants. As she shakily stood Win Ling up next to the bed, she pulled the scrub pants up around her waist. Having no extra time Chang pulled a scrub top over Win Lings arms and head leaving the patient gown she was wearing underneath the top.

Win Ling is too unsteady to walk let alone run. Nurse Chang stands in front of Win ling and grabs her arms around her neck and across her chest. Shuffling slowly to the door Chang carries Win Ling out of her room. Leaving by the back door, Nurse Chang drags Win Ling out to the open back door of the rover. Propping the medicated woman up against the door Chang pulls down one of the large packing cases. She opens the case and dumps the plants out. She then throws them under the raised dispensary platform. Quickly emptying another case in the same fashion Chang was finally ready for the desperate gamble. She placed Win Ling in one case and told her to be very quiet. Nurse Chang climbed into the other and pulled the lid closed from the inside. She prayed that no one would notice the cases are unlocked.

Chapter 73

OUTSIDE THE FORTRESS

FIGHTING in armored pressure suits is nasty business. The suits will self-seal small punctures but the larger type common in battle will leave the being inside dying from explosive decompression. John Phillips now understands why besides energy and projectile weapons the Demons also fight with knives, swords and spears. Whatever makes the holes, you're just as dead. The advantage the Marines have is after the initial assault they turned defensive. The Demons boiling out of the fortress thought they are turning back an attack. However, systematically from cover to cover the Marines are slowly retreating towards the shuttles. The hope is that the D'mon won't realize the Marines outside are buying time for the Platoon rescuing the women.

The Banshees flying above took out the large defensive cannon that crowned the fortress. They also swept the area of what few fighters rose to meet them. They now flew back and forth impotently looking for targets of opportunity. Unfortunately, the figures engaged below were too close to each other for area strafing or bombing runs. The guns on the combat shuttles even had difficulty shooting over the slowly retreating Marines. A meter back at a time, when a Marine falls, another will grab a strap on his armored suit and pull them back to the shuttle. They won't leave anyone behind on the airless moon, dead or alive. The floating blood of the dead and wounded splashes the loading ramps and walls of the shuttles. The blood splattered as dark crimson, and then in the vacuum, quickly turning sticky black. Outside, they're doing their job, because, it's their job.

Chapter 74

EGAS DAUNTLESS

COLONEL Kellogg stands on the Bridge of the Dauntless next to the Commanding Officer. The Skipper of the Dauntless is a grizzled veteran of the EGA Fleet. Captain James Bossian is short and rather stout with a generous paunch that has defied all types of Fleet physical training. The Fleet Command in a very wise move ignored the mandatory physical standards and allowed Bossian to stay on duty. They allow Captain Bossian to Command, not only the Space Carrier Dauntless but give him overall Command of the rescue operation. Captain Bossian's experience, knowledge and leadership are just too valuable to lose.

Both Officers calmly listening to the communications chatter of the battle below wondered the same thing. *What is taking them so long?* Both Bossian and Kellogg know the operation's success depends on speed. The ship's resources and the Marines involved cannot sustain a long battle. The troops on the moon outside the fortress are already retreating close to the shuttles. Time is against them. The longer the engagement takes the more that can go wrong! The Communications Officer turned from her console and reported, "Captain, I have a flash comm. from Lieutenant Hall. The prisoners are all alive and are now fully suited. They are now working their way out of the fortress, resistance is heavy." Bossian calmly answered, "Very well," and thought, *finally!*

Just then, the Ensign at the sensor console announced, "Captain, we have multiple vessels just entering the system." Bossian walked to his bridge chair and sat before asking, "What direction and how many?"

"Sir, I estimate sixty plus vessels lying two eight zero. They just entered the rim of the system. The ships will be within weapons range in approximately five, five, point eight minutes."

Bossian swiveled his chair to face Kellogg, "Well Colonel, it looks like we have company. I believe it's time we got this dog and pony show on the road!" He quickly swiveled his chair forward again, "Communications!"

"Yes sir?"

"Flash message to Lieutenant Hall. You have thirty minutes then I pull the plug." Kellogg stepped up next to Bossian's chair and commented, "That's cutting it pretty close isn't it Captain?" Bossian answered dryly, "Not in my judgment. I believe that when it's time to go, my, ships will outrun anything they've got." Kellogg stood impassively her face a calm mask as she thought. *Come on Hall; get them the hell out of there!*

Chapter 75

A CONVIENT END TO A LITTLE PROBLEM

Alpha spoke quietly and apologetically to the irritated Colonel at the gate of the station. He apologized for the rude manner of his employees, and had the Colonel communicated with him prior to coming all this way he would have told him of the unusual fungus that his scientists found in the soil here. He assured the Colonel that normally he would have full access to the station but he was sure that the Colonel was aware of the EGA regulations regarding possible foreign contamination and the need to quarantine all areas where new organisms have the potential to spread. He also assured the Colonel he would send a representative to Camp Mills to set up liaison as soon as the quarantine is finished. The Colonel appeared suspicious but according to his own regulations, he can do no more.

Alpha was pleased as he watched the Colonel and his baldy Marines troop back aboard their shuttle for the trip back south. He knew the "Quarantine" story couldn't last long but it will be long enough to tie up the three loose ends of "Operation Gabriel". Once the loose ends are gone, all he has to do is now wait patiently until the Defender emerges from the dome then whisk him away to Earth. Alpha walked back to the dispensary. Last night he called Dr. Dau to his office to give him an update on the health of the woman. With the Doctor away from his room, it was easy for one of his men to add strychnine to the opiate in the Doctor's bag.

A thin smile on his face, Alpha entered the dispensary and met the guard he had left outside the door. The guard smiled with pleasure and led Alpha to the Doctor's room. Alpha glanced inside the room to confirm that the fool Doctor had indeed used the contaminated drug. Continuing down the hall, they walked into the room where the woman slept. Seeing the bed empty, Alpha pulled out his pocket communication pad and punched in his private code giving him access to the stations security cams. With the guard looking over his shoulder he watched as Nurse Chang emptied the two cases and after putting the woman in one, climbed into the other. The guard asked, "Do you want me to go and get them?"

"No, I want those cases put on the next autopilot shuttle going to the Harvest Moon. In my office is a small remote controlled explosive device. Put the device on the shuttle with them. I will be able to set off the device with my handheld communication pad when the time is right. An explosion in space is a convenient end to our little loose end problem." The guard nodded and left the room. Alpha walked back to his office whistling an ancient tune that is his favorite, it was something about dirty deeds . . .

Chapter 76

DANCING IN THE DARK

MARYANN received the message from the Dauntless as her group started down the dark passageway towards the intersection. Maryann and the female Marine that extinguished the lights in the corridor took the front. The Defender took the last place in the line. The suited women walked along one after another one hand on the shoulder of the person in front. Maryann had the Giann Marines staggered on the sides to keep the women moving and protect them from bumping into the metal support beams that ran in intervals. The D'mon female in the bloody suit was the first in line. She explained that her large eyes could see fairly well in the dark. Angela was next, since the other women didn't want to touch the D'mon.

At the intersection, the fighting is quieting down to intermittent sniping. Since the passageways went dark, the Demons had charged twice. After the second attack with many more warriors killed the Demons realized the Marines could see fine in the dark. Stopping her column, a few meters short of the intersection Maryann crawled forward on her stomach behind the female Marine that was at her side. The Marine took a covering position across the corridor from Sergeant Hill. Maryann slid up next to him. With their infrared lenses down, the helmeted Marines reminded Maryann of bees she saw in a nature program when she was a child. Whispering Maryann asked, "What's the situation Sergeant?"

Hill instinctively ducked as an energy bolt hit the metal beam he was using for cover. "I've got two wounded and one dead. The Demons are holding back for now, why? I don't know. With the pile of bodies getting closer they could crawl forward and then rush us any time now."

Maryann rolled to her side and pumped her arm with fist closed up and down signaling to the first Giann Marine to start the women crawling around the corner down the last corridor. The Giann with their increased strength found it a lot quicker to pull the women lying down around the corner. The women huddled next to the Marine wounded behind some barricaded debris. As the last woman traversed the corner, and all the Giann had joined them, Maryann turned back to Sergeant Hill, "The Defender will stay here with you. He will take charge of the rear guard action. We will need about five minutes, and then you people pull out. We're taking the wounded and the dead with us. Good luck Marines." Maryann crawled across the corridor avoiding the occasional shot from the Demons. The Giann picked up and carried the wounded and the dead Marine as they quietly left in the darkness.

Hill fired at movement he saw down the body-filled corridor. Glancing to his left, he was surprised to find the Defender kneeling next to him. He hadn't even heard him arrive! An energy bolt hit the Defender in the chest and dissipated with no effect to his armor. Hill fired back heard a satisfying grunt and a body toppling to the stone floor. The Defender stated, "In two minutes Sergeant, you take the remaining Marines and run as fast as you can back to the exit hatch."

"But sir, shouldn't we fall back in stages keeping up a steady stream of fire?"

"I will hold them here until you are out of the hatch. The D'mon can run twice as fast as you can. Without someone to hold them here they will just run you down and kill you."

"But what about you, how will you get out?" Michael gave Hill a sly smile, "I believe I'm a little faster than they are."

Two minutes later the Marines slid backwards on their stomachs into the back corridor. Once they were about three meters down the corridor, they paused and waited. The Demon fire was increasing as the Marine fire had stopped. The Marines saw the Defender get up, walk to the center of the intersection and then kneel facing the passageways that led to the D'mon. Shortly after, with the energy bolt and projectile weapon fire concentrated on him the Defender shouted, "NOW! SERGEANT, GO!"

The remaining Marines leapt to their feet and ran as fast as they could back down the corridor to the hatch. The D'mon warriors seeing them run, gleefully charged down the two corridors hoping to catch them from behind.

The Defender knelt with saber in one hand and dagger in the other. The running Demons didn't see him kneeling there until they were within three meters. Michael jumped to his feet and started a twirling dance of death. Both saber and dagger glowed with fire as they cleaved through armor weapons and bone. Demon body parts began filling up the intersection. The air vibrates with the continuous scream of those charging and those dying. Blood drips from ceiling and walls pooling between the bodies. The faster they poured into the intersection the faster they died the ones in the back pushing ahead not knowing the grim death they face. Michael leapt and danced faster and faster his armor and helm glowing bright from the weapon hits, illuminating the macabre scene in stark white light. His face set in neutral mask of serenity. After all, he is last Defender of the Anjiils, Romeo's Defender.

He finally stands amid the bodies and blood alone. The last few D'mon are fleeing as fast as they can back the way they came. Michael feels the tired let down that always follows battle. In his mind, Michael hears Teacher remind him. *Refresh Defender, refresh!*

Backing slowly down the corridor to the hatch Michael takes a flask from a pocket at the back of his armor. He drinks all of the water and Element suspension in the flask. His weapons are gone and now his armor reverts to a pair of shorts without enough of the Element available for his armor. Staggering with fatigue walking barefoot down the dirty stone corridor Michael drops the empty flask and wonders if the suspension he consumed would be enough to refresh his Elemental level. He also wondered if his body would absorb enough of the Element in time to reform his armor so he can exit the airlock.

Maryann boarded the shuttle with the Platoon, the women, the wounded and the dead. The nervous shuttle pilot quickly prepared to lift off. When he started to raise the loading ramp, Maryann ordered him to hold. When the pilot asked why, she told him she needed a few more minutes that there was still one man left in the fortress. After two minutes with no movement coming from the airlock, she grabbed the water bag off the bulkhead and ran back to the hatch. As Maryann reopened the hatch, she found Sergeant Hill and two Giann marines right behind her. Putting her helmet to Hills to avoid a communicator transmission she demanded, "Sergeant why aren't you on the shuttle?" With a grin, Hill replied, "Sorry ma'am, I always have to go before a long trip!" Maryann just shook her head and the four of them entered the airlock.

Maryann, Hill and the two Giann Marines took positions at the doorway of the room just inside the airlock. Down the right corridor, which led to the intersection, came the last sounds of battle. Suddenly the corridor was dead quiet. The four Marines pulled down their infrared visors and peered down the passageway weapons ready. Finally, they saw the Defender walk soundlessly out of the gloom. He staggered within a couple of meters and then collapsed. Maryann and Hill pulled Michael into the room and propped him sitting against a wall. The two Giann took up positions covering the corridors. Hill propped Michael up while Maryann pulled the tabs opening the water bottle. Noting Michaels fatigue the smeared blood but no obvious wounds Maryann asked. What happened back there?" Michael slowly raised his head, "They won't be following us for a while." Michael's head slumped back down to his chest as he mumbled, "I'm just so tired."

With the cap and the vent open, Maryann brought the water bag up, "Sergeant, hold him up we've got to get as much of this into him as fast we can." Maryann poured the fluid into Michael's mouth. He coughed once then greedily began to drink as much as he could of the suspension that Maryann had brought along on the Shuttle. Suddenly Maryann's helmet comm. came to life. "Lieutenant Hall, this is Lieutenant Mays your shuttle pilot. We're running out of time here! The other shuttles are already leaving and the Dauntless say's we have boogies in the system coming fast!" Maryann handed the water bag to Hill, "Keep him drinking." Sergeant Hill nodded and continued to ease the suspension into Michael's mouth as fast as he could swallow. Maryann keyed her helmet mike, "Listen to me Mays, this is Hall, I've got a man down here and we're not leaving without him. So don't get your panties in a bundle we'll get there as fast as we can, Hall out!" Maryann moved over to where the two Giann stood watch on the corridors. "See anything?"

"No ma'am."

"Good."

Moving back to Michael and Hill she now saw Michael holding the water bag taking long sips on his own. Between sips, Michael asked, "Why did you bring an extra bag of the suspension?" Maryann smiled, "Just in case!" In a few minutes, Michael was able to stand up. Shortly after, he could initiate his armor. When Michael stood, Maryann stated, "Ok guys enough of a break. What say we get the hell out of here?"

Hill nodded to the Giann and they once again exited the hatch. On the outside, Michael was able to activate his saber and cut through the outer part of the air lock. As they loped to the shuttle, Michael explained, "The inside of the lock won't cycle now that the outer hatch has been breached." Once the group boarded the shuttle, Maryann slapped the button to close the ramp and looked for a place to strap in. With the back cabin of the shuttle pressurized, the Co-pilot opened the door to the cockpit and exclaimed, "About time! It seems the whole damned Demon Fleet has just arrived. Strap in quickly, we've got to get the hell out of here!"

The shuttle was already rising from the moon as the Marines strapped in. There is no extra room in the bay of the shuttle. The two wounded Marines are strapped to portable stretchers in the middle walkway of the Back Bay. Maryann scooted up to the small fold down jump seat between and just behind the pilots. As she is strapping in Maryann can see the other three shuttles slowly rising and backing away from the fortress with fore and turret guns blazing. The pilot Mays commented. "They had a much harder time leaving. They wouldn't leave their dead and wounded and the Demons just kept coming."

Maryann could see the blood blackened by the vacuum splashed all over the closing ramps of the other shuttles. Looking past the dead rock planet that the moon orbits Maryann can see hundreds of small flashes. She realized it is the system's sun reflecting off shiny areas of the approaching Demon ships. The sight brought a cold shiver up her spine. Then the shuttle turned and headed full speed towards the Dauntless.

On their way, Maryann unbuckled and pulled herself over to the mid-shuttle ladder to go up and glance out of the gunner's turret. The gunner sat calmly with his twin guns facing behind the shuttle. From this position, the D'mon ships looked quite far away but they were closing fast. Maryann just hoped that once on the Dauntless, they would get away in time.

Chapter 77

THE ESCAPE

NURSE Chang sweated in terror inside the plant case. The case is hot and humid from the plants she had removed and smelled of fertilizer. She is terrified that Win Ling might make a sound and give them away. After what seemed like hours, she heard the crunch of boots at the back of the rover. She heard a bump as something slid in beside her in the rover, then the loading doors slammed shut. She bumped her head on the side of the case when the rover lurched into motion for the short trip to the shuttle pad.

There is another lurch as the rover stopped next to the pad and the loading doors opened with a bang against the sides of the rover. Nurse Chang dared not even breathe as she heard what sounded like two men sliding the case next to her out of the rover. A few minutes later, the men returned and her case followed the others out of the rover. She feels her case carried up a ramp then set down. The waiting is almost unbearable as she heard case after case stacked around her. Then she heard a gruff voice say, "This is the last one where do you want it?" Nurse Chang thought she would faint when she felt a case placed on the top hers.

She felt her heart jump when she heard the pneumatic sound of the shuttle doors closing. She felt another lurch as the shuttle lifted. Nurse Chang pushed against the top of the case but it wouldn't move! She pounded on the lid but no one came. Finally, she lay on her back and braced her feet on the lid. Pushing with all her strength the lid began to rise, then the case on top slipped to the side and fell. The lid of her case slammed open against the side of the container! Feeling the cool air rush into the container, Chang took a deep breath. Dim red light is illuminating the case from the small grate enclosed cargo lights.

Sitting up in the case, Nurse Chang can see the cargo hold of the shuttle is only half-full. She shuttered as she looked down at the case on the deck that had fallen when she pushed open the lid. If the hold were full, she would have never opened the case! Climbing out she began to call out in a low voice. "Win Ling, can you hear me? Where are you Win Ling?" She heard a pounding noise from one of the cases toward the front of the hold. Pulling off a stacked case Nurse Chang finally opened the lid of the case that holds Win Ling. Still somewhat groggy Win Ling asked, "Where are we?"

"We're in a shuttle heading off of that miserable planet." Sitting up Win Ling pointed and asked, "What's that blinking light over there?" Nurse Chang turned quickly and looked at a square metal case sitting next to the shuttle bulkhead. She ran over and kneeled next to the box. She sees what looks like a little window in the box that is blinking the word "Armed". Nurse Chang steps back in fear next to the case where Win Ling still sits. "I think it's a bomb!" Win Ling lays her tired head on her arm. "Why would they put a bomb on the shuttle?"

"You silly girl, it's us! If the shuttle blows up there will be no one to tell about what happened to Dr. Dau or what happened to your baby!" Win Ling began to cry, "What happened to my baby? Nurse Chang grabs Win Ling by the shoulders and gives her a shake. "Not now, we've got to get out of here! Win Ling lifts her head tears streaming down her face, "B . . . but how?"

Nurse Chang ran to the door that leads to the cockpit of the shuttle. Pounding as hard as she can she shouts, "OPEN UP, THERE'S A BOMB BACK HERE!" After pounding and shouting to no avail she finally turns around. "I don't think there's anyone there. This must be an automatic shuttle. I must find some way to open this door! Win Ling once again put her head on her arm. "What good will that do can you pilot the shuttle? As she searched around the hold Chang answered, "Well, yes and no. My brother is a shuttle pilot for Singapore Shuttle Service. I have flown with him many times. At least I know which buttons to push! Ah this might do it." Nurse Chang pulled out a long metal bar from behind some crates and cases.

The small magnetic lock on the cockpit door really wasn't much security. Chang swung the metal bar and hit the little keypad box next to the door as hard as she could. The box broke and fell to the floor leaving stripped wires hanging out of the bulkhead. Nurse Chang put her palms against the door and slid the door back easily. Chang and Win Ling stepped through the doorway into the small cockpit.

Since a computer operates the shuttle, they didn't find much in the cockpit. Looking out a small forward port, they saw they are flying across the expanse of Romeo. Below the port is a small access station so personnel can operate the shuttle manually if needed. There is no pilot's seat with safety straps only a small metal bench bolted to the deck. Nurse Chang sat on the small bench and said. "I think this button will disengage the autopilot, and then I use this little joystick handle to adjust direction. Each of these buttons controls the jets for up and down and these levers control the thrusters. Yes, I think I can do this!"

Chang turned to Win Ling and advised; "Now you go back to the cargo compartment and strap yourself to one of the bulkheads. It may get rough when I turn off the autopilot. Once we land the hatch doors will open automatically. Run as fast as you can to get away from the shuttle. The further you go the better."

"What about you? You have no safety seat up here."

"Don't worry about me, just remember, when the hatches open run as fast and far as you can. I will catch up with you as soon as I can. Now go, yell to me when you are strapped in." Win Ling turned and walked back into the cargo compartment. She wrapped a cargo strap around herself and clicked the end of the strap into one of the many slots in the bulkhead. She pulled in the strap and felt it is secure. Win Ling said a small prayer to the Great Creator then yelled, "Ready!" Nurse Chang leaned forward and pressed the button to disengage the autopilot.

Chapter 78

EGAS DAUNTLESS

THE Dauntless has her largest Landing Bay in the stern. There are two smaller Landing Bays on the side's amidships one port and one starboard. Captain Bossian turned the Dauntless so the stern faced the returning shuttles. The EGAS Stalwart was a couple of thousand kilometers above sitting perpendicular to the Dauntless. With nothing to see out the front armored view ports all eyes on the Bridge look to the aft view screens. Bossian had recalled the Banshees from the moon. Refueled and rearmed they now sat motionless in the space between the two huge ships. The twenty-four Banshees are in three ship triangles. There is one ship above two, then two ships above one, with about one kilometer between the floating ships. The Banshees sit and patiently await orders.

Colonel Kellogg watched the oncoming ships, standing next to Bossian. She suddenly said, "Crap!" Along with everyone on the Bridge, Kellogg saw hundreds of fighters spewing out of the enemy ships. Bossian turned to the Communications Officer and directed, "Inform the shuttles, Alpha and Beta are to land in the Starboard Amidships Bay and Charley and Delta in the port Bay." Bossian waited patiently while for the message transmissions than he asked, "Could you please get me Captain Zin of the Stalwart?"

Captain Zin's face appeared on the comm. view screen. Bossian asked, "Captain Zin is the Stalwart ready?"

"Aye sir, the long range missile broadside is ready for your order." Kellogg looked over at Bossian. The Captain could see the confusion in her face, "Captain certainly the long range missiles won't stop all those fighters!" Bossian turned to her with a small smile, "Have a little faith Colonel. We've got a little trick up our sleeve the Demons haven't seen yet." Calmly sitting down in his command chair Bossian buckled himself in and suggested, "Colonel, perhaps you might want to buckle in too."

Kellogg glanced around and noticed that she was the last one on the Bridge still standing. She quickly sat in one of the extra jump seats on the Bridge and secured the straps. Bossian advised Captain Zin. "Captain you may fire as soon as the shuttles are recovered, Bossian out."

Bossian then pressed another comm. button on his chair that connected him with the Dauntless' Air Group Commander. Commander Sandra Rushing was currently sitting in Banshee 1 awaiting orders, "CAG are the Banshees ready?"

"Aye sir, we're locked and loaded!"

"CAG, the Banshees will follow the Stalwart's broadside. Half way to contact with the enemy fighters you will initiate the M-101 reverse maneuver. After the M-101's are deployed the Banshee's will then catch up with the Dauntless where we shall high speed recover. Remember the Dauntless will be going to full speed as soon as possible. Any Banshee that cannot high speed recover will be expendable. Is this understood?"

"Aye sir, understood. After M-101 deployment, the Banshees will be high speed recovering. Any Banshee missing the team's bus will have to walk home, CAG out."

Bossian then pressed a ship intercom button to speak with the Dauntless' Damage Control Officer when the phone picked up he stated. "Mr. Grass, prepare the Aft Landing Bay to high speed recover both of our Squadrons of Banshees." Lieutenant Joshua Grass taken by surprise interjected, "But sir, we've only practiced high speed recovery with only one or two ships! We've never recovered a whole Squadron, let alone both at once!"

Bossian frowned towards the intercom and responded dryly, "I'm sure Lieutenant you'll do your best. I will be highly inconvenienced if we return without all of our Banshees, Bossian out." Josh Grass paled as he looked at the silent phone in his hand. Hanging the phone back in its cradle he shook his head and muttered, "Creator, help us!" Josh then pushed the button for the crash and collision alarm, calling all the Firefighters and Landing Bay Damage Control Personnel to their stations.

Chapter 79

BANSHEE ONE

COMMANDER Rushing sat patiently, one hand idly doing a slow tap on the knee of her pressure suit. Through the tinted lens of her helmet, she watched the agonizing slow progress of the shuttles. In space, the appearance of speed is deceptive. The shuttles appeared to be slowly approaching the Dauntless although Sandy actually knew they were flying thousands of kilometers per second. In the distance behind the shuttles, she could see hundreds of metallic flashes as the enemy poured it on to make contact with the EGA ships.

Sandy knew that her Banshees with their black non-reflective coverings would be virtually invisible to the approaching fighters. The EGA in fact had spent a lot of time and money perfecting their stealth technology. Sandy's Banshee has the sensor signature about equal to that of a fist-sized rock. In space that was like a grain of sand at the beach. Sandy knew the enemy fighters wouldn't see the Banshees until she wanted them to.

Sitting in Banshee 9, Tommy Chin felt the sweat rolling down his neck into the collar of his suit. He glanced nervously several times at Tan's ship up to his right but could see no movement in the dark cockpit. He ached to talk with anyone to relieve the tension but with communication silence, that is not an option. Like everyone else in the Squadron, he just sat and watched the drama of what appeared to be a slow speed chase. Finally, as the shuttles neared the Dauntless, Tommy saw the small white puffs of the shuttles front thrusters signaling the decrease of speed for their docking.

Commander Rushing watched the tail of the last shuttle as it eased into the Dauntless. As the large blast doors on the side Bays began to close she turned her attention to the Stalwart above and on her left. Within seconds, waves of missiles began to erupt from the Stalwart's launchers. With the launch of the last missile, Bossian's voice came through her helmet, "You are a go CAG, good luck and good hunting!" Sandy keyed her comm. to the Squadron's channel, "Ok boys and girls it's time to dance! We burn in three, two, and one, NOW!" As she felt the punch of the thrusters she added, "Remember turn everything on, and lots of chatter! We want them to see us!" As one, the Banshees turned on cockpit lights and all their sensors, and then sped after the missiles at full power. Sandy thought. *Now all we need is a band playing "Garry Owen!"*

Far ahead of her Sandy watched as the missiles reached the closing enemy fighters. They leapt back and forth, easily avoiding the missiles. Then they kept coming. She mumbled to herself, "That's ok boys; those missiles aren't for you anyway!"

Chapter 80

DWS PREDATOR

THE Elevated Prime watched in anger as the fighters maneuvered to avoid the missiles, "Those fools! Why are they avoiding those missiles? They should try to destroy them! Don't they realize that those missiles will continue on to our Fleet?" Darwak, the Prime that is the commander of the Predator replied, "But Elevated Prime! You only gave them orders to take out enemy ships, specifically the troop shuttles!"

"Quickly," The Elevated Prime commanded. "Screen the Predator with lesser vessels. Have all batteries in the Fleet open fire, TAKE OUT THOSE MISSILES!"

As the Predator headed for the middle of the Fleet three smaller vessels sped to screen the flagship. The lead ship spewing energy cannon fire managed to destroy two missiles before a third hit amidships blowing the small ship in two. Following missiles collided with the debris causing a short spectacular chain reaction. Missiles claimed two more ships and damaged four. All other missiles succumbed to the intense Fleet cannon fire.

The Predator tucked itself into the center of the Fleet and the Elevated Prime ordered. "All fighters forward, let them destroy the Fighter Carrier!" Darwak looked at the sensor screen and exclaimed, "Elevated Prime! Twenty-four fighters just appeared on sensors! They are flying straight at our fighters! The Elevated

Prime grimaced, and then growled. "Their fighters may be good but they're no match for the numbers they now face. Signal our warriors to destroy those fighters first. They'll have plenty of time to catch that Carrier."

Chapter 81

DELTA SHUTTLE

MARYANN climbed down from her peek out of the gunner's turret. At the bottom of the ladder, she paused and checked on the wounded. The Corpsmen were doing their best but obviously one of the men would need surgery aboard the Dauntless. Glancing around the compartment, she found most of the Marines were sleeping. Maryann knew that extreme fatigue was common following the stress of combat. The women looked thin and ragged but they appeared healthy. There will be full medical exams when they reach the Dauntless and psychological support for the trauma ensued as captives.

Maryann looked at Michael and noticed he appeared to be meditating, sitting up straight with eyes closed. Angela Stil sat leaning against Michael asleep. She slept with one hand around Michael's arm. As Maryann watched, Angela stirred and opened her eyes. Angela saw Maryann looking at her and said with a yawn, "He's my Guardian Angel." Angela then snuggled against his arm and went soundly to sleep. Maryann thought to herself. *Once we get back to Camp Mills, we have to have a talk with Michael and Mrs. Stil about those ID tags that Michael wears.*

Feeling suddenly fatigued herself; Maryann went back to her jump seat and buckled her harness. As the fatigue washed over her before her eyes closed, Maryann thought. *With his helmet field engaged, Michael does appear to have a golden glow around his head. I don't know much about Angels but he sure saved our bacon again.* Maryann drifted off to the deep sleep of a combat survivor.

Chapter 82

LANDING THE SHUTTLE

WIN Ling felt the straps hold her weight as the shuttle suddenly dived. The now unsecured crates in the cargo compartment slid back and forth, as Chang struggled to stay in her seat and maintain control of the lumbering shuttle. When Nurse Chang decreased the thrusters, the shuttle fell like a rock. Over compensating, the increased thrusters shot them back into the air at a dizzying speed. Chang held in to her bench with one hand and used the other to try to control the runaway shuttle. Peering through the small forward port Chang can see the many large craters that cover the landscape. She sees she must avoid the crater ridges and drop into a valley in the middle of one of the larger craters.

Flying over the ridge of a large crater Chang pulled back on the handles killing the thrusters. Her fingers danced over the buttons to the jets as she fought to slow them down and land before they flew into the ridge on the other side of the crater. She is going much too fast! The wall of the crater looms up before them and she quickly presses the lift jets as the shuttle scrapes over the top of the rim tearing out rust colored trees and bushes that were growing along the top. The shuttle careened down the other side of the large crater the burning jets leaving a trail of fire in their wake as the dry brush and stubbly trees ignited as they passed. A large formation of boulders stood in their path and

Chang quickly pressed the left lateral and the lift jets at the same time. The jets fired but sputtered, clogged from the debris that the shuttle blew through at the rim of the crater.

Nurse Chang screamed in frustration as they hurled towards the wall of boulders. The forward lift jets kicked in and the bow of the shuttle rose as they plowed through the top of the pile of boulders skidding sideways throwing rocks and trees before them. The backside of the shuttle hit a rock formation whipping the front of the shuttle back around in a half circle. The Nurse thrown around the small cockpit like a broken discarded doll bounces from wall to wall her bones continuing to be broken even after she is dead. The shuttle continued skidding through the brush gouging a lazy circle of destruction. It finally smashes into another rock formation wedging the shuttle between two large boulders.

Win Ling awoke hanging from a bulkhead by a cargo strap. Her head hurt terribly as she must have hit it several times as the shuttle collided with numerous things during the uncontrolled landing. She pressed the release on the cargo strap and fell to the floor. The pain in her head makes her nauseous and unsteady on her feel so she crawls on her hands and knees around the jumbled crates and cases in the hold. She peeks into the cockpit of the shuttle and sees blood splattered all around the compartment. Win Ling sees a bloody pile of what looks like torn clothing in the corner. An arm that is broken at an unusual angle, sticks straight up out of the bloody pile. Win Ling vomits on to the floor of the cockpit.

Win Ling wipes her mouth on her sleeve and crawls through the chaos of the cargo hold to the hatch that automatically opened when they crashed. She feels another wave of nausea as she stands in the doorway. She remembers the bomb and begins to stagger away from the burning shuttle. She makes her way through the prickly scrub bushes tearing her clothes on protruding thorns. As she remembers more, she runs faster, her arms up in front of her face keeping the thorny bushes away from her eyes.

Minutes later, she reached the line of boulders that the shuttle hit. Win Ling sees what looks like a cave or passageway that leads through the bottom of two huge boulders. She picks up a spindly brown piece of wood about a meter in length to help steady her weaving body and heads towards the cave. After several stops to climb around broken bushes and trees, she began to climb up to where she saw the cave. Win Ling finally reaches the opening when suddenly she feels a massive hand push her forward! The blast throws her into the opening of the cave like a loose leaf on the wind. Her head hits the side of the opening as she falls inside unconscious. The small cave helps to protect her from the expanding fireball of the shuttle explosion.

Chapter 83

BANSHEE ONE

As the Banshees sped towards the enemy fighters, they slowly spread their formation. Sandy noted with some satisfaction that the enemy's fighters are actually grouping closer together! She was watching her sensors closely. They were almost at the point to initiate the reverse maneuver. The Fleet calls it the M-101 reverse maneuver. The pilots call it the junk in the trunk flop! Sandy counted down, "Ok guys, time to flop in three, two, and one, NOW FLOP!"

As one, every Banshee in the formation hit both front reverse thrusters and rear elevator thrusters. This caused the fighters to flip head over heels. At the start of the flip, the pilots hit the release of their M-101 launcher. Each fighter released thousands of tiny steel ball bearings in the direction they had been traveling. Upon completion of the flop, each fighter turned and went to full power heading back towards the quickly retreating Dauntless the doors of the M-101 launchers closing.

Chapter 84

DWS PREDATOR

THE Elevated Prime saw the enemy fighters suddenly turn and release some kind of dust. As the Bridge Crew watched, the cloud slowly expanded hiding the running enemy ships. The warrior at the main sensor station commented. "It must be some kind of sensor smoke screen." The Elevated Prime stated. "Well it won't do them any good our fighters will be through the dust in a moment and they'll quickly run them down.

As the D'mon watched, the cloud expanded past the width of the fighter formations. Then the Elevated Prime watched in horror as the first speeding fighters hit the cloud. The fighters shredding like rotten fruit thrown at a screen! One after another flying so fast there was no stopping each shredded ship adding more debris to the cloud! The Elevated Prime screamed, "STOP ALL THE FIGHTERS! RECALL ALL FIGHTERS TELL THEM TO STAY AWAY FROM THE CLOUD! REVERSE THE FLEET; GET US AWAY FROM THAT CLOUD!

The warrior at the communications console was franticly yelling for the fighters to reverse! The Prime commanding the Predator was yelling, "NO, CONTACT THE SHIPS OF THE FLEET FIRST! HAVE THEM ALL TAKE A COURSE TO THE RIGHT! The Elevated Prime just stood there trembling in rage as one after another the fighters flew to destruction in the cloud. Finally, towards the end of the massive group of fighters individual pilots began to pull up and reverse course back to the Fleet.

That was just the beginning of the catastrophe. As the Fleet also watched the fighters destroyed by the advancing cloud, each individual Prime decided to turn his own ship away from the certain destruction. Instead of the entire Fleet going in one direction, the ships turned in every direction imaginable. The Elevated Prime watched helplessly as one ship after another collided. Finally the Elevated Prime roared, "BROADCAST ALL STOP! STOP ALL SHIPS!"

It took a while but finally most of the ships finally stopped. A few fighters and other ships on the edge of the Fleet were still moving, however, little by little, the ships stopped colliding. The D'mon were totally dumbfounded when the deadly expanding cloud finally reached the stopped Fleet. Since the ships were no longer moving and the bearings had lost a lot of inertia, the tiny balls bounced harmlessly off the thick-hulled ships!

The Command Prime of the Predator inquired, "Elevated Prime. Do we go after them?" Shaking his head the Elevated Prime looked at the carnage, "Not this time, we've lost three-quarters of our fighters and a fourth of the Fleet has damage. We will have revenge but not today. We will rebuild re-arm and then crush them! We will wipe these species off the face of the galaxy, SO I SWEAR!"

Chapter 85

HEADQUARTERS

(Camp Mills)

Lieutenant Colonel Silverton sits at his desk composing a report concerning the reported fungus contamination at Greenleaf Station. He didn't trust the head of the station even with the follow up documents they had sent him showing the unusual laboratory results they said they encountered. Silverton has suspicions, but according to EGA regulations, he must respect the quarantine. So, as per the regulations he will submit his report with all supporting documentation up the chain of command. He is just finishing as Lieutenant Hernandez knocks urgently at his door. Without looking up Silverton responds, "Enter."

Hernandez walks quickly up to Silverton's desk and states. "Colonel we have a report from the Harvest Moon that one of their automated shuttles has crashed on Romeo. The crash site is about halfway between Camp Mills and the Greenleaf Global Station. I have authorized a couple of Banshees from the CAP to do a flyover and the telemetry should be coming through by now." Pressing a button on his desk console to retrieve the pictures from the Banshees, Silverton asked. "Did the Harvest Moon say if there were any personnel traveling on that shuttle?" Hernandez shook his head. "They stated the shuttle was totally unmanned."

Silverton waved the Lieutenant around his desk so they could look at the monitor screen together. "Geeze, would you look at that!" The pictures show what look like the results of a very large explosion. "The blast area must be at least a kilometer wide! The skid trail is almost five kilometers long so it looks like the shuttle at least tried to land. It looks like the shuttle must have had some type of explosives on board for such a big explosion after the shuttle crashed."

Hernandez glanced down at some papers he is carrying in his hands. "I asked for the Harvest Moon to send down a copy of the manifest and it just has agricultural tools and plants listed."

Silverton looked at all of the footage and frowned. "Whatever destroyed that shuttle it sure wasn't just the crash. Lieutenant, I would like you to take Sergeant Major Min and two Squads and investigate the crash site. Something really smells here and I would like to find out what it is. I don't trust any of these large corporations any more than I trust freighter Captains. This whole business with Greenleaf Global makes the hairs on my neck twitch."

Lieutenant Hernandez, Sergeant Major Min and the two Squads left by shuttle within the hour. It didn't take the shuttle long to cover the five hundred kilometers to the crash site.

Chapter 86

BANSHEE ONE

COMMANDER Rushing made a slow turn with her fighter to observe the effects of the maneuver. Watching the carnage and confusion caused her to smile. Sandy mumbled to no one particular, "Well how's that for season's greetings fellas?" Turning her Banshee and going to full burn to catch the fleeing Dauntless Sandy keyed her communicator, "Dauntless, Banshee One." She heard the voice of Bossian reply, "Go ahead Banshee One."

"Dauntless it looks like the Demons have one hell of a cluster copulation going on! Their surviving fighters have given up pursuit and their Fleet is at a standstill."

"Roger that Banshee One, catch up as fast as you can. Good job, Dauntless out."

At four times the speed of the Dauntless, it didn't take Sandy long to come in behind the ship. The problem was at that speed, she had about exhausted the Banshee's fuel supply. Now the Dauntless was steadily increasing speed. For high-speed recovery, Sandy had to bring the Banshee in the Bay at exactly five meters per second faster than the speed of the Dauntless. She keyed the data quickly in the flight computer so the Banshee would automatically compensate for the fast increasing speed of the Dauntless.

Lieutenant Grass and his damage control party had rigged catch nets across the Bay of the Dauntless in case she came in too fast. The figures told her if she were too slow, she would run out of fuel before she was safely in the Bay. Unfortunately, she knew the nets were there to help protect the Dauntless. Hitting the nets too fast with the light composite Banshee would be like a swatter hitting a fly in mid air.

Sandy was one thousand kilometers out and closing on the Bay when her red low fuel warning light came on! With her remaining fuel, she would have to catch the Dauntless faster than she would like. The CAG knew the ships were still too close to the D'mon Fleet for the Dauntless to stop and pick her up. Missing the Bay was not an option. A Banshee was expendable the Dauntless was not. Keying her comm. straight to Lieutenant Grass in the bay Sandy relayed, "Aft Landing Bay, Banshee One. I'm going to be coming in just a little faster than desired. Red fuel light is on and I only have one shot at this," She then flicked off the flight computer and took manual control.

Josh Grass watching her approach responded immediately, "We see you CAG, acknowledge your low on fuel and coming in hot." Josh once again hit the collision alarm and broadcasted to all personnel in the Bay. "Attention in the Bay! Clear the Bay! Repeat, clear the Bay! We are recovering a Banshee under speed duress. Damage Control Parties prepare to vent the Bay to vacuum in case of fire or explosion!"

All Landing Bay personnel quickly left the Bay sealing the exit hatches behind them. The two pressure suited Damage and Fire Control Parties took cover in specially designed bunkers sunk into the hanger deck. The bunker windows protected by armored glass half a meter thick, is the same glass used in the ports on the Bridge. When he saw all was ready, Josh keyed the comm., "We're ready CAG, bring her on in, good luck."

Sandy increased her speed aiming for what looked like a tiny square opening rushing at her at a frantic speed. Her display counted down the decrease in distance to the Bay, like an elevator falling down a shaft. At about ten Kilometers out from the Bay the Banshee's twin engines sputtered then stopped. They were out of fuel! Sandy still watched the display countdown knowing she still had a lot of forward inertia. However, the Dauntless was still accelerating and she had no way to increase her speed!

It appeared agonizing slow. As the distance decreased, the Dauntless' speed was slowly increasing. One hundred meters out the Banshee dropped below five meters per second faster than the Dauntless. Sandy sat strapped in helplessly as the speed dropped to four, then to three, then two and finally one. The nose of the Banshee was less than ten meters from the entrance to the Bay when the Dauntless slowly began to pull away!

Sandy knew she was all out of options. Then she saw pressure suited figures push what looked like two ancient whaling cannon to the corner edges of the bay. As the distance began increasing slowly, the suited figures were securing the bases of the cannon to tracks in the deck. Sandy could see Josh in a pressure suit walk up just as the crew secured the bases. He checked the angle of the first cannon then hurried to the second.

With the distance to the Bay about twenty meters and expanding Sandy saw a white puff of air discharge from each cannon! Two cables trailed past her cockpit and over the Banshee's wings. At the ends of each cable are stubby cylinders that spring open to three inverse fingers. As the Banshee drifted backwards, the cables pulled taunt as the grapples caught behind the curved wings.

Sandy could hear the airframe of the Banshee groan as the cables pulled taunt and began to drag the Banshee behind the Dauntless. She watched the computer display as the Banshee matched speed with the Dauntless! Over the comm. link, Sandy heard Josh say, "NOW!"

The grappling machines began to move backwards on the tracks. By the time the machines reached the back of the Bay, the Banshee floated inside. Lieutenant Grass slowly increased the artificial gravity inside the Bay bringing the Banshee to rest as the Bay blast doors closed.

By the time Sandy turned off all systems and opened the cockpit, the Bay was again pressurized. She gratefully removed her helmet and wiped the sweat from her face on her sleeve. Climbing down the small ladder a crewman had attached to the Banshee, Sandy saw Josh with his helmet removed standing by the Banshee's wing. He had a large grin on his face. With a smile matching his, Sandy put out her hand to shake. Pumping his arm with enthusiasm, she said, "Nice catch Lieutenant!" Grass replied, "Well CAG, the Captain said he would be highly inconvenienced if we lost a Banshee. I would certainly hate to inconvenience the Captain!"

The CAG headed for the bridge as Josh and his team checked the Banshee for damage. Finding no damage he ordered the Banshee refueled and rearmed. Josh knew that from here on out the Banshees might have to launch at any moment.

Chapter 87

SURVIVOR

THE woman awoke in great pain. She opened her eyes to find she could see across a rock and dirt floor and an opening filled with light. The light hurts her eyes and the view gets blurry as her eyes produce tears. She tries to move but movement brings pain. The dirt from the floor coats her mouth and tastes slightly bitter. She tries to spit out the dirt but the movement causes pain and her world turns black as she slips into unconsciousness.

The combat shuttle landed gently up wind of the slowly drifting smoke. The first two Marines off the shuttle, wearing full environmental suits wave hand held sensors checking the air for dangerous contaminates and radiation. The shuttle had already completed three flyovers checking the area with its onboard sensors but Lieutenant Hernandez is a very careful man. The Sergeant in charge of the Nuclear, Biological and Chemical warfare contingent on the shuttle verified all the readings displayed on the hand held sensor then keyed his helmet mike. "It looks pretty clean Lieutenant. The smoke of course carries hydrocarbons and poly-carbons from the burning debris but that's about all."

By the time, Hernandez and the rest of the Marines retrieved their gear and exited the shuttle's rear ramp; the NBC warfare people had removed their helmets and were removing their environmental suits. The Marines landed about one hundred meters from the crater caused by the explosion of the Harvest Moon's shuttle. Hernandez turned to Sergeant Major Min. "Sergeant Major let's split up the search. We'll start by the crater and I'll take half of the Marines and sweep east. You have the rest and sweep west. Give me a holler if you see anything unusual." Sergeant Major Min gave an, "Aye sir", and moved out with his Marines.

The woman moaned as she wakened for the second time. The pain stabbed through her mind. She opened her eyes and once again looked toward the light. She tried to listen but she can hear no sound. She very slowly moves her head the movement bringing another wave of nauseating pain. She can see an arm. The arm has charred remains of clothing stuck to the burned skin. She tries to move away from the arm but passes out from the pain.

Sergeant Major Min slowly moved on line with his Marines. He is in the center of the line with the Marines about twenty-five meters apart. They stop and examine every piece of the destroyed shuttle and fill out a small tag noting its location in relation to the explosion crater. Specialists from the orbiting Ship Repair Facility will later retrieve the pieces after the crash site mapping is complete. The heading that Min and his Marines follow is slowly taking them back along the shuttles skid trail. The Sergeant Major looks back along the long path of destruction and can see where the shuttle plowed through a line of boulders. At the base of two large boulders, he sees what looks like a dark opening perhaps a cave.

The woman opens her eyes again. She coughs and a small cloud of dust rises from the dirt before her. She tries to mover her hand to wipe dust out of her eyes and realizes the burned arm she saw earlier is hers. She is so thirsty. Her tongue feels swollen in her mouth. A shadow blocks the light from the door of the cave. She tries to cry out but her swollen tongue doesn't seem to work right. Then she sees a large form blocking the light at the entrance. She thinks it's a man but the shape isn't right! The head is too long and the limbs are too slender. The monster approaches her and kneels beside her. The large diagonal eyes look down at her and long slender hands reach for her. She tries to scream but nothing comes out. The pain brings the welcome darkness again.

Sergeant Major Min pulls the emergency blanket from his pack and wraps it around the burned woman. "Lieutenant Hernandez, I have found an injured human woman in a small cave. I have wrapped her in my emergency blanket and I'm bringing her out. Please send the Corpsman with the large shuttle medical kit."

"We're on our way Sergeant Major!"

Min gently picks up the woman and carries her out of the cave. One of his Marines places his blanket on the ground in the shade and the Sergeant Major places her on the blanket. He listens carefully at her mouth and watches her chest rise and fall. Her breathing appears slightly labored. Min hears running feet approaching. Lieutenant Hernandez and the Corpsman arrive with the large medical kit. The Corpsman springs into action putting together the pieces of two IV sets. He quickly starts the IVs with one in each arm. As the Corpsman works on the woman, Hernandez and Min step back towards the cave. "Have you found anything else in the cave Sergeant Major?"

"No sir, just pieces of what look like burned clothing. I couldn't even tell you what the clothing looked like. It's in charred pieces now." Hernandez watched two Marines heading towards the Corpsman and his patient carrying a stretcher from the shuttle. Where do you think this woman came from? She couldn't have been on the shuttle. That crash obliterated the shuttle."

"That's assuming sir that the shuttle exploded as it crashed. What if the shuttle exploded after the crash?"

"Do you mean the shuttle power plant?"

"No, the power plant is designed to automatically shut down in case of a crash. I think I'll have the NBC people check for explosives residue around the site."

The two of them walked back to where the Corpsman worked on the injured woman. The corpsman finished with the placement of the IVs is adding medication to one of the IV lines. "I'm almost ready to go here sir. I've have the two IVs going and I'm giving her some morphine for the pain. She's going to need hyperbaric treatment for these burns and I think the explosion blew out both of her eardrums. On a quick check, I can find no broken bones but the sooner she gets a MRI to check for internal injuries the better."

"Thanks Doc let's get her down to the shuttle as quick as possible and I'll get clearance to take her straight up to the hospital on the Ship Repair Facility. They can do hyperbaric treatments up there. Sergeant Major have the Marines pack it up for today. We'll be back tomorrow I think there's a lot more going on here besides the simple crash of an autopilot shuttle. I'm going to suggest bringing a criminal investigation team out with us tomorrow."

Chapter 88

EGA FLEET HEADQUARTERS

(Orbiting Repair Facility Romeo)

Rear Admiral, Lydia Barker stood looking out the large view port of her new office. The office is aboard the new EGA Fleet Support and Repair Facility that now orbits the planet called Romeo. Before the D'mon attacks Admiral Barker was in what many would say, was the twilight of her career. Lydia enlisted in the Fleet as a young woman barely out of her teens. An assertive intelligent woman Lydia learned leadership from the bottom up. Possessing a gift for languages, she started in communications and cryptography. Before the end of her first enlistment, she attained the rank of Petty Officer Second Class and cross-trained in both ships tactical systems and basic Human and Giann Medicine.

By the end of her second tour, the then Petty Officer First Class gained selection to the Fleet Officers Academy. Graduating third in her class at the Academy, she joined the Fleet as Communications Officer on one of the old Explorer Class vessels that started the EGA exploration of the galaxy. Two tours later as a Lieutenant, Lydia met and married a brilliant Engineering Officer, Ronald Barker who would work with the Giann in developing the new EGA stellar drive.

Captain Lydia Barker's first Command was the EGAS Relentless. The Relentless along with her First Officer, James Bossian had carried Captain Kellogg and her Marines to the aid of the miners on Spiegel 2. Following her command of the Relentless, Lydia had a tour on Giann as a Liaison Officer. With promotion to Rear Admiral, Lydia secured a seat in the Admiralty at EGAF Headquarters.

With the onset of hostilities, now called the D'mon war, the Admiralty dispatched Commodore Ronald Barker to build the orbiting Support and Repair Facility at the planet Romeo. Following the placement of the Facility overall command of Fleet operations in the area fell to Admiral Lydia Barker. Tactically commanding operations from all the way back at EGAF Headquarters would have been ludicrous. History has shown that Commanders in the field without the interference of other possibly politically motivated entities have better success with their missions.

The Admiral watched as the Dauntless and the Stalwart docked at the facility. In the distance, she could see a Squadron of Banshees heading out on their deep space patrols of the area. Three more Space Destroyers and a Cruiser had joined the Starfury in the system. The Starfury is undergoing major repair at the Facility. The Admiral received word just that morning that another Fighter Carrier the Victorious was in route with five of the new Interceptor Class Reconnaissance and Patrol ships. These ships replaced the unarmed Searcher Class exploration and mapping vessels. Armed with energy cannon and missile torpedoes the EGAF would do its scouting with ships that could now pack a punch. Hearing the quiet buzz of the intercom at her door Lydia turned and responded "Enter."

Lieutenant Cin, her aid entered and spoke, "Admiral, Captain Bossian and Colonel Kellogg are en route to brief you on the rescue operation. The women are in transit down to the Base Dispensary. The Surgeon on the Dauntless stated they were in good physical shape but he will defer psychological evaluations to the Fleet Specialists. The Dauntless also has a D'mon female, um—guest. Captain Bossian stated he will explain along with a personal issue concerning the Defender, Second Lieutenant Grade."

The Admiral turned from the view port and nodded, "Very well. I will meet with the Captain and the Colonel in the conference room. Please provide coffee and sandwiches." Lieutenant Cin came to attention stated, "Aye ma'am," turned and left the office. Turning back to the view port hands clasped behind her back Lydia mumbled, "This Defender, I've got to meet."

Chapter 89

GABRIEL

Every planetary cycle Alpha waited outside the dome. He has cameras and sensors watching the spot where the door had opened around the clock. It is past eighteen lunar cycles now and the time is near. Alpha could be anywhere and notified immediately if there is an appearance but he chooses to be right here when it happens. This operation is his crowning achievement. He is procuring for his benefactor the most valuable machine of war there is in the universe. He wants to ensure he is the first one to make contact with the Defender. He must mold the Defender's mind in his own image.

Alpha has always been very good at recognizing real power. The reason he works for Marrt is that Marrt has the resources to let Alpha work to his full potential. However, Marrt has one fatal weakness his devotion to Wingate Toath. Of course, Toath and Marrt make excellent partners. Toath has his political and business connections and Marrt has his underworld connections. For Alpha, the relationship is highly valuable. Since Toath and Marrt have very public faces, they rely more and more on Alpha to take care of the messy jobs. Nevertheless, as they rely more and more on Alpha, he in turn finds more and more of their weaknesses. *Yes, the relationship is working out very well,* thought Alpha.

Cycle in and cycle out Alpha waits across from the dome in the shade of an awning, he had erected for the purpose. Alpha patiently waits and plans. *How do I use the association with Marrt and Toath? What will make them turn on one another? I can't kill them they are the goose laying the proverbial golden egg. They must want to support me. The best way to do that is by having the Defender bent to my will. Yes if they can only access the Defender through me then they will have to support me, or die!*

Then one bright morning Alpha sipped spiced coffee sitting in the chair under the awning. He had heard of the investigation by the Marines into the crash of the shuttle. Toath had already put roadblocks in the way of the investigation and there was a terrible accident on board the Harvest Moon. It seems a view port on the Bridge of the ship failed venting the bridge to space. The Captain of the Harvest Moon and most of his bridge crew died of explosive decompression. Alpha thought, *the last loose end neatly tied up.* One moment he was in quiet reflection and in the next moment, the door to the dome opened!

Alpha placed the cup in his hand on the small table next to the chair. Standing slowly his eyes watched the open doorway. The guards came to port arms as he rose from the chair. He made a small movement with his hands indicating that they should stay where they were. Alpha walked slowly forward and stopped five meters from the doorway. The Defender walked silently out of the doorway he stopped two meters in front of Alpha looking at him curiously. Alpha gave his biggest smile and stated. "Welcome Defender, I am known as Alpha. Your name is Gabriel. I shall be your new Teacher. You have many new things to learn and I will help you. The tall muscular oriental man in the golden armor of a Defender smiled brightly and stated. "Thank you Alpha, I shall be happy to learn new things, but first you must tell me how the battle goes with the Evil Ones."

Alpha gestured towards the Greenleaf dispensary. "Please walk with me. We fight the D'mon valiantly and we need your help. But first you must go to Earth for further training and education." Gabriel walked slowly next to Alpha. "Why must I go to this place called Earth? Do not the Evil Ones threaten us right here in our own quadrant?

"Yes, that is true but, you are also part human. To work with the Humans there is a lot you have to learn. If your education is not completed correctly you could turn out like the other Defender." They stopped at the doors of the dispensary and Gabriel asked. "What do you mean turn out like the other Defender?"

Alpha looked around like there were others that might be listening. In a low voice, Alpha began. Gabriel this is a secret just between you and I ok?" Alpha was pleased to see Gabriel nod his head in agreement. The people I work for have found evidence that the other Defender named Michael is secretly working with the D'mon!" At the news, Gabriel whirled his saber in his hand. "Show me this traitor and I shall kill him myself!" Alpha took Gabriel by the arm and soothing said. "It's ok Gabriel, put your saber away. You will have plenty of time to kill the traitor Michael after you go to Earth and complete your training."

Gabriel placed his saber back in the scabbard and the scabbard absorbed back into his body armor. Alpha looked at Gabriel's golden armor. "From now on, you should wear this uniform. After all you're one of us now." Alpha pointed to one of the PTS guards by the door. In just a moment, Gabriel stood in black body armor with the silver PTS shield on his left breast. Alpha nodded with a big smile, "very well done Gabriel, very well done." Alpha knew that anyone that now saw Gabriel would assume he is part of the PTS security contingent. He once again gently took Gabriel's arm and guided him into the dispensary. "Let me show you where you will stay until Mr. Toath comes to take us to Earth."

Chapter 90

FAMILY

SINCE returning from the rescue operation, the Marines had many duties to catch up on particularly the Platoon Leaders. Since Michael had no Platoon responsibilities, he continued with his daily weapons training and physical fitness. At Maryann's insistence, Michael started training in the use of the longer-range energy and projectile weapons. With the ever stoic Sergeant Hill at his side Michael attended classes teaching the use and maintenance of automatic weapons and even the larger mortars and the use of artillery.

Michael surprised the Armory Officer one day. The subject that day was grenades and explosives that the Marines commonly used. The Officer was instructing Michael how to use a shaped charge of explosive to blow a hole in twenty-centimeter thick steel sheet representing a closed hatch or side of a ship. After setting up the charge the Armory Officer checked for all clear then blew a nice neat hole in the large sheet. He said the drawback is the noise and that if entering a compartment with let us say hostages inside they would not survive the blast. Michael calmly produced his saber and quickly and quietly cut a hole of the same size right next to the demonstration hole. As the Armory Officer stood there scratching his head a Corporal brought Michael a message. It was from Lieutenant Cin at the Admiral's office directing him to report at 0900 the next morning.

Michael was not surprised when taking the shuttle up to the station, Sergeant Hill was right there with him. Michael liked the older man and appreciated his silence. Sergeant Hill would eloquently answer any question Michael presented however; he just wouldn't speak unless asked. Michael found Sergeant Hill's economy of words as enjoyable as his companionship.

Michael knew Maryann wanted Hill to go with him and accepted the company without question. After all, Maryann is his friend, and he likes her. Michael felt warm inside when he thought about Maryann but he felt uncomfortable telling her, since they were just friends. Michael read all he could about human relationships but found there was a big difference between what books said and how he felt. He thought about that on the shuttle ride to the station but just couldn't seem to make any more sense than when he thought about it before. As the shuttle docked, he once again put it to the back of his mind for another time.

Michael reported to Lieutenant Cin by 0845. Sergeant Hill explained he had other duties waiting and Lieutenant Cin released him with a nod. Michael took a seat and at exactly 0900 entered the Admiral's office. Michael was surprised when Admiral Barker rose to meet him from a comfortable chair one of three surrounding a low coffee table set with a tea service and two cups. Michael came to attention and saluted as proscribed by the Officer's Manual. The Admiral returned his salute her inquisitive eyes twinkling along with a warm matronly smile. She then offered her hand to shake and stated, "Defender, Second Lieutenant Grade, I've been looking forward to meeting you."

Michael shook the offered hand and noted that the Admiral seemed to evaluate his every move. The Admiral gestured towards the chairs and table and added, "Please, let's have a seat." Waiting until the Admiral was seated Michael took one of the chairs waiting for the Admiral to speak. As proscribed in the Officer's

Manual, Michael sat at attention on the first 1/3 of the seat. The Admiral noted his posture and gently smiled. "Defender you appear well versed in the correct etiquette as written in our manual. However, this is an informal meeting. Please sit back and make yourself comfortable."

Michael sat back and relaxed in the soft chair as the Admiral continued. "I have heard about how quickly you learn. Can you tell me about it? I have also read your historical file compiled by Lieutenant Hall. However, I would really like to hear your account first hand, from when you first awoke inside of Romeo." Michael looked at the Admiral's kindly face and gentle eyes and felt as comfortable with her as he felt with Maryann.

Michael began when he first awoke and met Teacher. He explained how Teacher recorded anything he viewed or read and that it was always available for immediate recall. He explained his development with the Element and his training as a Defender. Michael summarized how he prepared for the battle with the Evil Ones the ancient enemy of the Old Ones. The only thing Michael had omitted from his story was the name of the ancient beings of Romeo. The name given to him in his memory wasn't his to give to others. The Old Ones known by many names to many cultures would rest quietly. The secrets of Romeo were not Michaels to give.

When he had finished, Admiral Barker asked if she could see the identification tags, he wore. Handing her the tags Michael waited for a response or question. The Admiral looked at the tags then slowly returned them to Michael without comment. Finally, the Admiral rose from her seat and spoke, "Defender, I would like you to come with me."

With the Admiral in the lead, they left her office and walked through the station. Lieutenant Cin joined them when they passed his office. The Admiral led them to the heart of the facility that Michael noticed was the Station Sickbay. The Admiral led Michael to an observation window that overlooked a counseling room. In the room, a Psychologist sat patiently with Angela Stil. Angela was furiously working on a picture with crayons. Through the speaker on the wall, they could hear Angela speaking. She was saying repeatedly, "My Guardian Angel, My Guardian Angel." Michael looked through the window around the room. There were crayon pictures taped to all the walls. Michael realized they were rough semblances that looked like him fighting the Evil Ones. In the pictures though, the glow of his Elemental force field helmet looked like a halo. The Admiral watched his face carefully then spoke.

"Defender, Angela Stil has been like this since her return from the rescue on Harrak's Moon. The Psychologists call this Post Traumatic Stress Disorder. It's common in people exposed to prolonged mental or physical danger associated with captivity. It also happens in both Humans and Giann during warfare, with long periods of life threatening stress. The other women that survived say Angela kept up their spirits protected them as well as she could and served as their leader while they were in captivity. The additional stress and responsibility wear down a person over time and then the mind sort of shuts down." Michael watched through the window sadness showing in the muscles of his face. "Will she get better?"

"Only time will tell. We are supporting her here but she needs to go back to Earth for definitive treatment." Michael straightened turned to the Admiral and asked, "why are you telling me this?" The Admirals face softened as she explained, "Defender, your identification tags. Those same tags belonged to Lieutenant Commander Michael Stil. In route from Earth to the planet, Romeo, Angela Stil gave birth to a baby boy on the EGAS Inquisitive. We have learned from Angela that when the

D'mon attacked Romeo she placed the baby Michael in the cradle located in the dome. Angela also said she placed her husband's identification tags around the baby's neck before she left the dome. Defender, we think that you were that baby. If you like we can do a simple swab of your saliva and compare your DNA to Angela's and confirm the theory."

Michael turned back to the window and once again watched Angela drawing. Speaking quietly to himself Michael queried, "Teacher?"

Yes Defender?

"Is this the woman that brought me to the dome?"

Yes Defender. That is the woman.

With his eyes suddenly growing moist, Michael turned back to the Admiral. "That won't be necessary Admiral. I believe Angela Stil is my Mother."

Admiral Barker turned with Michael to face the window so she wouldn't see the tears in his eyes. She coughed once to clear her throat, and then quickly wiped her own eyes. She continued in a low voice. "Defender, it may be some time before Angela understands that her son is alive let alone that the grown man that helped rescue her was her child." Michael nodded and sighed deeply. "I understand Admiral."

Michael and the Admiral turned away from the window and walked slowly back towards her office. Barker noticed Michael straighten as he walked then his face brightened. "Admiral, I've just realized that there was something missing in my life. Up until now I was the last Defender, alone, different and one of a kind. But now I have a family!"

"Yes Defender you do. I promise your mother will get the best care we can offer. Hopefully one day you both will be reunited." Michael thought. *A family!*

Chapter 91

QUESTIONS

Aᴅᴍɪʀᴀʟ Barker stands with her hands clasped behind her back watching the movement of the ships out of the observation port of her office. Lieutenant Colonel Silverton and Lieutenant Hernandez sitting on the low couch by her coffee table slowly sip on the tea brought in by Lieutenant Cin. After reflecting for a few minutes, the Admiral finally turns and addresses the Officers. "I believe it is in our best interest to keep the woman under wraps for the moment. How many people know the woman is here? Silverton placed the cup back in the saucer on the table. "Less than thirty ma'am, they are all active duty Marines. The Sergeant Major has already passed the word to the enlisted Marines to keep silent. Lieutenant Hernandez gave the same orders to the shuttle crew. Lieutenant Cin has briefed the medical personnel up here."

The Admiral nodded and asked. "So what have you found out?" Silverton looked a little uncomfortable as he spoke, "Unfortunately, not too much. The shuttle belonged to the Harvest Moon. Due to the unfortunate accident, the Captain is not available to give a statement. The computer logs of the shuttle flight are missing. There is no record of the woman at the Greenleaf Station or on the Harvest Moon. We have no idea how the woman got to the cave or even if she is involved with the shuttle at all."

"The Criminal Investigation Team found the residue of military grade explosives on some of the pieces of wreckage and one more interesting item. They found minute traces of another female body blown all over the crash site. They suspect the other female was very close to the explosion. The woman brought here is currently receiving hyperbaric treatment for the burns she received in the explosion and even with all these lunar cycles of treatment, it is just the beginning. The concussion of the blast damaged both her middle ears and she will need prosthetic surgery in the future to hear. She has had trauma to her head and her mental status is unknown. The woman has been in a medical induced coma since we brought her here but the surgeons say she has a good chance to survive." The Admiral proposed a question, "Have they run a DNA identification request?

"Yes, the DNA identification was negative. The woman is oriental but that is all we know. If she comes from one of the poorer regions of the orient, she may not be in the world database. There is one more thing, her medical examination shows she had delivered a child perhaps last solar cycle, so she may have a child on Earth." Barker raised an eyebrow and commented, "If she delivered on Earth."

Silverton poured himself another cup of tea from the service on the table. Taking a tentative sip from his cup, he then continued. "So we know something, possibly something illegal, happened but we have no idea what. The Security Chief at Greenleaf Station states they use military grade explosives to clear large rocks so if there were some on the shuttle it wouldn't be very unusual. He stated it is just a terrible accident."

Admiral Barker sat wearily down in the large chair behind her desk. "So after all this time and investigation we basically have zip. Gentlemen what I am about to tell you doesn't leave this room." Both Silverton and Hernandez sat up straighter in their chairs. "As you know PTS Corp. provides security for the Greenleaf Global Station. What you may not know is both Greenleaf Global and PTS Corp. are subsidiaries of Toath Enterprises. Councilman Toath has pulled many strings to set up Greenleaf Global on Romeo. Why, I don't know. However, this unusual crash and the accident aboard the Harvest Moon smells to me of corporate intrigue."

Now, Wingate Toath is one of the staunchest supporters of the Fleet and the Fleet Marine Corps. He is also one of the leading members of the EGA Council. If, and I do reiterate, if Councilman Toath is involved in anything untoward the proof would have to be irrefutable. I feel the small pieces we have uncovered here may be parts of a larger puzzle. To what end I don't know, so as of now this investigation is closed." Lieutenant Colonel Silverton looked like he swallowed a vile cocktail. "But, Admiral . . . !"

Barker sat forward in her chair, "Colonel this is not open for discussion. This decision came directly from Fleet Command. I am not happy with the decision either, but we have no recourse. The Fleet has a war to fight and to do that they need support from people like Councilman Toath. Do I make myself clear?"

Silverton sat up straight on the edge of his chair like a Midshipman called to task. His face turned a deep crimson but all he said was, "Aye, ma'am." The Admiral sat back in her chair and pointed to the investigation documents on her deck. "Lieutenant Cin, please remove these documents and put them in the safe. They will be classified top secret and forwarded to EGAFC with the next available courier. Now gentlemen, I have a Space Liner to meet. Councilman Toath and Mr. Justin Marrt of PTS Corp. are arriving on Toath's personal Liner for a fact-finding tour of this station. Are there any questions?" The Officers rose and came to attention. "Then you are dismissed, thank you." Admiral Barker rose from her chair and watched the two men file out, her face an impassive mask.

Chapter 92

THE COUNCILMAN ARRIVES

A DMIRAL Barker accompanied by Lieutenant Cin walked into the VIP receiving lounge of the VIP hatch. This hatch is for visiting dignitaries such as the Councilman. The Councilman's personal luxury Liner had an escort of two Space Destroyers to the Romeo system. The Destroyers have orders to accompany the liner to the Romeo system and back.

The Admiral is surprised to find the head of Greenleaf Station Security standing next to the docking hatch with six of his security staff in the black PTS combat armor. Admiral Barker walked straight up to the thin man in the long black leather coat. "Good afternoon Mr. Alpha."

Alpha pulled himself to attention and responded with a glowing smile. "Good afternoon Admiral." Looking over Alpha's shoulder Barker commented, "I wouldn't think Councilman Toath would need a security detail aboard my repair facility." The Admiral noted that while five of the men appeared to be older veterans and stood looking straight ahead, the tall young oriental guard was looking around as if all this is new to him. The thin smile never left Alpha's face as he replied. "Oh, these men are just due for rotation back to Earth. Councilman Toath has been kind enough to offer us transportation on his liner."

The Admiral glanced once again at the tall oriental man then said, "You said "us", Mr. Alpha are you going back to Earth too?"

"Yes, Admiral, my work here is completed. The Station's security is set up and running to Mr. Marrt's specifications. The Security Captain can now handle the day to day events." Barker turned her attention back to Alpha and said dryly, "I hope you and your men have a comfortable trip back Mr. Alpha, now if you will excuse me I believe the Councilman is ready to disembark. The Admiral turned and walked with Lieutenant Cin to the now open hatch to the liner.

Councilman Toath strode out of the hatch bubbling with enthusiasm. It was almost as if he were expecting the press to be waiting so he could stump his favorite issues. "Admiral Barker it's so great to see you again!" He stepped forward and grabbed her hand pumping it up and down as if she were a long lost friend. Dropping her hand he asked, "How are you doing? In addition, how is that brilliant husband of yours? I hear this station is the cutting edge of ship repair technology!" Before Barker could reply, he turned to Marrt that was following a few paces behind. Admiral have you met my associate Mr. Justin Marrt?

Marrt stepped forward and offered his hand. Taking his hand Barker stated. "It's a pleasure to meet you Mr. Marrt. I have heard about all the good things that PTS Corp. has done for the Fleet." Dropping her hand a little too quickly, Marrt offered, "The pleasure is all mine Admiral. The pleasure is certainly all mine." Avoiding the temptation to wipe her hand off on her uniform leg Barker asked. "Will you be coming along on our little tour of the facility Mr. Marrt?" Marrt with a pained expression on his face sadly shook his head. "Business Admiral, unfortunately I have too much business to take care of here."

Marrt made a sweeping gesture with his arm towards the hatch and Alpha led the PTS personnel through the hatch to the liner. The last in line is the tall muscular oriental man still looking everywhere as if on a great adventure. "I must get these men settled aboard Mr. Toath's liner then take care of a multitude of communiqués. I'm sure you understand Admiral. A Corporate Head never has a life of his own." Marrt quickly shook her hand again and added. "But it was a real privilege meeting you Admiral." He quickly turned and hurried after the men boarding the Liner.

Admiral Barker glanced at Lieutenant Cin as she turned to face Toath. Cin gave a slight questioning shrug of his shoulders at the quick exit of Justin Marrt. "Well Councilman, shall we proceed with the tour. In about an hour my husband will join us for lunch so he can bring you up to date on the more complex aspects of the Facilities capabilities."

"Indeed Admiral; I always enjoy seeing the fruits of the Councils endeavors. Now that we are at war with these "Demons", the capabilities of stations like this are of the most import. The military outposts here at Romeo are crucial in the defense of our home world." Admiral Barker walked slowly next to Toath as he spoke animatedly about the defense of Earth and the great crusade launched for Humans everywhere.

Lieutenant Cin followed the Admiral and the Councilman a few paces behind them. He walks with his long hands clasped behind his back in careful attendance. He followed the two of them for an hour before they stopped for lunch then for another three hours before the tour was completed. As Lieutenant Cin quietly followed, he noticed a few things. The first, that Councilman Toath talked extensively for the whole time of the tour. During the Councilman's monolog, Admiral and Commodore Barker had little chance to tell him very much. Second Lieutenant Cin noticed that in the whole time on the station Councilman Toath never once mentioned Giann or referred to any Giann personnel. It was as if they didn't exist.

The Admiral finally led Toath back to his Liner. She had offered quarters aboard the facility for Toath and his crew if he could stay longer but the Councilman declined. He spoke of pressing business back on Earth and the need to be at the next meeting of the Council. At the hatch, Toath promised they must get together socially at the next opportunity. He promised dinner with his wife should the Barkers get back to Earth and thanked the Admiral for the wonderful tour. Toath continued to wave goodbye to the Admiral as the hatch to the liner closed.

Admiral Barker and Lieutenant Cin stood there looking at the closed hatch for a minute or two. Heaving a great sigh of relief Admiral Barker started to pat the pockets of her uniform. Confused, Lieutenant Cin asked the Admiral what she was doing. The Admiral dryly answered, "After an afternoon with that guy, I had the sudden compulsion to check if I still had my wallet!"

Chapter 93

EGA GRAND COUNCIL CHAMBER

(Earth)

THE projected holographic image of Admiral Lydia Barker stood in the center of the vast round chamber. Even with the new star drive, the information that Admiral Barker had for the Council was too important for the delay of ship travel. The Admiral appeared to look up from her podium and around the chamber as she spoke.

"Esteemed Alliance Council Members, I speak to you today from the outpost at the planet Romeo. I do this by projection only because the information I relay for your consideration is so dire that it may affect the very survival of our species. Each of you by now has several information disks that contain all of the current information we have about the nomadic species the D'mon. The disks contain coverage of the defensive battle at the planet Romeo and the rescue operation at Harrak's moon."

"Along with the Human women rescued at Harrak's moon an elderly D'mon slave was also rescued. The intelligence gained from debriefing the female D'mon is invaluable. The quick thinking and sound judgment of the EGA Marine Officer that made the decision to bring her out of the fortress is phenomenal. In a few lunar cycles, we will have compiled a full social and sociological report on the D'mon. What we have gleaned so far is the D'mon is a nomadic space faring species. They have a warrior society and live off the spoils of warfare. They reproduce rapidly using biologically compatible females from defeated species. Any non-compatible defeated species are used as slave labor for their Fleets."

"At the Battle of Harrak's moon the Fleet we faced had from eighty to one hundred ships. We were lucky, lucky indeed! I don't believe I need to point out to you that this Fleet was the size of the whole Alliance Fleet including some of our old ships that are so small they barely make it back and forth to Europa. I believe the Fleet we faced at Harrak's moon stopped only because of lack of intelligence. When we destroyed a good number of their fighters and ran, they had no idea if we had other ships waiting on a chance to ambush them. If in Command, I would have been cautious with my Fleet also. Yes, I believe we were very lucky."

"However, the most astounding piece of information we recovered from the D'mon female is that this Fleet is just one of many! The female D'mon relayed to us that these D'mon Fleets could come together at any time to defeat a stubborn enemy and then share the spoils. If these Fleets come together in our section of space and find Earth and Giann we can easily be facing annihilation! I have spoken with the Fleet Staff at EGA Fleet Headquarters and we have the following recommendations."

"First, we are at war and need to produce military ships quickly and in large numbers if we are to survive. Second, we must create small bases between here and the planet Romeo confusing the enemy as to our home world's locations. Third, expand the Fleet and the Fleet Marine Corps. Fourth, all Fleet offensive operations must run out of the Romeo system. Once again, we must protect our home worlds. Last we must fortify the Earth and Giann systems."

"Thank you for your attention. Start building and start recruiting, for we know they're coming, Barker out." The Admiral's figure disappeared and the Council at first sat there stunned. Then everyone began to talk at once.